With Me

by Lucy Keating

Clarion Books
An Imprint of HarperCollinsPublishers

ISBN 978-0-35-846831-8

The text was set in Bembo Std.
Cover design by Celeste Knudsen
Typography by Karina Granda
22 23 24 25 26   PC/LSCC   10 9 8 7 6 5 4 3 2 1

First Edition

To my mother, Marty Keating, who makes us see the humor
and magic in everything
♡ ♡ ♡

Chapter 1

IF YOU WERE TO ASK ME ABOUT MY HOME, CHESTER Falls, Massachusetts—though I'm honestly not sure why you would, because that would mean you somehow knew it existed in the first place—I would direct you, first, to the town paper. The back page of the *Chester Falls Gazette* gives a rundown of every crime that has happened in our tiny town that week, and has included the following incidents:

On October 22, a geriatric sheepdog from a nearby farm wandered into a woman's home and refused to leave. The police were unable to get the animal out, so it remained there on her love seat for the next three hours, watching daytime TV, until its owner came and lured it home with a piece of turkey bacon.

On February 19, a prized alpaca got loose from its pen and went slipping and sliding out in the middle of frozen George's Pond, and had to be rescued by a four-person team.

On April 20, a frantic caller claimed that a dangerous person was breaking into her home with a weapon. Turned out it was her husband, who had misplaced his keys after one too many beers watching the Stanley Cup Finals with his club league and brought a hockey stick home with him.

And, my personal favorite, May 5, when a travel advisory went out via SMS warning of slick road conditions after a truck carrying three thousand pounds of buttermilk overturned on Route 2.

Riveting stuff. I know.

There is *one* reason you might know of Chester Falls, actually: it's the original maker of the Maple Pudding Pie, which was created by Maddie Baker in 1892, and is now sold in supermarkets across the country. If you've never heard of a Maple Pudding Pie, then I should tell you two things. One, it is delicious beyond words, with a layer of molasses-cookie crust, maple custard, and whipped cream, and two, it is pretty crucial to our town's economy. Every year, nearly one hundred thousand pies are shipped nationwide. And I would know, because for the past five years, my dad has been in charge of all of those packages being on schedule—when he's not watching TV, reading spy novels in a cozy chair in our living room, and pretending that one of these days he's going to get back to making the wood sculptures that once made him famous. I can't say I really blame him, though, for sitting around. Chester Falls is great. But there isn't a whole lot to do here.

♡ ♡ ♡

"You are *going* to this party, Charlie," Sydney says to me on Friday night as we take a left onto Route 102 and start driving north toward the lake. Sydney has been my best friend since kindergarten, since her dad became our town doctor and I was rushed into his office having just eaten an entire bottle of chewable Tylenol, only to barf all over the rug before anyone could pump my stomach. Instead of laughing at me, Sydney, who was playing in the office, came over and gave me her stuffed turtle. This, I like to think, explains why we're *still* friends, even though we're more different now than ever. I enjoy taking long walks in the woods, making trips to the modern art museum in New Winsor to sketch, overthinking my problems to the point of nausea, and listening to all the obscure music I can get my hands on. Sydney prefers to stay at home learning complicated nail design techniques, watching videos of people cooking miniature-sized food, and doing butt sculpting workouts on Instagram Live.

We don't always see eye to eye, but I'd do basically anything for her.

"When did I say I wasn't going?" I ask her now as I fiddle with the AC. It's the first week of April, and it feels like summer. I prefer the fall, when the trees of our mountain town change to nearly all the colors of the rainbow. Before the cold sets in and stepping a foot outside is like a shock to the system, like you might as well be diving into a frozen lake in a bikini. Which people actually do in this town. They call it the Happy Penguins Club. "I'm literally driving us there right now," I tell Sydney.

Sydney looks out the window. "You used to love going to parties," she sighs, like we're a married couple on the brink of divorce.

"I still do!"

"Really? Because the past few we've been to, you hardly say a word, then leave early to give someone a ride home."

I open my mouth to reply, but don't know what to say. The truth is, I have been feeling a little over it. Like I'm waiting for my web browser to load. Like I've just finished season one of a great TV show, and season two still hasn't come out.

"May I chime in?" Reggie, my fourteen-year-old neighbor, says from the back seat. He's so small, I forgot he was there.

Sydney turns around to look at Reggie. "No," she says. "You may not chime in."

"Why not?" Reggie wants to know.

"Because you're a freshman, that's why," Sydney replies as if that explains it. And, honestly, it *should* explain it. Nevertheless, I have to step in.

"Sydney. Reggie is a paying customer, just like you. If he wants to participate in our conversation, he absolutely may." I give her a look to communicate the following: *Let's just ignore whatever he has to say.*

"I liked it better when the app first came out, and you could only take one rider at a time." Sydney crosses her arms in front of her chest. The app she is referring to is Backseat, and it's the only way that Sydney, one of the most popular girls in our junior class, and Reggie, would ever end up in the same car in the first place, let alone on their way to a party together.

Backseat was developed as a class project by a group of seniors two years ago. They said it was an effort to reduce emissions. A small, meaningful act. Maybe people around here, who drove mostly SUVs and pickup trucks, would use less gas if they had other modes of transport. But everyone knows what it's really for. The year before, a group of seniors were in a bad accident on one of Chester Falls' many mountain roads, and one of them almost died. With Backseat, people are always guaranteed a safe ride home.

The app quickly became a local necessity in our town, which may have once been said to have "the quaintest main street in America," but where the big grocery store is almost forty minutes away. Teens love Backseat because they can get wherever they want, whenever they want, without depending on their parents, or their own car, or even having to wait until they can get a license. Parents love it because they can finally have some semblance of a life again, without schlepping their kids all over town, to school, practice, and sleepovers. And, most importantly, they trust their kids will find a safe way home after a night out.

I love it because, as one of the top drivers for Backseat in our town, it's paying my way toward the summer of a lifetime.

"But single riders made the rides twice as expensive," I tell Sydney. "This way, everyone can use it."

"Yeah, but now I'm showing up to the hottest spring party with a minion," Sydney mutters.

"I resent that," Reggie says from the back seat, peering up at her through his thick prescription glasses.

"Well, I've got a near perfect rating, and I'd like to keep it that way," I say to Sydney. "Speaking of. Reggie, can I offer you a mint?"

"You may." Reggie leans a skinny arm into the front seat and takes one. Then, unfortunately, he keeps talking: "Hoping to smooch someone tonight."

Sydney and I grimace at each other.

"You drive a lot, Charlie?" Reggie continues.

I nod. "I try and turn the app on whenever I get in my car. Easy money."

Reggie pops the mint in his mouth. "What do you need so much money for?"

Normally I'd tell Reggie he asks a lot of questions. But I need to keep my rating high. Backseat provides a bonus to the top drivers in town at the end of every quarter, and I could really use it. Besides, last month I had an unexpected thing happen behind the wheel, something that wasn't even my fault. It should've just been a bad rating, but instead I got a full-on safety violation. You only get two, and you get suspended.

I study Reggie in the rearview mirror. He's itty-bitty, and wide-eyed, and totally comfortable in his skin. I'm not even sure how he got an invite to this party. He hasn't been messed up by high school yet. Maybe next year. Next year he will certainly be questioning his own existence.

"Allow me." Sydney smirks. She turns back to Reggie. "Charlie is saving up for the Big Trip. The journey to the great beyond, if you will."

In the rearview mirror, I see Reggie frown. "Death?"

I snort.

6

"No!" Sydney exclaims. "Jesus. She's going on an *actual* trip. A road trip."

"Cool!" Reggie says, talking around the mint in his mouth. "Where?"

I lean over the steering wheel, like I'm trying to follow the signs, even though I could probably drive around Chester Falls blindfolded.

"Yeah, Charlie." Sydney tears her eyes off her phone to look at me with mock intrigue. "Where?"

I clear my throat. "I don't actually know where. All I know is, I want to travel for a bit. Experience life beyond Chester Falls."

Sydney sighs. "Charlie is just looking to find out who she is. And she thinks going somewhere else will help her figure that out."

"That's not true!" I shake my head. "I love Chester Falls! I just want to see how other people live. What other cities are like. From New Orleans to Seattle."

"Charlie wants to be an architect," Sydney explains. "So, she wants to see every building on earth."

"Not all of them. Just the most interesting and important," I tell her. "You can always come with me, you know."

"No thanks, I'm good here." Sydney lowers the passenger mirror and checks her lip gloss.

"Can I come?" Reggie finally asks, after a long pause.

"No," Sydney and I both say at the same time. Then we look at each other and burst into laughter.

Chapter 2

"YESSSS!" TUCKER EXCLAIMS, ARMS RAISED ABOVE HIS head, when we walk in the door of his party, which is already filled shoulder to shoulder with people. Tucker's mom and dad own an antique business that takes them all over the country distributing ancient milk cans and century-old doors, which means Tucker throws a lot of parties. Like, every weekend. He'd never admit it, but I think he's afraid of being here alone, all the way out in the woods.

Now, he gives me a double high five, then adjusts his beanie. "Thank god you're here. Thought you were off painting a giant mural or knitting another weird sweater or something."

I give him a light shove. "You didn't think that beanie was weird when I made it for you," I say, pointing to his hat. "In fact, I'm pretty sure you wear it every day."

"He definitely does," Sydney says, running her hand over a giant wooden bird sculpture.

"Don't touch that," Tucker warns. "It's from 1952. It's worth, like, seven thousand dollars."

Sydney looks like she could throw up. *"This?"*

Tucker shrugs, turning back to me. "I love my hat," he says, wrapping an arm around my shoulders. "You're so creative, it makes my head spin. Is that what you want to hear?"

I nod. "Yes, actually."

Tucker chuckles. "But more importantly, we have a situation."

He points to the corner of the party, where Tessa and Marcus are having another one of their fights by the pool. Tessa's mascara is smudged like some kind of *Bachelor* contestant, whereas Marcus just looks exhausted.

I heave a heavy sigh. "Oh boy."

"Yup," Tucker mutters. "Can you handle it? It's *really* harshing the vibe."

I look at Sydney, who rolls her eyes, like, *what choice do we have?* After all, she's our best friend.

"Could he *be* more into you?" Sydney says under her breath as we walk away.

"That was forever ago," I say dismissively as we speed toward Tessa and her sobs. Tucker and I kissed once at a party, which is the longest relationship I've ever had. He's cute, and has a heart of gold, but he'll always just be the guy who takes a giant bite of my hamburger before I have any for myself. The guy who lights his farts on fire for a laugh.

"Not for *him*," Sydney says. "Not everyone can have Charlie Owens's cold, cold heart." She raises an eyebrow at me, but our attention is drawn back to the pool at the sound of Marcus's annoyed tone.

"I. Wasn't. *Doing*. Anything," he is saying through gritted teeth.

"Yes. You. *Were*. Marcus! Do you think I'm an idiot? Like I haven't seen all her likes on your pics? Like I haven't seen your comments on her finsta? That's right, I found it." Tessa takes a step forward and pushes him.

Marcus closes his eyes, a prolonged blink. Then he turns our way, just as we reach them. "Can you do something about this?

"*This?*" Tessa says. "Oh, because I'm the problem now? The thing that needs to be dealt with. Have you ever considered the fact that I wouldn't be such a bitch if you just treated me nicely in the first place?"

And have either of you ever considered the fact that you should've broken up years ago? I think silently to myself. Why do people constantly push their relationships past their expiration date?

"Whatever," Marcus says, shaking his head. Then he walks away. But he doesn't get far before Tessa takes a long step forward and pushes him directly into the pool.

Amid a roar of cheers, and Marcus's indignant exclamations, Tessa turns back to us, her face softening.

"Hi," she says. "Marcus is definitely cheating on me."

"Hi," we say, circling around her in a big hug as she bursts into tears.

♡ ♡ ♡

"Don't say it," Tessa laments half an hour later, still sniffing as we rest, our legs entangled, on a red velvet couch in Tucker's parents' library. Tessa is the daughter of two farmers. She likes fresh-cut flowers, and vintage jeans, and every baby animal on earth. Tessa and I have been friends since we were practically born, since our moms met while floating their pregnant bellies in the local community pool.

Whereas Sydney is quieter and more calculating, Tessa wears her emotions on her sleeves. She is all fire. And she's particularly fiery about her boyfriend, who she's been with since the seventh grade. And it seems like Tessa and Marcus are the only ones who can't see that they've grown apart.

Directly next to where Tessa is propped up on the couch is a large taxidermy ostrich, which someone has put a baseball cap on. Beneath our bare feet is a shag rug. Tucker said it would be okay if I took over his Spotify for a bit, and this band I've been listening to from Northampton is floating out of all the speakers in the house. In this moment, in this tiny room with my two best friends, away from the keg stands and the football on TV and the loud talking of my classmates, everything feels perfect.

"Don't say what?" I shrug, playing dumb.

"You're going to tell me to break up with him. Again."

I shake my head. "I can't tell you how to live your life, Tess. It just doesn't really seem like he's making you happy anymore. It doesn't seem like he's made you happy for a long time."

Tessa buries her head in her arms. "I don't even know who I am without Marcus."

"None of us know who we are yet." I roll my eyes. "If we did, that would be *weird*. But we have to keep looking, right?"

Just as Tessa lets out a sigh, the face of a boy appears next to the polished wooden doorframe. I recognize Andre Minasian, a senior and star midfielder on the lacrosse team. He's also a serious skier, like a lot of the kids in our mountain town, so he only comes to about half the parties each year, because he's always traveling to meets. But when he does show up, he parties. Hard. Rumors about Andre Minasian abound, like the time he got drunk at a party, climbed into someone's little brother's tree house, raised the ladder so nobody could get in, and nearly froze to death. Or the time he set up an elaborate obstacle course for four-wheelers in the woods, got concussed, didn't tell anyone, and fainted during a lacrosse game. I've never been able to decide if he's purely an adrenaline junkie, or if he's just an idiot, but I doubt I'll be finding out. I'm pretty sure we have nothing in common.

"What band is this?" Andre asks, scrunching up his face to hear better.

"The Moors," I call out, surprised but also kind of pleased, glad someone around here likes my music.

Andre looks at me, nodding as he listens, and I'm just about to tell him that if he likes it, I can recommend some others, when he says, in a tone like he's given it serious thought and is just reaching his conclusion: ". . . it kind of sucks."

Sydney and Tessa try to hold back their snickers as Andre heads back out of the room, saying something about changing the music, because "We can do better than this," and I feel my cheeks flush. I want to chase after him and tell him that, in fact, *he* sucks, that he wouldn't know what good taste was if it bit him on his ultra-firm skier's butt, but I have a feeling he wouldn't care. Andre is one of those people whose good mood seems impenetrable. And that might be what annoys me the most.

Sydney refocuses us on the topic on hand. "You know exactly what you want to be, Charlie. A big fancy architect, with a sleek marble desk and an assistant that you use as a footstool."

I snort. "Okay, A, that is not the kind of architect I am trying to be at all. And B, I may know that I want to be an architect, but I definitely don't know how I'm going to get there."

"Cornell, *duh,*" Sydney says, bored, as she pops a ridged potato chip in her mouth. "The best five-year master's program in the country. Isn't that what you're always telling us?"

I hold up a finger. "With a really chill ten percent acceptance rate, don't forget."

They both look at me assuredly.

"You're going to get in," Tessa says. And, answering the question nobody asked out loud: "And you'll get a scholarship, too." Tessa is going to UMass, a little over an hour away, where she can take classes and still help out on the farm. Sydney has her sights set on Howard, one of the best HBCUs, where her parents met. With her grades, she's a shoo-in. And after growing up in Chester Falls, which has to be one of the whitest towns on earth, she's excited to get to DC.

I shake my head. "For now, I'm just going to the info session tomorrow." I glance at my phone, taking note of the time, when it goes off with a *ding!*

"Shit," I say, just as the music in the background changes to a Drake song. Andre.

"Don't take it." Sydney looks at me imploringly.

"Yeah, please?" Tessa asks. "We never hang out anymore."

"I have to." I look down at the map. It's a longer ride, taking me from the lake to the other side of Chester Falls. "At this time of night, it's at least a twenty-five-dollar fare."

"How about I just pay you twenty-five bucks right now, and you stay and hang out with us?" Sydney asks.

"You know I can't do that," I say, even though I could. But I hate taking Sydney's money. It feels like money is always falling out of her pocket. The other night I slept over at her house, and while I was peeing before bed, I looked around the bathroom and realized she has like six different types of each toiletry. Face masks, body lotion, tampons, conditioner. She doesn't have to squeeze the last drop out of everything, or worse, discover that her mother has used her favorite eyeliner to jot down a phone number or make an impromptu gestural sketch of a future painting.

"Hey, remember when she used to be fun?" Sydney asks Tessa now, like I'm not even there.

"It's ringing a bell," Tessa says idly, running her fingers along the velvet couch.

I look between them. "I'm sorry. I'll make it up to you. Text me if anything interesting happens. Maybe I'll get another ride back."

"No, you won't!" they both say at the same time as I walk out.

As I head toward the front door, I pass Tucker with Marcus, who's wearing a pink terry cloth bathrobe and looking emotionally bruised. "Off to make some kind of sculpture out of found objects?" Marcus mutters, and I don't bother responding, because he's not even worth it.

"You're really leaving?" Tucker calls out. "I was thinking we could hang for a bit."

"Another time," I tell him. I hold up my phone to explain.

"That's quite a business you've got going, Charlie," Tucker calls after me. "Seems like I have to book a ride with you if I ever want to get your attention."

"I'll take you wherever you wanna go," I call back, blowing him a kiss.

Chapter 3

THE WAY I FELT WHEN I FIRST GOT BEHIND THE WHEEL OF a car, all by myself, took me completely by surprise. Obviously, it wasn't my first time driving. I'd spent months learning the basics with my dad (and only my dad, because all it took was my mom gasping loudly before I had even pulled out of the driveway to make us want to kill each other). So my dad and I started in parking lots, then moved on to uncomplicated, flat, quiet streets in town. Eventually we began taking the beautiful roads that led in and out of Chester Falls, east toward Boston, north toward Vermont, or west toward New York State. I fell in love with it pretty quickly. The open road and my foot on the gas. The ability to see all these new places, all these buildings, to imagine what life was like for the people inside them.

And that was before I even understood the freedom that

came from taking off on your own. Suddenly, I could go anywhere I wanted. Anywhere and back, and nobody would even know.

So, as much as I hate disappointing Sydney and Tessa, I can't deny the sweet relief that washes over me when I hear the familiar alert of a ride request on my phone. When I head out of a place on my own with somewhere I have to be, *I'm* the one in charge of my destiny. Most of the time that high, that feeling of satisfaction, lasts for a while. It's not so much the destination as it is the journey itself. The promise of it.

That is, until a night like tonight, when I pick up someone like Michaela Sullivan.

I drive Michaela back to her house in the center of town for seven solid minutes of sniffling, seven minutes of soft crying so high pitched I can barely hear myself think, before she pauses long enough for me to ask her what's wrong. I do so while passing her a box of tissues I keep in the glove box for exactly this purpose. When you work for an app like Backseat, and you willingly drive teens home after parties, with all their hormones, and feelings, and poor decision-making, you are bound to encounter some interesting situations. Michaela Sullivan is a good example of what I like to call the Wailer.

"Whatever, you wouldn't even *get* it, Charlie," Michaela says between nose blows. Michaela and I are not exactly close friends. She is the queen of pep, the ultimate lover of high school, the first to raise her hand for any activity. Michaela is definitely never leaving Chester Falls, if she can help it. I have heard her say as much, on multiple occasions, as if someone is trying to kick her out. And, without a doubt she is *always* the last one to leave a party. Except for tonight.

"Try me," I say, carefully passing back a bag of Dove chocolates, which I have noticed also come in handy at a time like this. Because I know Michaela hates me, I have to try that much harder.

Michaela sighs, wiping her eyes. I hear the sound of crinkling tinfoil. "I snuck out tonight. I'm still grounded from that thing a few weeks ago . . ."

That *thing* was a party so epic kids came from two towns over to attend. Michaela's parents were on some couples retreat in the Catskills, making their own beeswax candles and talking about their feelings. I made almost two hundred bucks that night. Michaela's house was trashed, which didn't matter anyway, since the cops came, so her parents were going to hear about it regardless.

Michaela is still talking, now with her mouth full. "My mom says if she catches me out again, she's killing my allowance. Which would really suck, since I need it for our new dance uniforms."

"So . . . what made you risk it?" I ask, wondering if Michaela actually believes that the only way to make money is to have someone drop it into the palm of your hand.

Michaela sighs. "Grant."

I wrinkle my nose, glad that Michaela can't see the lower half of my face in the rearview mirror. Grant Chase is the captain of the Chester Falls High hockey team. He's also a supreme dickhead, in my personal opinion. At school he can be found cracking jokes in class to undermine the teacher's assignments, at parties he enjoys smashing beer cans into his skull, and his on-ice persona seems to be with a bloody nose and a tooth-chipped grin while some guy lies flat out next to the goal. It's like he's watched every bad eighties movie possible on how to be a douche and makes sure to brush up on the weekends.

"He's *really* cute," I say, because it doesn't matter if the mere sight of Grant Chase makes my skin crawl, what matters is that Michaela gives me five stars.

"Right?!" Michaela asks, her look changing immediately from disdainful to puppy dog. "We've been . . . talking. He told me to come out tonight. I gave my little sister forty bucks, and I waited until my parents went to sleep. If I'm caught, I am dead. But I risked it all for him."

I grimace inwardly, remembering the time I saw Grant pick a booger out of his nose and flick it across the all-school assembly, then high-five a friend with his booger hand. How do guys like that have so much clout?

"So I get to Tucker's, and I ask where I can find Grant, and everyone is all *weird* about it, and when I walk outside, I see why. Because guess what he's doing?" She looks at me, eyebrows raised, and I realize she actually wants me to answer.

Making out with Mia Harold on the pool furniture? I think to myself, because that is exactly what I saw him doing before I left.

"He's shoving his tongue into Mia Harold's big stupid

19

mouth," Michaela says, sniffing as she sits back in her seat. "I mean, seriously? Can you even believe that?"

Yes, I can absolutely, definitely believe it. And also, if you fall in love with a guy like Grant, what do you really expect?

"I *cannot* believe it," I say to Michaela.

Michaela will be fine. She has a new obsession every week. I've seen her crying in the hall more times than I have seen her *be catapulted into the air,* which is really saying a lot. Sydney says she's just a romantic. I think she should start meditating.

"I just thought he was special, you know?" she says, gazing out the window like a heroine in a period piece, thinking of her long-lost love. "I can't explain it. I just felt a connection. I thought we had a future."

At these last words, I feel the word vomit rising. *Nobody needs to hear this, Charlie,* I think. *Keep it to yourself.*

"But . . . this is high school, right?" I hear myself say. The silence that follows makes me wince outwardly.

Michaela's razor-sharp eyes cut up to mine in the rearview mirror. "Your point being?"

I think back to my conversation with Tessa earlier. "I just mean, you have your whole life ahead of you! Statistically, high school relationships don't last anyway . . ."

This was the wrong thing to say, and I can see it written all over Michaela's face. Her eyes scrunch together as she chews rabidly on a chocolate.

"My parents have been together since high school," Michaela points out.

Michaela's mother had an affair with the varsity wrestling

coach last year, and everyone knows this. This was the reason for their couples' retreat, after all. But I choose to keep this information to myself.

"Whatever. Like I said, I knew you wouldn't understand."

"Why do you keep *saying* that?" I ask as I take a left on Michaela's street.

"Because obviously you've never been in love!" she exclaims. "You're like, eternally single, no commitments to speak of."

"I have a *lot* of commitments," I say defensively. "It's just that none of them revolve around dating."

"And what, that makes you special? Because you'd rather be *alone*?" Michaela says, which leaves me speechless. Michaela speaks for me anyway. "Can you let me off up here? I don't want to risk my parents seeing me."

I swallow, pulling the car over and putting it into park. "Sure."

Michaela pauses on her way out of the car. "Sorry, that was kind of mean. What I said. But until you know the devastation of losing the one you love, I suggest you keep your comments to yourself on this one. Thanks for dropping me off here, though. It's true what they say, you can always count on Charlie Owens for a ride." After a second, she ducks back into the car. "Like, not in a gross way though."

I sit there, unable to move, as she walks away, and I keep sitting there until I see her shimmy up the back lattice of her house and fall through her bedroom window.

Next, I get an alert on my phone. Five stars, and a twenty-five percent tip. Michaela may be dramatic, but at least she's not unkind.

♡ ♡ ♡

After I drop Michaela, it's nearly nine p.m., and I have a text from Tessa waiting on my phone.

> **TESSA:** You coming back, or . . .

I take a deep breath, then type.

> **CHARLIE:** Got another ride! Then I think I'll head to bed.

She types for a moment and I see ". . ." before the dots disappear.

I could go back to the party. I know I won't be asleep for hours, anyway. But instead I take the winding road back through our picturesque little town with its food shops and its white steepled church and drive three miles east.

The Greek Revival farmhouse that my parents bought in 2002 is listed on the town's historical registry. It's a masterpiece of clean lines, columns, and hand-carved cornices perched on a hill, with a steep front yard, a carriage house, and a large chicken coop. My mom converted the chicken coop into her painting studio right after they moved in, and back when my dad was making art, he worked out of the carriage house. Our town has no shortage of old, beautiful buildings, but in my opinion, ours is one of the best. That is to say, it used to be. It has definitely seen better days. The paint is chipping off the right side, and there's a leak in the roof, and if someone leaves a light on in the basement, you can see it through the floorboards of the living room. There's a long list of things my parents have been saying they'll get around to fixing for years, partly because we don't have much extra cash, but mostly because they don't seem to really care, a fact that drives me crazy.

My mom met my dad at an experimental art opening in NYC in 1995, and after two years of living in a tiny walkup in Brooklyn, he convinced her to move to greener pastures. Literally. My dad, who had already made a name for himself for creating large-scale sculptures out of metal and wood, wanted to move back to his sleepy hometown of Chester Falls, and my mom went with him, even though her career in New York was just getting started. At first, they made more art than ever. Their work was covered in art periodicals, and even taught in some courses. They had me and got married.

Then, I don't really know what happened. Their friends started moving elsewhere, mostly west, to Los Angeles and Portland, and Mom and Dad just stayed. I guess maybe they fell out of love. They started spending more time apart, and my dad moved into the back of the house "because of his insomnia," but never left. So now they just live here more like roommates than partners. Together.

It's confusing. At least, it is for me. But apparently, not for them.

I take my time walking up the front path, then gently push open the front door and enter the front hall of the house. Through the doorway to the living room I can see my dad in front of the TV, a paperback book in his lap, his head back, his mouth open, snoring lightly.

When I was younger, I can almost never remember seeing my dad inside. He was always out on a hike, or working on some old car in the driveway, or in the carriage house, creating another one of his big pieces. I'd find him there when I got home from school, and then I'd bring him dinner and sit and watch him shuffle around, nodding his head as the long guitar solos of the Grateful Dead crackled out of an old radio in the corner.

When he had a major show coming up at a gallery in New York, he slept in the carriage house, too. I was worried, but my mom wasn't. He was happy. He was doing what he loved.

Then the review came out in the *New York Times*. I've never seen it, because my dad burned the copy we had, but from what I understand, the critic said his work looked like a middle school shop project.

At first, my dad raged on the state of the art world. How someone's life's work could be ruined by just a few sentences. He started going into the carriage house less and less after that. Instead, he comes to the couch.

I take an old wool blanket from the top of the sofa and fold it over his body, then sit down next to him and pull out my phone.

I pull up Instagram and look at pictures of the party. The keg stands and the fireworks, Tucker trying to wrestle Marcus, both now in bathrobes on the back porch. A shot of Tessa and Sydney eating pita chips in the kitchen, laughing, and . . . me. I'm there too, but I'm not laughing. I'm tucked into the corner, my hip against the counter, staring down at my phone.

And that makes you special? Because you'd rather be alone? I hear Michaela Sullivan's words echoing in my ears.

I glance back over at my dad, still sound asleep.

Whatever. Michaela barely knows me, and she has no idea what she's talking about.

I exit out of Tessa's photos and keep scrolling down my feed, till I land on an image that sparks something in me. It's a woman standing on a piece of packed dirt, a tiny, beautiful house behind her, palm trees visible in the distance. She's dressed in simple chinos and a lavender-colored tank top. Her tight coils of curls hug her head, her bright earrings hang down.

Ava Adams.

I click play on the video that was posted this morning.

"Hey, what's up, everyone, it's Ava. I'm traveling to the East Coast this week for a friend's opening but thought I would update you a bit on the status of our most recent tiny house!"

She begins panning the camera over the house behind her, the white stucco and natural wood, the dark metal windows and textured, organic materials. She explains the challenges with proper drainage, how they built the kitchen when they had run out of money, and how they sourced everything from no more than twenty miles away.

Ava Adams is my idol. She started her sustainable building company in New Orleans almost a decade ago, first going to work on small projects, like her own apartment. Now she gets commissioned by everyone to work in their spaces. Hotels. Museums. Private clients. She lives a simple and beautiful life filled with good things, plants, lots of friends, and a sense of community. She travels constantly. She gets shit done.

Basically, I would kill to be living her life.

I shut off the phone and lay my head back on the couch, staring up at the ceiling.

But instead, I'm here.

CHARLIE'S BACKSEAT REVIEWS

★★★★★ Best service in town, just wish she didn't work so much. Love u! 🫰
—Sydney

★★★★★ Dropped me off a block away from my house after curfew, no questions asked. And she packs snax! Kinda judgy tho . . . 🙄
—Michaela

Chapter 4

IF EVER I GAIN CONSCIOUSNESS ON A WEEKEND AND
don't know when or where I am, the smell of my dad's apple
flapjacks will always get the message across. Early on Saturday
morning, my nose wakes up before the rest of my body does as
the scent of cinnamon and butter wafts gently up the stairs and
into my room. I get dressed, mess with my hair until it looks
relatively normal, and head downstairs, where I find him leaning over the stove, a spatula in his right hand poised for flipping, his left arm bracing himself against the countertop. He's
wearing his favorite worn old Levi's covered in rips and paint,
and a scratchy-looking wool sweater.

"You need help?" I ask, nodding toward the pan.

"This is my duty and my right as your father," he says back,
barely looking up at me. Saturday pancakes are a necessity for
my dad. There is a steadiness to him, a habitual nature that

comforts. Sometimes I look at him and wonder where the wild man of his youth went. The one who lived in an unheated loft in the garment district and painted over billboards at night. "There's already a batch in the oven," he says.

I pour some coffee and grab a warm plate and join my mother at the kitchen table, where she has her head buried in the paper, her red hair flying out at all angles beyond the page.

My mom is a happy person, by most standards. She teaches art at the middle school and is well liked in town, if maybe a little eccentric, and sometimes I can see her dancing to Stevie Nicks through the window of her studio in the backyard. She also makes me laugh harder than anyone else I know.

But my mom's favorite pastime, for as far back as I can remember, has always consisted of talking about the past. The summer she spent in Rome. The little gallery she created in Brooklyn, before she moved here. How much fun she had when she visited old friends on their compound in Joshua Tree, and how cool their life is. I wonder if she thinks about what she gave up when she moved here for love.

I've tried to ask my mom about it, what happened exactly, but she always says I have to wait until I'm older to understand. But one thing I'm clear on: being beholden to someone creates far more problems than if you aren't.

"We should go to MaCA tomorrow," she says now, over the top of the paper. "The Mark Rothko exhibit is in. I think you'd like it, Charlie."

The Massachusetts Collective of Art is one of the best museums on the East Coast, and it's just a little over an hour away. I rarely turn down a chance to go. But these days I just have too much on my plate. "Can't, I have work," I say, mouth full of flapjack.

My mom watches me with a partially disgusted expression, but she knows better than to tell me to chew with my mouth closed this early in the day. I'm not rude, after all. I'm just excited for our visit to Cornell. Today could be an important step toward the rest of my life.

"Another time," she says.

I nod and catch sight of a house for sale on the back side of the paper. It's a little like ours, historic and on a nice piece of land. But unlike ours, it's in good condition, freshly painted, with a well-tended yard. I imagine that, unlike our house, there are no chipmunks scurrying through the walls at night. No vine growing through a hole near the back door that has to be trimmed periodically with a pair of kitchen scissors. No spoons holding windows up, replacing broken sashes.

"When do you think we're going to fix the downstairs bathroom?" I ask out loud, still staring at the house in the photo.

"Just use the upstairs," my dad says over his shoulder.

"I don't always want to use the upstairs," I say. "We have two bathrooms. Why can't both of them work? I looked it up. It's not expensive."

My mom looks back over the paper again, and my dad turns around slowly from the stove. "It works fine," my mom says. "You just flush it twice, and if necessary, you take some water from the sink and pour it in the bowl. That's what the red cup is for."

That's what the red cup is for. I say the words over and over in my head. Like it's the most normal thing in the world.

I blink. "It's just that, you know, maybe it would be cool to . . . not have to do that? To . . . just be able to flush it once?"

I take a big gulp of coffee and swallow as my parents share a look.

"If it means that much to you, we'll deal with it," my dad tells me as he adds more flapjacks to the oven plate.

"When?" I ask, looking back and forth between them, searching for anything. A plan. A direction. An idea of what's next. I realized long ago that this was a tactic I had to adopt. *If not now, when?* We've had this conversation a million times, about a million different things in the house. The leak above the stairway. The noise the kitchen sink makes if you turn the water on too high, like the pipe might explode right out of the cabinet. The oven that is either way hotter than it says or doesn't turn on at all.

"Look, honey," my mom says. "We know you wish the house wasn't so . . ." She waves her hand around, like she's explaining it. "But Dad and I are the adults here, okay? And you have a roof over your head. And there are more important things in the world."

I stare back and forth between them, my cheeks growing hot. I want to tell them that regardless of how I feel about the house, it's not the craziest idea to want more than one of the six outlets in my room to work. Or for the water in the shower to just be hot instead of going from hot to freezing every ten seconds. And oh, also, do they intend to live together and sleep in separate bedrooms for the rest of their lives?

Instead, I stuff more pancake into my mouth.

"How about you let us do the parenting, kiddo," my dad asks, straddling that line of firm and gentle he does so well. "Would that be all right?"

I stand up from the table, brushing past him to put my dish in the dishwasher.

"We should go, Mom," I say, glancing at my watch. It will take us nearly four hours to drive to Cornell, and the meeting is at one.

"Sorry I can't go with you," my dad says, running a hand through his hair, which has started to grow long again, like when he was young. My mom busies herself with finding her keys and purse. These are the moments when it's so clear that even though they want to pretend things are "fine," that the way they live is normal, it obviously isn't. Because if it was, and if they were really happy, he'd just come with us.

"That's okay," I say.

"Knock 'em dead." He comes close and gives me a hug.

"It's just an information session," I say, trying to pull out of his grasp.

"Knock 'em dead anyway," he replies, and messes up my hair.

♡ ♡ ♡

My mom is right. I do love our house. I love every post and beam, every piece of aged floorboard, the windows on the second floor that start at your shins and let in the best kind of light. All of it tells a story. And besides, this house is what led me to my love of architecture.

When I was growing up, wherever we went, my parents would always insist on going into every museum we could find. There we would walk carefully through each exhibit, observing, discussing, sitting in silence as we let the experience overtake us. But I was usually more focused on the spaces than the art itself. Old warehouses. Historic compounds. Repurposed shipping containers. New builds of glass and steel. The way light traveled across the room. The way people moved from space to space, and how that played into their experience of the art.

Then one day, one of my parents' friends visited and gave me a book on ancient Greece. I noticed that certain aspects of the temples—columns, cornices, an abundance of right angles—matched our home. How was it possible that all this time had passed, and yet a love for this specific style remained?

I took a book out from the library on American art and architecture, and learned that to early American architects, who were designing buildings just as ancient Roman ruins were being excavated, these styles represented the height of architecture. I was in awe that a language could be spoken through physical properties rather than words. That so much of what the farmhouse was designed to be was still what we lived with today.

It blew me away how much thought went into the things we interacted with constantly, on a daily basis, but at the same time, it couldn't have made more sense.

Like the way the house is situated at such an angle so it always catches the right light. Or how the interior of the house becomes less fancy the farther away you get from the front rooms, which were used for entertaining. Or, perhaps my favorite, the idea that farmhouses like ours were actually designed using the golden ratio, a mathematical sequence derived from nature itself, which is pleasing to the eye.

Last year, I found out about Cornell's five-year program. A college degree and a master's in architecture all in one, and only an extra year is needed to do it. To me, this is the ultimate. Why go to college and not study architecture, then spend three more years studying it somewhere else? I just need to find a way to stand out. And right now, I have no idea how. Maybe today will give me some ideas.

♡ ♡ ♡

Mom and I head west for an eternity, through the farm country of upstate NY, stopping only once for roadside coffees and a bathroom break, before dipping down to Ithaca. When I originally planned the trip, I found a sweet bed-and-breakfast in town, in a historic arts-and-crafts-style bungalow, but it was way too expensive. So we decided to do it all in one day, just us girls. A fun adventure.

Cornell is a big, looming campus, but the city of Ithaca is small, with beautiful gorges. I hear it's even colder than Chester Falls in the winter.

Still, when we enter the studio building, when I see all the worktables lined up in front of large windows, light falling across sketches and small models, I have a strong feeling that this is where I need to be. I take in the wide hallways, the cute student-run café downstairs, the stools in corners and comfy couches. I want to talk with my peers, as I watch a group of students do now, and make my ideas come alive, from my mind, to paper, to a 3D model. I feel myself leaning forward during the info session as they describe the professors who teach there. World-renowned experts on form, and space, on not just architecture but landscape design and urban planning. We watch slides of a beautiful home in India, deep in the forest, that students helped build last summer, where they collaborated with local artisans and used only local materials. We learn about a home in Sweden built entirely inside a greenhouse, which is completely self-sustaining. I know what it's like to really think about space. About where you live, and what you do there. I know what it's like to place value on a home.

I'm lost in this sense of weightlessness, this sense of belonging, when a boy in the info session raises his hand toward the end of the session.

"Yes?" the program director calls.

"I'd like to get to the more important stuff," he says, with an obnoxiously confident smile. When the director gives him a confused reply, he follows it with: "How do we get in?"

The director raises an eyebrow, clasping her hands over her knee. "This question was inevitable, I suppose. We seek out artistic merit, of course. Good grades in art, and an interest in the material. Excelling in physics and mathematics is really helpful, as it plays a critical role in the profession. And, of course." She smiles. "That extra something special."

The boy doesn't return the smile, he only nods repeatedly. "I'm spending this summer at RISD," he says. "Their youth architecture program. Last year I studied art history in Tuscany. I'm hoping that next summer, before Cornell, I can go to Japan."

I stifle a snort, casting a glance at my mother. *Is this guy serious?* She just rolls her eyes and shrugs.

But he still has the director's attention. "Wow. Impressive. Things like that can certainly add to your application." She glances around the room, adjusting her thick black frames. "I'm curious now. How many of you have pursued the study of architecture, design, or art history outside of the traditional high school experience?" she asks.

Nearly all the hands in the room go up, except one other boy and me. We exchange a helpless look. My throat feels parched, so I take a sip from my Cornell water bottle.

"My high school actually has a course on architecture," one girl pipes up to say. "I took that sophomore year, and this year I'm doing an independent study." I choke on my water, and my mom pats my back.

The director shares a wry look with one of her contemporaries. "I'm sure each and every one of you would make a great addition to our program." But as I look around the room, I'm not so sure that I would.

♡ ♡ ♡

"So, what did you think?" my mom asks on the dark drive home, after we stop for fries and milkshakes. I pull the last burnt bits of fry out of the Styrofoam to-go box and drop them into my mouth.

"It was . . . intimidating," I admit, when I finish chewing.

"I mean, I never thought it would be easy to get in. But those other students . . ." I shake my head. "They've done . . . so much. They've been everywhere."

"Oh, please," she says. "You've always been a talent. Cornell would be lucky."

"Mom, I'm serious." I shake my head. "Did you hear what they said? The things they've been *doing*. How could I possibly compete with that?" I gaze out the window. "It's probably not the right fit anyway."

We drive on in silence a bit longer before my mom says, "Well, if it doesn't work out, it doesn't work out. There are plenty of other programs in the country."

I know she's just trying to be nice, but deep down, all I really want her to do is tell me to go for it.

Chapter 5

"OKAY TRY *THIS*," THEO SAYS, HANDING ME A MUG. I'M leaning against the counter of Wild Oats health food store and café a week after our trip to Cornell, gazing out the window at a group of teens our age who are laughing, sunglasses on, as they devour the biscuits and pastries Wild Oats is so famous for. The couple who own it, Roger and Kit, were into health food and clean living long before it was cool, and the menu of matcha, almond flour, and grain bowls, plus supplements, bulk herbs, and clean skin-care products, brings people from all over the Berkshires.

This particular group of teens, who showed up in a Land Rover Defender, are probably from New York City. I wonder what kind of places they return to when they leave here. Immaculate apartments on the Upper East Side of Manhattan? Renovated lofts in Tribeca? Brooklyn brownstones? Or those new, towering skyscrapers that I've been seeing on Instagram, with views that make me dizzy just thinking about them?

I'm about to take an absentminded gulp of what Theo just handed me when I look down and notice it's filled with fluorescent blue liquid.

"What have you done?" I ask her, raising an eyebrow.

"Oat milk, vanilla bean, Earl Grey, and spirulina," she says, grinning. "I call it the English Coastal." Theo and I have been friends for a year, since I drove her from the café to a dentist appointment. We spent the whole time talking about how over high school we both are. Theo and her girlfriend, Sam, can't wait to graduate and move somewhere bigger, like Austin, or Atlanta. When it was time to pay, the app wasn't working, and I told her not to sweat it. She's supplied me with free beverages and pastries ever since. Long past what she owes me.

"It's actually . . . *good*," I tell her, after taking a reluctant sip.

"Good enough to tell Roger about?" She fixes me with a serious stare. "Be honest with me." Like me, Theo's got plans for herself. She considers herself a beverage wizard and is always looking to concoct something new. She feels she's ready to take on a bigger role at Wild Oats, she just needs to prove herself. I love that Theo thinks outside the box, I just wish she'd think bigger, try and start her own thing instead of working within Roger and Kit's rules. I even got her some pamphlets from a few local farmers markets, but she says until the customers of Chester Falls start tipping better, it's going to be a while. Something like that require a lot of investment.

I hesitate. "I'm just not sure he's going to love how . . . blue it is?"

"But the blue is all natural!" She makes a face. "I think?" She pulls a package out of a drawer and squints at it, running a hand through her short hair, which changes color every couple of weeks. These days, it's a deep mauve.

"Really? Because it looks like pool water in a David Hockney painting," I tell her, just as one of the girls from the porch comes inside to throw out their coffee cups and the rest of the group starts heading toward the car.

"Thanks!" she tells Theo with a big smile. "This town is so beautiful. Wish we didn't have to leave!"

"It's a paradise!" Theo calls after her with a grin, her smile disappearing when the door shuts behind her. We share a look. The truth is that Chester Falls *is* beautiful. It's just a whole lot cooler if you're visiting. If you get to be somewhere else first. Which neither of us ever have.

I'm so distracted watching them drive off that I don't notice a new customer walk in and examine the chalkboard. When I finally take note, I almost drop my neon latte.

Standing in Wild Oats café, wearing a large sun hat, copper-colored linen blazer, signature turquoise earrings, and bespoke leather bag slung over a shoulder, is Ava Adams.

"Hi!" she says to Theo, and as she steps closer to the counter, I notice she's more tired than she looks on camera. I try not to stare. I wonder if I'm dreaming, or if I won some contest I don't remember entering.

"Do you happen to know of a reliable taxi service?" she asks. "My rental car broke down, and they're sending someone to pick it up, but I have to get to my friend's show at MaCA. I can't get a single Uber out here."

Theo nods. "Yeah, it's almost impossible to get those in this area. It's actually one of the reasons our town made their own."

Ava's brows go up. "Your own ride share service?"

Theo nods. "It's pretty cool actually. Charlie—"Theo starts to turn my way, and before I can think, I duck behind the back of the bar. A woman waiting for the bathroom gives me a look. "Was right here . . ." Theo finishes. "That's weird. Anyway, it's called Backseat. It's supposed to be just for high school kids, but my mom takes it to her book club sometimes when she wants to get a little loose, if you know what I mean."

I hear Ava laugh. "Hey, I'm willing to try anything. Thank you so much."

"Not a problem," Theo says. "Can I get you anything for the road?"

♡ ♡ ♡

"Wait, *who?*" Theo says a few minutes later, after she's sent Ava off with an almond flour scone and a green tea, and I have stepped out from my hiding place near where they keep the high chairs to her raised brows.

"Ava Adams! She's like, my *idol.*" I pull up Instagram and show Theo Ava's profile, and all her tiny properties.

"Her life looks like a magazine," Theo says. "Where does she do her laundry?"

I balk. "Who cares?"

But Theo is serious. "You know a person can't live in a five-hundred-square-foot open-plan house without laundry somewhere."

I ignore her, pulling up a story from last month, a party Ava threw at one of her remodeled properties, with her roof deck and little studio outside. People were spread out everywhere, drinking, laughing, leaning heads on each other's shoulders.

"Look at this," I say. "This is where I want to be. This is what I want my life to be like. Art, culture, design. People who love it all as much as I do."

"So why were you *hiding* from her?" Theo asks, putting a hand on her hip.

I swallow. "I dunno. I was afraid, I guess?"

"Afraid of what?"

"Screwing up my one shot?"

"Doesn't sound very *Charlie* to me." Theo crosses her arms in front of her chest.

I shake my head. "Well, it's over, she's gone anyway."

"You sure about that?" Theo asks, nodding at my phone, where I see a new ride alert.

From Ava Adams.

And I almost drop my phone into my latte.

♡ ♡ ♡

Be cool. Be cool be cool be cool, I tell myself as I pull my car around in front of Wild Oats, where Ava is waiting, her tea in one hand, a straw bag and sleek canvas duffel over one shoulder. For a split second, I wonder what she will think of my giant Prius, but she has her hand on the door before I can run with the thought very long.

"Hi!" She beams. "Cool if I sit up front?"

I swallow. "Mm-hmm," I say. But Ava is already getting into the car, not looking at me, so she doesn't notice that I appear to have lost the connection between my brain and my body.

How, I wonder, as she buckles her seat belt and I pull her destination up on my phone, do you explain to a person that you've adored them from afar for years, when until six seconds ago, they didn't even know you existed?

Ava sighs, letting her head fall back against the seat.

"Long day?" I ask, and she smiles, before filling me in on what I heard her tell Theo.

"Anyway, I'm headed to my friend's show at MaCA, and then on to Hudson from there. Have you seen the Sol LeWitt exhibit? I hear his murals are something else."

"So many times," I tell her. "But he's only one of the reasons to go. Make sure you check out Marielle Lombard while you're there too. Her portraits will blow your mind."

Ava nods, eyeing me. "How old are you? And where did you get that incredible sweater?" She nods toward my chest.

"Thanks," I tell her, looking down at the shawl that's wrapped around my waist like a vest. "I'm seventeen. And I made it."

Her eyes widen. "You *made* that?"

I shrug. "I saw one like it in *Little Women*. I thought it would look cool. My friend's parents own an alpaca farm, so they gave me the wool. I like your bag," I add, before blushing.

"Thanks," she said. "I made it."

I laugh and bite my lip. "I actually know. I've followed

your whole career. I think I have every one of your houses and designs memorized."

Ava blinks. "Wow. I didn't get into design until college. What sparked the interest in you?"

As Ava sips her tea, I tell her about my parents' house, the way so much has changed and yet so little, how it affected the way I see the spaces we live in. I'm surprised by how easy it is to talk to her, someone who is technically a total stranger.

I drive Ava through Chester Falls pointing out historic landmarks, some of my favorite old houses, and the factory at the edge of town that some recent college grads just turned into a coworking space.

Ava listens intently.

"So, if you could build something here, what would it be?" she asks, which is something nobody ever asks me, but something I've always wanted to answer.

"I think it would be cool to have a hotel. But not one of the stodgy old inns we have around here. Something sleek and modern. Something that would stand out against the landscape. Especially in the snow. Plus, it would do a lot for our town economy."

"I love that idea," Ava says. "It always feels like East Coasters are trying so hard to hold on to what's old. But when you combine that with more contemporary design, it can be really striking."

"Exactly!" I say loudly, and when Ava asks me if that's what I want to do, design things, I tell her about Cornell, how I have my heart set on it, but how it may be out of my reach. "Hmm," she says, when I tell her this, like she's thinking about something.

♡ ♡ ♡

"Well, it was really great meeting you," Ava says when I pull up in front of the museum. And, maybe I'm crazy, but it feels like she is looking at me like she can really, actually, see me.

"Charlie," I remind her.

Ava has already stepped out of the car and grabbed her duffel when she turns around.

"Do you have plans this summer, Charlie?"

I nod. "Hoping to take a road trip, but not really sure where."

Ava bites her lip, frowning. "How about New Mexico?" At my confused look, Ava continues. "It's just that we've been talking about getting interns. We've been hired to rehab this collection of old cabins . . ." She looks me over admiringly. "We don't have much money, but I think it could be great to have another pair of hands."

The busy street outside MaCA seems to quiet around me. "I don't know what to say." My body suddenly feels like it's covered in shining, shimmering glitter, or lit up with neon lights. Ava Adams wants *my* perspective.

"How about we start by you sending me your stuff?" she asks.

I clear my throat. "My stuff?"

Ava laughs loudly now, a beautiful laugh. "Your portfolio! Some examples of your work. I know you're probably too young to have *built* anything yet, but sketches, inspiration, anything will work. It will help determine if you're a good fit and if you're ready for something like this."

"My portfolio . . ." I start to say, before changing my tone. "My portfolio! Totally. I would love that."

"Excellent." Ava gently shuts the door. "Be in touch, okay Charlie?" she says through the open window.

And just like that, Ava Adams walks out of my life, possibly after changing it forever.

♡ ♡ ♡

After I get back from MaCA, I'm just stopping in to Wild Oats again to use the bathroom when I hear my name called.

"Charlie?"

I turn to see my mom's friend Elaine standing next to the passenger door of her car across the street. She waves me over.

"How are you, honey?" she asks. "How are your parents?" Something about the way she says it, with a tilt of the head and a slight frown between the eyes, sends an alarm bell off in my head.

"They're fine." I picture my dad shuffling around the house in his slippers, and my mom cursing loudly at herself as she stares at a painting she's unhappy with. "Same as ever. Why?"

"I've been trying to get in touch with your mom, but I think she's avoiding me." Elaine smiles good-naturedly.

"Can I give her a message?"

"I'm doing a show at the gallery on local artists, and I just had someone cancel." She hesitates. "I know she doesn't like showing her work these days, but I would really love to get her involved. Is she working on anything new?" she finishes hopefully.

I purse my lips. My mom is always working, but never showing. "I'm not totally sure . . ."

She nods. "Well, have her call me, okay?" She pauses. "It would be low key, nothing for her to freak out over. Her stuff is so gorgeous. I just want the world to see it."

I nod. "You and me both."

"I knew you'd get it," she says. "You're a good girl, Charlie."

I watch Elaine get into her car and pull out onto Main Street, thinking about my mom and all her beautiful creations hiding away in her little studio. I shake my head. She may be willing to let opportunity pass her by, but I'm not. I'm going to figure out how to get to New Mexico.

A text from Tessa pops up on my phone. I open it to find a selfie of her and Sydney in sunglasses, snuggled up on either side of an alpaca . . . also in sunglasses.

> **TESSA:** How's the busiest driver in Western Massachusetts?

I smile.

> **CHARLIE:** High on caffeine and questioning her life, like always.

> **TESSA:** . . .

> **TESSA:** Same old same old, then?

Next arrives a video, teens laughing, talking loudly, and standing on bales of hay, flecks of light shining down on an old barn and a small pond and a beer pong table.

> **TESSA:** Lucky for you, we have the ultimate distraction. Get over here.

I tilt my head up to feel the sun on my face. It is a beautiful Saturday, after all. Plus, there will be plenty of paying customers who need a ride home.

> **CHARLIE:** Be there in ten.

CHARLIE'S BACKSEAT REVIEWS

★★★★★ Cool girl with a bright future ahead. Thanks for the ride! —Ava

Chapter 6

TESSA'S ANCESTORS, THE WALKERS, CAME HERE DURING the Great Depression and started working the land. They've owned a massive farm out on Old State Road for generations, where they do practically everything: grow crops, raise beds of colorful flowers, and harvest maple syrup, goat's milk, and farm-fresh eggs. They grow pumpkins in the fall and offer snowy carriage rides around the holidays. The only thing they don't do is raise animals for meat, which Tessa is relieved about, because she's an environmentalist and an animal lover through and through. Her parents used to find her sleeping in the barn at night. Tessa is the ultimate badass who can put on the cutest party outfit at night, then suit up in overalls and milk a barn full of cows by the time the rest of our school is barely shoving Cheerios into our mouths.

With a farm that's been around as long as the Walkers' on so many acres, there's a lot of history, and a lot of unused land when they move the fields each year for fresh soil. Way at the back of the property, so far back you have to take a separate, rocky road to drive there, is the original settlement that was used when Tessa's relatives bought the land. There's a small pond and the remnants of an old cabin.

And then, my favorite part of the property: there's the old barn.

Two stories high, with lofted spaces, a tall ladder, and a sliding door that runs half the length of the longer side, the barn is perfect in its form and its simplicity. Which sounds crazy, since even though it's held up really well, the inside is a mess, filled with old wood and dust and bent nails. But I still love it. I love to stand inside and imagine the possibilities for the place. What some repairs and a nice coat of paint would do. I'd live in it, if I could.

These days, the back part of the property is reserved for Tessa and her brothers. We've been coming out here since we were little for sleepovers, telling ghost stories, roasting marsh-mallows, building forts, pretending the world had ended and only us kids were left. They are by far my favorite memories.

Now, so many years later, it's where we come to party.

"She's here!!!" Tessa practically screams, standing up on the bed of a truck in jean shorts and a bathing suit as I round a grouping of trees and emerge in the open space.

"And I brought treats." I hold up a heavy brown paper bag of leftover baked goods. Sydney appears out of nowhere, im-mediately taking the bag out of my hand and shoving a flaky biscuit into her mouth without so much as a hello.

"Mmmmf suh gohd," she mutters with a full mouth. Then

she swallows, noticing the look on my face. "Sorry. I've been here for hours and I forgot to eat lunch."

"How was your day?" Tessa asks when she finally makes it over, and I open my mouth to tell them about Ava, about her proposition, when someone calls Tessa's name from the doorway of the barn.

"Oh boy," she says. "I told them to stay out of the hay loft. Who knows what's up there?" She goes running off to see what the commotion is.

"Is Marcus here?" I ask Sydney, who nods, making a face.

"Did they make up yet?" I take the bag from her and pull out a biscuit to nibble on.

"She won't say." Sydney raises an eyebrow in suspicion, which basically means *yes*. "They aren't talking to each other, but they also aren't screaming at each other, so you know that means they are probably back together and she's just trying to hide it."

I sigh, taking note of the little pond, its surface like a mirror, its cool waters beckoning. Nobody else is even in there. Where are their priorities?

"You wanna go for a swim?" I try, already knowing the answer.

Sydney scrunches up her nose. "You must be joking. Do you know how long it took me to do this contour?" She waves a hand over her face as if revealing a magic trick. "I'll go make you a beverage for when you get out." She turns back, holding up a pointer finger. "No alcohol. I'm sure you're on the clock."

I strip down to my bathing suit, which I grabbed on my way over here, and wade in a few feet before taking a shallow dive. I feel the water come up around me, soothing me instantly and making my mind go blank, if only for one precious moment. I keep thinking about Ava's offer. The spark I felt when she mentioned it. I think about what it would feel like to be somewhere else. And then, just a for a little while, I close my eyes and picture it.

I hear someone else dive in after me, and think maybe Sydney changed her mind after all, or maybe Tessa saw me from the barn. But when I rise to the surface, it's not Sydney who I find gazing back at me.

"Look who finally showed up," Tucker says, his hair slicked back with water, his freckled skin already starting to get some color.

"What did I miss?" I ask.

"Oh, serious stuff." Tucker wades toward me. "Vince Mahony got a new truck for his birthday, and it looks like our baseball team is going to be pretty strong this year. Oh, and Eleanor Olson would like all of us to strongly consider going vegetarian, for environmental reasons."

I put one hand on either side of my face. "Can't believe I missed those groundbreaking revelations. If only I had gotten here sooner."

Tucker takes a step closer in the shallow water. "It feels like I never see you. You're always working or something."

I move my hand through the flat water. "It's not intentional." Though as I say the words, I know I'm lying a little bit. "I just like to keep moving."

"But look around," Tucker says, and I do. The sun has lowered in the sky, just over the tops of the trees, and everything is lit with undertones of pink. "Shouldn't you actually be slowing down? Isn't this supposed to be the best time of our lives?"

I let my eyes roam over the crowd, kids talking loudly to each other as they play drinking games or shoot videos for social media. I watch my friends at a distance, Tessa standing in the doorway to the barn with her back to Marcus, who is having a conversation next to her. He leans back and nudges her butt with his. Yup, they are definitely back together. I pan over to where Sydney is talking to a handsome boy from the swim team, laughing with her hand to her chest.

I watch these people I grew up with, having the time of their lives . . . and I don't really feel anything.

Before I can respond to Tucker, he keeps talking. "I was thinking maybe we could take a hike tomorrow."

I frown. "Since when do *you* hike?" I ask warily.

Tucker snorts. "Come on. I hike!" He makes a face. "Maybe not as much as I'd like to, but I thought this would be a good opportunity." He gives me a little nudge. "Okay, *you* hike. I just wanted to hang out. There's something I want to talk to you about."

Tucker is buzzed. I can see it in the redness of his eyes, the openness. *Could he* be *more into you?* I can hear Sydney say. Tucker is handsome, and he's kind, and if I recall, he's also a pretty great kisser. Maybe it wouldn't be the worst idea to just give him a chance.

But he's still Tucker.

I inhale a deep breath and let it out. Tucker is a great guy, but we've never been on the same page. Over his shoulder, I see Sydney is now watching us carefully.

"It's been a pretty busy weekend. Rain check?"

He nods.

I climb out of the water and realize I haven't eaten much today besides the scones Theo gave me, so I grab a towel and head over to a table filled with chips, seltzer, and cookies. I pull out my phone, sifting through some of my old artwork, landing on a multimedia piece I did last spring, part photograph, part paint, part organic materials. I wonder if it's good enough for Ava, or if I need to start from scratch.

Nicole Meyers walks up, dropping some pieces of popcorn into her mouth and leaning over to look at my phone. "No way. That's yours? I saw it in the student center." Nicole is the captain of the lacrosse team, and a straight-A student. She's exceptionally nice, but I don't think we've had a conversation since freshman bio. I feel that brief stabbing pain of terror in the pit of my stomach, the one that happens when someone is about to tell me what they think of something I've made. Did they love it, or hate it? Will they try to pretend they liked it when it's obvious they didn't?

"I *loved* it," she says. "Seriously, I'd hang it on my wall if I could."

"Thanks," I say, breathing a sigh of relief and feeling genuinely flattered.

"I'm hoping to get into AP Art next year," she continues. "You already took it, right?"

I nod. "Yeah, it's great. I'm doing an elective now, actually." I pause. "So, you've taken Intro to Studio and Art 2?"

Nicole nods enthusiastically. "Yeah, I'm in Art 2 now. It's so good. Miss Jamali is a genius."

"I'm obsessed with her," I say. "I want her to be my best friend. What's your favorite medium to work with?"

Nicole shrugs. "Sort of everything? But I'm really interested in sculpture." She grabs more popcorn off the table and puts it carefully in her mouth, chewing thoughtfully. "I was super interested in Daniel Winters's work at MaCA last summer. Did you see it? His use of found objects with local resources?" She shakes her head. "Incredible."

I feel a sort of shiver run through my body, like someone just sprinkled me with fairy dust. The only person I ever have conversations like this with is my mom. I'm just about to ask Nicole if maybe she wants to go to MaCA together sometime when a guy comes barreling out of nowhere and throws her over his shoulder.

An "Eeep!" escapes Nicole.

"Too much chatting. More swimming," he says, before running with her, fully clothed, into the lake.

"Nice talking to you, Charlie!" Nicole cries, her words vibrating with every leap the guy takes.

I shake my head, turning back to the snacks. As much as I want to pretend that we are somewhere else, somewhere we can talk about art, and sculpture, we're still in Chester Falls. And someone is still going to get thrown into the lake.

As I look around for my friends, I hear a ding on my phone.

A ride.

"Perfect timing," I whisper to nobody but myself, and head off to find my car, somehow feeling lonelier than I did when I arrived.

At least I have work to do.

♥ ♥ ♥

But my usual feeling of purpose diminishes when I emerge onto the side road by Tessa's pond, to an area packed with cars and shaded by trees, and find my new rider waiting for me. Except I'm not sure you could call it waiting, since it's not even clear if he's conscious. He's slumped between two of his friends, his arms hanging around their shoulders, his head forward. I walk up just in time to hear him mumble:

"I don't feel so good."

"Lucky me," I say.

Drunk kid, whose name is Chris, according to my phone alert, raises a head and squints up at me. "Who is this?" he asks.

His friends share a glance over the top of his head. I recognize Nick, who's in my ceramics class, and Carter, who helped me paint backdrops for the town play during community service week last year.

"I'm your driver, Charlie," I tell Chris. "You called a ride?"

"Charlie is a boy's name," Chris states, his eyes unfocused.

And I know what rating you're going to get, I think to myself. But I only smile. The sooner I can get Chris moving, the sooner this ride will be finished.

"Sorry about this," Nick tells me. "But he's ruining our whole day. He just threw up in Tessa's alpaca field.

"They were not pleased," Chris says, then he starts to laugh. "The looks on their faces!"

"Whose faces?" I ask.

"The alpacas. They were all, mehhhh." Chris makes a kind

55

of mopey, sour face, turning his smile into a weird frown and flaring his nostrils, before erupting in more laughter.

Nick sighs.

Chris laughs harder, then stops abruptly.

"Are you going to throw up again?" I ask.

"Like I'd tell you," Chris says. Then he turns around and heaves into the bushes.

"I know there's a no barfing policy in Backseat," Carter says. "Maybe we should just see if we can get him to pass out in the grass somewhere . . ."

"I wanna party!" Chris announces, his head still in the bushes.

Carter groans, and I picture the twenty bucks from Chris's ride disappearing into nothingness, not to mention a tip. Twenty fewer dollars in my bank account. Twenty fewer dollars to get me to New Mexico. Besides, I don't want him doing anything stupid that gets the cops called on Tessa.

I shake my head. "No, it's fine. I can handle it."

"Really?" Nick asks.

"You don't know Charlie?" Carter says to Nick. "She's a legend. She'll pick up anyone, anywhere."

"I'm just that kind of gal, I guess," I say brightly, and smile at Chris again, who looks at me distrustfully, and I wonder where he got such a bad attitude from. What's been going on behind the scenes to make him act out like this. People change when they're drunk, though. That's one of my biggest take-aways from being a driver for Backseat. Some get happy, others get mean. Others just wanna keep going until their feet won't hold them anymore.

"I'm not going anywhere," Chris says. "Andre did a beer run. I gave that guy eighteen bucks. He should be back any minute."

His friends roll their eyes.

I sigh heavily, crouching down in front of Chris. "Hey. Do you like Bob's Burgers?" I ask, in a tone I'd only use to speak to a child.

Chris's ears perk up. His unfocused eyes try their best to look at me more clearly. "Yeah. But that's, like, a town over."

"You got cash?" I ask.

Chris nods.

"How about we stop on the way home," I tell him. "You know how good those curly fries are after a late night." It's only six thirty. But Chris doesn't need to know that.

Chris watches me a moment longer. "Fine," he agrees.

I stand up, pleased with myself. Carter and Nick breathe audible sighs of relief as they walk Chris over to my car.

"Wow, I didn't even know they made this model anymore," Carter says, referring to my Prius V, which is either a giant Prius or a tiny minivan, depending on how you look at it. That may be why nobody really bought them. I heard they were big in Japan, though.

"Toyota discontinued them in 2017," I say as I unlock it and open the back door for Chris.

"Wow, that late?" Carter asks, which I'm pretty sure is offensive. The car was a hand-me-down from Aunt Helen, my dad's sister. It's also almost ten years old. But with any luck, the old gal's still got at least twenty thousand miles left in her. She's sturdy, and reliable, and super spacious on the inside, while still being fuel conserving. Driving around, I spend a lot of time thinking about how, as consumers, we spend so much time obsessing over what our cars look like on the outside, when we never even see that part of the car when we're driving. So really, the exterior of the car is for someone else. Don't get me wrong, I love elegant design, but all that should really matter is comfortable seats and a quick engine. Neither of which the Prius V actually has.

"It gets me better mileage on gas," I say, like I need an excuse. Like I need to explain to them why I have this particular car when I'm lucky just to have wheels at all. "What's the point in driving for this app if I spend it all filling up my tank?"

"Making friends!" Chris says, his eyes closed. At this, I can't help but laugh, which makes him smile. "Are you single?" Chris follows. He turns to his friends. "She's hot, right? Or do I have beer goggles on."

"You're an idiot," Nick says.

"An idiot who's got a ride home with a *hottie*," Chris calls out loudly as they get him in the back of my car.

I take out some towels from the trunk, and also a beach bucket. Then I lean inside the car and grab Chris gently by the face. "Listen to me. If you are going to puke, you puke in this. Got it?" I hold the bucket in front of his mouth.

Chris looks at me a moment too long, then he nods. "Aye-aye, captain."

I turn back to Carter and Nick. "You guys are free to go," I tell them, before they gratefully wave goodbye and start walking back to the party.

I hop in the driver's seat and buckle my belt, plugging in my phone and handing a water back to Chris, who takes it and promptly tosses it on the floor. Tessa's property is vast, but in order to stay out of sight of her parents, the cars have to pack all the way into the back, and it's tight on this little road. Where there aren't cars, there are trees, so maneuvering out isn't going to be a piece of cake. Just when I'm trying to carefully reverse, Chris's head comes forward between the two front seats.

"So, you got a boyfriend?" His breath reeks of beer.

"Yes," I lie.

"Damn," he breathes, as I try and peer around him to see out my rear window.

"Could you sit back, please?" I ask, before I notice a look that suddenly comes over his face.

"Uh-oh," he says.

"Are you okay?"

"I think I'm gonna—" he starts.

"USE THE BUCKET," I yell, grabbing it from the seat behind me and shoving it in front of his face to catch his puke. And just when I'm wondering if this is all really worth it, my body is jerked forward and I hear the sound of my car slamming into something. Metal on metal.

Chapter 7

OH NO. OH NO OH NO OH NO. LEAVING CHRIS ALONE
with his face still buried in the bucket, I race to remove my
seat belt and, hands shaking, hop out of my car to survey the
damage, throwing my head in my hands when I confirm what
I did: hit a parked car. If you can even call it that. It's an ancient
Saab painted a kind of barf-brown color that is all but taped
together. In fact, as I look more closely, I see that parts of it *are*
taped together. The side mirror, and the front bumper, which
I have just nearly taken clean off.

Someone else is surveying the damage, too. At first, all I
see is a T-shirt draped over wide shoulders, and olive skin on
the back of his neck, a pair of car keys dangling from his fin-
gertips. As he turns, and our eyes meet, I realize whose car I
just hit.

"Nice work," Andre Minasian says, his tone coming out
not quite mean, exactly. But it's not kind, either.

"I'm *so* sorry," I tell him, my hand to my forehead. "I've got a drunk kid in the back, and he was going to puke, and I didn't want him getting it all over my car."

Andre's brows go up. "So you thought you'd trash mine instead?"

I frown. "No . . . I got distracted." I pause as Andre walks closer to me. His face, like his tone, is neither unkind nor friendly. It's easy. Confident, like it always is. Is this not a big deal to him? "I'm a really good driver, I swear. I drive for Backseat? I have, like, the highest rating in the county."

Not anymore, I think then.

"Not anymore," Andre says out loud, looking at the bumper. "This thing is barely going to be drivable."

Something inside me twitches. "I mean, to be fair, was it drivable before?"

Andre turns back to me and makes a face. "What's that supposed to mean?"

"It's literally held together with duct tape. It's from, like, 1989. It's older than both of us combined."

Andre surveys me. "How do you know it's an eighty-nine?"

I roll my eyes. "It was a guess. GM started buying out Saab in 1989, after which all their design went to shit. This was one of the last good ones." I pause. "My dad and I like cars."

Now Andre frowns, opens his mouth, closes it, and opens it again. "And I suppose you can really tear up the open road in that massive Prius?" he says, looking at my car, which, surprisingly, is fine, thank god.

"Maybe not, but I can go three times as far as you can with that gas guzzler."

Andre rolls his eyes. "Whatever. I just hope you have insurance."

This makes me stop smiling. I *do* have insurance, of course. Everyone who drives in the state of Massachusetts has to have it. But if we call my insurance, they will alert the parent company that owns Backseat. And that will not be good.

"Isn't there some other way we can work this out?" I ask.

"You could just pay it out of pocket," Andre says, opening the back passenger door of his car.

I swallow. "For a foreign car like this? It'll take me months to pay for." My stomach turns. And I can basically forget about my road trip.

Andre rummages around in his back seat. "Well, I really need a set of wheels right now, and this is all I've got. You should probably move your car, by the way. You're blocking the road."

As I turn back to my car, my heart sinking, Chris hops out of the back, still clutching his barf bucket.

"Hey bro," he says. "You're back. Did you get my beer?"

Andre nods at Chris in response, and something clicks in my brain. *Andre did a beer run. I gave that guy eighteen bucks,* Chris said earlier. Now, Andre has just emerged with two twenty-four-packs of beer, with a big brown paper bag stacked on top.

"*He* bought you beer?" I ask Chris, just to be sure I heard him right.

Chris looks at me like I'm an idiot as he wavers. "Of course. This is Andre! I thought everyone knew him?" He looks at Andre. "I thought everyone knew you?"

Andre shrugs.

"No, I know who he *is,* but . . . just to be clear, did Andre also buy you beer earlier?"

I see a look of understanding come over Andre's face and he opens his mouth just as Chris laughs. "No, he bought it last weekend," he says. "Andre buys everyone's booze. I bet seventy-five percent of the party over there is drinking because of him."

Andre closes his eyes tightly and takes a breath.

"Is that so?" I tilt my heard toward Andre. "What a good Samaritan."

"He's making a bigger deal out of it." Andre starts walking toward the opening in the woods. I reach out a hand and stop him.

"Well, isn't this just classic," I say.

"What?" Andre asks. "What exactly is so classic about this?"

"You just waltzing into the situation, here to get the party started, and yet you're untouchable. Others have to suffer the consequences."

Andre's brows go up and then he looks pointedly at his car. "Are you serious? Did we both witness what just happened to my car?"

I sigh. "The only reason I hit your stupid tuna fish can of a car was because one of the kids you got irresponsibly drunk, and then, might I add, went to buy *more* alcohol for, was about to vomit in the front seat of *my* car."

Andre shakes his head. "So?"

This makes something flare up inside me, and it's hard to keep from raising my voice. "So, had you not bought him that alcohol in the first place, none of us would even be standing here."

"Um, guys?" Chris asks. He leans an arm on Andre, who gently pushes him off.

Andre looks at me like I'm crazy. "Says who?"

"Don't be dumb," I say.

"Guys . . ." Now I am the one who has to wiggle out of Chris's grasp.

Andre leans in closer to me. "Maybe you're a bad driver. Or maybe you were distracted tonight. Maybe hitting my car had absolutely nothing to do with the fact that Chris was about to puke in yours."

"What a cop out!" I tell Andre. "What difference does it even make to you? The price of my deductible would literally be the cost of what it would take to buy this trash heap from you right now!"

"What is your *problem*?" Andre says, getting closer, his eyes wide in exasperation.

"Guys like *you*," I say. "Who only care about getting drunk, and having a good time, when some of us actually want more for ourselves. But why would you worry about that?"

Andre pulls back and squints at me. "Is this because I told you your music sucked?"

"No!" I practically scream.

But just when I'm really leaning into it, Chris leans in too.

And he barfs on both of our shoes.

Andre and I look down at our feet, and when our eyes meet again, his are stone cold. "You're paying for my car," he says.

"At this rate, you're lucky I don't make you pay for my shoes, too." With that, he heads off into the woods.

♡ ♡ ♡

"Wait!" I call, after hastily pulling my car back into its original spot and following Andre through the woods as he hustles around partygoers, his arms weighed down with the two cases. He sets them heavily on a table with a loud clink and looks around with a satisfied expression. The crowd cheers.

"We love you, Andre!" a girl exclaims.

I grimace.

Andre forces a smile, then, after casting a sidelong glance at me, takes his puke-covered canvas shoes off and carries them in one hand as he walks with purpose toward the pond. I follow. The entire walk down, it seems like not a single person can help acknowledging Andre in some way. He asks after their parents, checks in on their game scores from the previous day, inquires as to how their violin lessons are going.

"I didn't realize you were the mayor of Chester Falls High," I say as we reach the water's edge, and a boy hands Andre a book, tells him it changed his life, and thanks him for loaning it out.

Andre stuffs the book in the back of his jeans, ignoring my observation, and dangles his canvas sneakers into the pond and shakes them off. Clouds of barf loosen in the water. I decide to follow suit, dunking my own shoes in and out.

We stand there for a moment, sloshing and sloshing, until I finally break the silence.

"Look, I really am sorry," I say. "Trust me, I didn't want this to happen any more than you did."

Andre turns and looks at me, and I never noticed how warm his brown eyes are.

"I'm sorry that Chris puked in your car and you lost control," he says. "But you are going to have to pay for damages, one way or another."

I nod, my heart rate rising, as I sit down at the edge of the pond. "It's not that I don't want to help you fix it . . . it's that I can't let you report it."

Andre frowns. "Why?"

I swallow. "Because I really, *really* need this job." Before I can stop it, a vision of my parents at home, my dad in front of the TV, pops into my head. It's funny when the mind pulls stuff like this. Takes you to places you had no intention of going, and you scramble to catch up. But you almost always know how it got there. *Reminder: I'm not going to get stuck here* is what my brain seems to be telling me right now. "It's a lot to explain," I tell Andre. "But I already got one violation earlier this year, and if I get two, I'm done."

"Don't you have a job at Wild Oats, though?"

I give him a wary look. "Are you obsessed with me or something?"

Andre looks bored. "Please, Charlie. Our town has like two people in it. My mom likes their gluten free carrot cake. I've seen you there."

"I don't work there. I just hang out there a lot. Backseat offers me tips, and it also offers me the added bonus of working while I'm doing other things, like driving to school, or parties, or going to do errands." I turn to face Andre now. "I really can't afford to lose it."

Andre picks up one of his shoes, looks it over, then places it back in the grass again. "Well, I can't afford to lose my car. I have places I need to be."

"Like on beer runs?"

Andre raises an eyebrow. "Make jokes all you want, but it's not going to help your situation."

I bite my lip. This is not going well. Tears start to form behind my eyes as I imagine my bank account, which I've been working so hard for, getting whittled down to nothing. How is this really happening? How did this go from one of the best days of my life to one of the worst?

Andre seems to notice, and he looks suddenly flustered, too. "Tears aren't going to help, Charlie," he says, looking away.

"Charlie?" I hear a voice call, and Andre looks behind me, smirking.

"Looks like your problems are just beginning."

I turn to see Chris leaning against a tree, looking green. "Charlie?" he calls again. "I really need to go home now."

"On my way," I call back, standing up and wiping a tear from my eye, grateful to have an excuse to leave before Andre sees me cry.

"Hey!" Andre says, and when I turn back to him, I find him standing, his arms out wide. "Are you serious right now? You can't just walk away, Charlie. We have to figure this out."

I swallow, feeling desperate. "Look at him, Andre. He's a liability. I *really* need to get him home." As terrible as all this is, I can't help but see dark humor in the fact that Chris is the reason I got into this in the first place, and he's also getting me out of it.

"And how am *I* supposed to get home?" Andre wants to know.

"Right. That . . ." I pull out my phone, look Andre up, and send him some Backseat credits.

His phone goes off with a buzz, and he scrutinizes the screen. "What is this?

"It's enough to get you home later tonight." I turn back around, heading in the direction I just saw Chris stumble off. "I'll figure out how to fix it," I call back, trying not to let my voice shake. "I promise."

♡ ♡ ♡

Later that night, after Chris and I pick up burgers to give him time to sober up, and I drop him off at his parents' house, I'm out in my mom's studio, admiring her work.

My mom's painting studio is a perfect little haven on my parents' property. Mom says that when they first bought the house, it was just a large, run-down chicken coop that hadn't been used in years, with a broken door and rotting wood and old hay strewn all about. So she opened the windows wide and cleaned it up, and she patched the holes in the roof, fixed the hinges. She painted the interior the palest, grayest lavender, a color she says brings out her most inspired self, and the exterior she left as natural gray shingles, with white window trim and a turquoise door.

In half of the old hen cubbies she put painting supplies,

old oil tubes, brushes, water mixers, and rags, and in the rest, she added objects that inspire her. Fresh flowers. Postcards and photographs. Blue medicine bottles. Old eggshells she found nested in the rafters.

It smells like acrylics and oil paints, and in the afternoon, it gets hit with the most amazing light. And she is generous enough to share it with me.

My mom says whenever you're stuck, don't force it. Go for a walk, take a deep breath, and think about what really inspires you. How do you invoke that feeling of inspiration in your own work, to inspire others? She's really good at that part, the inspiration. She teaches art part time at the middle school, and she's applied for a job at a few nearby colleges, but nobody will hire her without an advanced degree.

I let my gaze travel over her canvases: abstract landscapes painted in the most unexpectedly beautiful colors. When I was growing up, my dad always tried to look at them and figure out where they were in Berkshire County.

"They are nowhere, Hank!" she'd always exclaim. "That is not the point!"

"I still think this is Round the Bend Farm, though," he would say, more to make her laugh than because he meant it. I remember the way they used to laugh together, heads thrown back and in on the same joke, as though surrounded by some bubble or connected by an invisible current. I remember it because I would always look at them and think, there is so much love in laughter. I haven't seen them laugh that way in a long time.

"What's happening out here?" a curious voice asks now, and I find my mom standing in the little doorway in her pajamas, watching me with her arms crossed.

I sigh, kneeling down to browse her vast collection of art books and museum catalogs. "Do you know how to make a portfolio?"

My mom laughs. "Of course. And I'd be happy to teach you."

I shrug. "I'm just not sure what I have to show for myself."

My mom sits down on an old wooden chair. "Well, that's definitely not true. You've been making stuff since you were a little kid. I set you up with an easel out here with me and you just started churning stuff out. And remember all those incredible wildflower bouquets you made last year for graduation? They could've been in *Vogue*. A portfolio is to show that you have talent and taste, no matter how you use it."

"But I need something to show I can *make* stuff," I say. "Real stuff. For the real world."

My mom lowers her gaze to my shoulders. "Well, how about you start with what you are wearing?"

I glance down and remember the knit vest Ava admired earlier today. "Not this."

Mom's brows knit together as she studies me. "What's gotten into you, doubting yourself like this? You've always been proud of your art."

I reluctantly explain to my mom about Ava, about her offer today. When I'm done, my mom shakes her head. "What an opportunity. Someone you admire so much." She's happy for me, I can tell, but her tone says something else. It's relaxed, and almost . . . removed. Like at the end of the day, this isn't that big a deal. Like life will go on if it doesn't work out.

I bite my lip. "It will be . . . if I can get it . . ."

My mom moves past me toward her painting table, studying all the books she has stacked one on top of the other. "You know, I might be able to help. I was accepted to that visiting artist . . ."

"Yes, the visiting artist program at RISD, I know," I say. "But you didn't go."

"I didn't go. But you will." She steadies her gaze on me. "I get if you don't want your mother's help. But will you at least let me give you a few books? Some things to help inspire you?"

I study my mom in her old robe and the Birkenstock clogs she wears as slippers. She and Ava could not be more different. But she's also the closest person I have to a creative ally in this town.

"Okay," I say. "Thank you."

My mom does a small wave of the hands, a little victory dance. Then she scoots down on the floor with me and starts opening up books, showing me artists and architects she thinks will inspire me.

Later that night as we are heading to bed, I stop my mom at the edge of the stairs. "I ran into Elaine today."

She raises an eyebrow. "So now she's hounding you, too?"

"She just wants to show your work, Mom!" I say. "This could be a big deal for you. A chance to get back out there again."

My mom takes a deep breath. "Charlie, I appreciate that, but I get to decide where and when to show my work."

"But right now you aren't showing it anywhere at all . . ." I push.

"Let me come to this on my own time, sweetheart," she says, closing the discussion and walking off down the hall to bed.

CHARLIE'S BACKSEAT REVIEWS

★★★★★ ILY CHARLIE MARRY ME. Thanks for the burger. YuM — Chris

Chapter 8

ON SUNDAY MORNING I PICK UP LULU COOPER OUTSIDE her home, a low ranch house on a road that runs perpendicular to mine. Lulu gets in the car, says a polite hello to me, shuts the door, and then we're off, just like always. I have picked her up here at exactly nine thirty a.m. and delivered her to the same location every Sunday for the last six months. I now consider it a commitment I can't miss. Yes, there are some Sundays when I want to sleep in, when I want to eat toast in bed and finish up the book I'm reading with no bra on or surf Instagram until my brain feels like Jell-O. But it's nice to be able to count on the income from this ride, and also, I have a weird feeling that Lulu needs me. Just for this one simple task. I had to miss our pickup once, in the beginning, to visit my aunt in Boston. The next time I saw her, Lulu seemed relieved. I never missed a ride again.

This, I think, is because she knows I don't ask a lot of questions, even though there are so many I could ask. For example, what is in the unmarked municipal building just past the town center that I always take her to? Why is she always so nicely dressed? And, most importantly, what is in the little suitcase that she always carries on top of her legs in the back seat, making no effort to explain what it is?

I have my own private theories about this. Maybe she's attending some kind of workshop, or a youth group she'd rather not talk about. Maybe she's working on a public art project that has yet to be revealed. Maybe she's an alien masquerading as a human being, and this building is her secret headquarters where she conducts all her bizarre experiments. Or *maybe* she just wants to be by herself, away from her parents —who can be kind of controlling, I've noticed—and all that's in the little suitcase are paperback books and a pillow to rest her head on.

"Lulu?" I ask her today as she carefully climbs out of the car.

She pauses in the open doorway, looking at me with wide eyes, like she's afraid of what's going to come out of my mouth. Like whatever I say has the potential to disrupt our perfect setup.

Where are you going? I want to say. But I don't. Instead I shake my head, as if trying to make the thought disappear like an Etch A Sketch. "Um, if you need a ride home, just, you know . . ." I hold up my phone in the air and wave it back and forth.

Lulu's mouth forms a small smile. "Thanks, Charlie, but I'm going to meet my mom in town, like always. She thinks I'm at the library. But it's nice to know I can count on you."

And with that, she hops out of the car and walks toward a staircase at the edge of the parking lot.

The other thing I wonder, before she disappears, is why she's so confident I'll keep her secret.

♥ ♥ ♥

After I drop Lulu, I'm just pulling up to a stop sign in town, taking a sip from the water bottle I always keep in the center console, when the passenger-side door of my car opens and Andre gets in.

"Um, excuse me?" I say, looking around, like someone should be present to explain what is happening here.

"Excuse *you*," Andre says. He buckles his seat belt and waits.

"What are you *doing*?"

Andre smiles knowingly. "I'm glad you asked. I *was* waiting for the local bus, you know, considering my car was totaled yesterday? And you just left me there, stranded?"

"I didn't leave you stranded!" I try. "I made sure you had a way to get home."

"Oh, and thanks for that, by the way." Andre nods. "Apparently Emily Jacobson believes that when she drives for the app, she can also give a free ride to six of her closest friends. It was like a clown car in there."

"She shouldn't do that," I start to say. "That's a violation of the rules—"

Andre continues like he doesn't hear me. "And then, lo and behold, while I'm waiting for my severely delayed bus, I see the *very* person who put me in this situation to begin with!" Andre morphs his face into one of mock excitement, before releasing it. "So, I thought, *there's* my solution to a problem I shouldn't be dealing with in the first place."

I cringe, feeling terrible. "Look, I know we still need to figure all this out, but I'm supposed to meet Tessa Walker so I can help her with some stuff on the farm. She hates it when I'm late."

"Correction. *We* don't need to figure out anything. *You* do. You hit *my* car."

I close my eyes for a second. "I know that. I just need a little time."

Andre makes no moves.

"So . . . are you going to get out?"

Andre tugs at his buckled seat belt. "Yeah, good luck with that . . ." He glances down at his watch. "I think church should be letting out in just a few minutes. I'm sure the mayor would love to walk out of those double doors and find you trying to tear me out of your vehicle at a four-way stop sign out front."

I squint at him. "Is this amusing to you?"

Andre leans his head back against the seat. "I try to make light of shitty situations. But, you know, I could always just call Backseat, get this handled, since you seem to be taking your sweet time . . ." He holds up his phone in warning.

I sigh. "Fine. Just tell me where we're going."

♡ ♡ ♡

Ten minutes later we pull up outside Rick's Diner, a streamlined silver building on the edge of town, right near the on-ramp to the highway. Rick's is known for its giant pancakes, funky music, and a ridiculous hamster mascot that often welcomes guests with a dance. Dewey, named after Rick's first beloved childhood pet. It's totally insane, and I love it.

"You're a waiter here?" I ask. "This place is great. We come for my birthday every year. I actually applied for a job once, but they said I was too young." I steal a glance at Andre. I was here with my mom a few weeks ago. On a Sunday. I don't remember seeing Andre anywhere. Just some salty Massachusetts ladies. My favorite.

Andre is already getting out. "I'll see you in five hours," he says.

I hold the door open before he can shut it. "Uh, no, you will *not*."

"Uh, yeah, I *will*," he says back, making his voice sound weird and annoying, which I assume is an impression of me.

I give him a pleading look. "I'm going home after Tessa's. It's Sunday. I already work six days a week plus Sunday morning."

Andre leans into the car, his elbows resting on the window frame. "And now you work Sunday afternoon, too. Until you figure out what you want to do about my car, Charlie, you are going to get me where I need to go," he says. "Don't be late. My mom's making Armenian food tonight. And it is—" He kisses his fingers like an Italian chef.

♡ ♡ ♡

"Sally, I swear to god, you move your hairy butt or I will turn you into a pair of mittens," I hear Tessa say loudly, a little

77

while later, as I round the corner of the Walkers' big main barn, where I find her wrangling a very fluffy, very disobedient alpaca toward the food trough.

"Sally causing trouble again?" I lean over the wooden fence as the animal jerks its ridiculously giant head back and forth. Alpacas look like sheep from an alien planet.

Tessa gives me a tired look. "She wouldn't be so testy if you'd showed up on time. You know she likes you better than me."

I pat Sally on the head. "I'm here now."

Tessa reaches into the pocket of her overalls and throws me a pair of sturdy work gloves. "Let me guess. Another ride?" Then she cringes, touching the lower part of her back like it's tender.

"What's wrong with you?" I ask, pulling on the gloves and moving around into the pen, where Sally now watches me with a curious expression.

"Slept in the barn last night," Tessa mutters. "Not great for the body. Those old cots are from the dark ages."

I pause, trying to make eye contact with Tessa over the top of Sally's fluffy head. "Oh, really?" Tessa only ever sleeps in the barn when there's someone to share it with. And the only person she has ever wanted to share it with is Marcus.

She gives me a wary look. "Don't start."

"So, I take it you and Marcus are back together?"

Tessa blushes, a small smile creeping over her lips. As much as they fight, I can see she really is crazy about him.

"I don't know." She shakes her head. "Maybe this is just what's meant to be. Yeah, we have our problems. But I have a feeling it's gonna be us, forever. Even if we do break up every now and then."

"But what about his cheating?"

Tessa shrugs. "He says he didn't."

I watch her. "And you believe him?"

But Tessa doesn't get defensive. Instead, she bites her lip. "I think I do, yeah. I mean, I'm not saying he's a freaking angel, but I don't think he'd hurt me like that." She fiddles with Sally's rope as Sally makes a slight groan and leans her head over toward me, examining my face.

"Where are your manners, Sally?" I tell her. "It's rude to stare."

These are the moments with Tessa when I don't know what to say. Not because I feel so strongly that she and Marcus shouldn't be together, but because I'm just not sure how to weigh in. I've never felt this way about anyone before. As Michaela Sullivan so clearly noted, not that it's any of her business, I've never been in love. I don't know what it feels like to know a person so well, inside and out. To believe in your future together. Sometimes, I'm not sure I want to. So how could I ever know what kind of advice to give?

"Speaking of boys." Tessa interrupts my thoughts. "What was with you and Andre Minasian at the party yesterday? I didn't know you were even friends," she says. "He left his car here. It looks kind of beat up . . ."

I groan. As I lead Sally out of the barn and start pulling the rest of the alpacas in to eat, one by one, I relay what happened to Tessa, starting with driving Ava Adams, and ending in my ultimate predicament.

"I have no idea what I'm gonna do, Tess. I can't get another strike with Backseat. But I can't just leave him stranded."

"We don't talk for a day, and I miss a lifetime," Tessa says, shaking her head as she puts fresh hay into the alpaca trough. Then she dusts off her work gloves and leans against the fence. "You know what? I'm really happy for you."

I pick some hay off of a furry back. "I'm confused. Did you hear anything I just said?"

Tessa laughs, shaking her head. "Not about the car accident, obviously," she says. "I don't envy that. Though I think a lot of people at school wouldn't mind being stuck in a car with Andre Minasian."

I make a face. "Then they are welcome to take my place. I find him far too insufferable to flirt with."

Tessa raises an eyebrow but continues. "Anyway, I just mean I'm happy for you about Ava. You haven't really seemed like yourself lately. At first, I was kind of hurt, like maybe you didn't want to be around us. But I see now you're just kind of unsettled. You're seeking something. And really, I just want you to be happy."

Tessa has always been proud of her life in Chester Falls, what her family has built. She has big plans for the future of the farm, once it's hers. It's still a lot of hard work, and the reason they have to try so many new crops is to see which one will stick. But they're doing well enough that Tessa has the flexibility to dream. She sees possibility here. And I really envy that.

I look around, over the gorgeous fields and up at the mountain ridge. "It's not necessarily a good feeling, you know. To feel attached to a place but also kind of suffocated by it. It makes me sad."

"Which is exactly why you need to get out. So you can really see the beauty here again." Somehow Sally has found her way back over. She mews loudly in my ear, startling me, and then tries to lick me in the face.

"She is *obsessed* with you," Tessa observes.

We both laugh, just as Tessa's eighteen-year-old brother, Corey, comes following their mother out of the house, pissed off.

"Come on, Mom," he's in the middle of saying. "You don't want to be driving me around any more than I do! The dealership on Route 7 is having a special, and there is a perfect red pickup right out front. What do you say?"

"And please explain to me why we would buy you a new car, Corey, when you totaled your last one by off-roading it in the gorge?" She turns to me, gives a big warm wave. "Hi, girls!"

"Hi, Mrs. Walker!" I call back.

Tessa's mom turns back to Corey. "Just get in the damn car, Corey. You'll have to tag along with me like always until we figure out a better option."

Corey groans. "Fine, but next time I'm using Backseat. I'd rather use that than have to tag along with you like some middle schooler."

I shake my head as I watch Corey amble around the side of his mom's SUV, completely oblivious to his sheltered antics. Apparently to him, owning a car that you can't take care of is a right, not a privilege. Having to ride with his mom for a little while will do him good.

And then I realize, I might have an idea.

♥ ♥ ♥

A little under five hours after I dropped Andre off, I show up at Rick's with a peace offering: a small carrot cake I picked up at Wild Oats on the way. I'm early, so I park and order a coffee while I wait. I don't see Andre anywhere, so I ask one of the waitresses, Lindy, about him as I sip from a big heavy diner mug at the counter.

Lindy looks at me a second too long, her eyes blank. Then she rolls her eyes. "Oh, honey, he's not a waiter."

I frown. "I just dropped him off here this morning! Is he a busboy? Dishwasher?" I crane my head around, trying to peer into the kitchen from my seat.

Lindy raises an eyebrow, motions out the window with her chin, her lips pursed like she's trying not to laugh. There on the side of the road, doing a ridiculously embarrassing dance for passersby, is Dewey the hamster. As if feeling my gaze, Dewey finishes his dance and looks up, locks onto me through his giant hamster eyes, and then hangs his giant hamster head in defeat.

♥ ♥ ♥

Minutes later, I'm seated across a booth from Andre, who has changed back out of his costume into his usual T-shirt and jeans. Next to us, on the table, is a costume hamster head. I stare into its empty, soulless face. Noticing my discomfort, Andre takes the head and quietly puts it on the bench next to him.

"You told me you were a waiter." I frown.

Andre shakes his head. "No, you made an *assumption* that I was a waiter. I let you *believe* I was a waiter, rather than an oversize hamster that dances in front of the diner every Sunday and Thursday."

I grin.

Andre frowns. "What?"

"I'm surprised, that's all. Delightfully surprised."

"Well, my dad says there's value in hard work, whatever that work looks like."

I raise my eyebrows. Chester Falls' biggest party boy has a strong work ethic? I did not expect this.

Andre gestures toward the box on the table. "Thanks for the cake," he says. "Super nice, but you shouldn't have bothered. You're not going to get out of this."

I shake my head. "I'm not trying to get out of it. I have an idea that I think will solve all of our problems."

Andre looks genuinely surprised. "Okay . . ."

I take another sip of coffee, steeling myself. "You need to get your car fixed, which is going to take a while. Most importantly, you need a ride."

Andre nods.

"And I need to keep driving people for Backseat, so I can keep saving money."

"What for?" Andre asks. He leans forward on the table and rests his chin in his palm, still listening intently as I grow increasingly uncomfortable. It feels weird to be watched so closely.

"Same stuff as everyone else." I decide to look out the window while I explain the rest. "So, I figured out a way for us to do all of those things. While we wait for your car to be fixed, I'll drive you where you need to go. I'll pay for half of your repairs, and you can pay for the other half."

Andre's brows knit together. "And why would I pay for any of it, when you hit me?"

I swallow. "Two reasons. One, because you're the one who got my passenger drunk, and I'd hate to have to report the Kegger King to the local police."

As Andre opens his mouth to protest, I cut him off. "And two, because I won't just be giving you free rides. I'll be saving you money on gas, mileage, and extra wear and tear on a car that, let's face it, isn't going to last that much longer anyway."

I force myself to finally look into Andre's eyes, ready for him to call my bluff and say no. After all, I'm the one who wrecked his car, and he'd be doing me a huge favor. Besides, why would he want to be tied down to me?

"You'll take me anywhere I wanna go, anytime, no questions asked?"

"Will you agree not to report me to Backseat?" I shoot back.

"I asked you first."

I sigh. "Fine. Yes. If you agree to keep this between us, then I will drive you anywhere you want to go."

Andre frowns, tapping his foot as he thinks. "Okay."

As I let his words sink in, I feel relief slowly wash over me. This is going to be okay. I am not going to lose my job. I am not going to lose Ava. And I can get back to more important things, like my portfolio.

I hold up my hand in the air, forcing a smile.

Andre looks at it suspiciously. "What is that?"

I look at my hand. "It's a high five."

Andre doesn't move.

"Don't be a jerk," I tell him.

Andre shrugs, slaps my hand, then picks up the hamster head in one hand, and the cake in the other.

"Hey, maybe you won't even notice that you're not driving your own car?" I try.

"Somehow I doubt that." He stands up straight.

"Well, sir," I say. "Time to return to your residence?"

Andre gives me a look.

"Get it?" I ask. "Because I'm your chauffeur now?"

Andre sighs and walks out, leaving me standing there.

"You need to work on your sense of humor," I call after him.

CHARLIE'S BACKSEAT REVIEWS

★★★★★ Transported 30 cartons of farm fresh eggs to the market when the truck broke down, didn't bat an eye. Also, she's hot. 😉
—Tessa

Chapter 9

ON MONDAY MORNING, MY MOM COMES DOWN TO find me on the back porch, flipping through a book she gave me on female artists of the twentieth century. I can feel her pause with the screen door half open, unsure of whether to interrupt me or not.

"Anything interesting?" she finally asks as she leans against the doorframe with her coffee.

"Susan Rothenberg is pretty cool," I tell her, turning the page and showing her Rothenberg's paintings, most of them done in pastel or muted colors with direct, clear imagery. Her most famous early work included large-scale horses; big, bold, physical creatures on giant canvases, which she never thought people would really care about, but ended up causing a frenzy. But when she moved to a ranch in New Mexico with her husband, sculptor Bruce Nauman, her work became more narrative, more lifelike. Like, the experience of being bitten by a snake. Or watching her elderly dog rest its head after a long day. Two bluebirds making a nest. They're striking and moving in unexpected ways.

"Do you know Bruce wasn't allowed to enter her studio unless she gave him permission?" my mom asks as she comes over and takes a seat next to me on the bench.

I look up from the page. "Really?"

My mom shakes her head wistfully. "She was kind of ambivalent about him at times. She loved him, and you can see that in some of her work, but she also was very focused on her own craft."

"I can understand that," I say. "Why let someone get in the way of your vision?"

"Oh, *you* can understand that?" My mom smirks at me.

"I think sometimes love can hold you back." I pause, regretting how loaded the comment sounds as soon as it leaves my mouth.

But my mom doesn't seem to notice. She takes a sip of coffee, then says: "She was like Georgia O'Keeffe in that way. Georgia's relationship with Alfred Stieglitz was more as working partners than lovers."

"Now *that* sounds familiar." I turn a page, not looking at my mom. "Two people living together, under one roof, with no romantic relationship to speak of."

"Ha-ha," my mom says, not taking the bait. "This was very different."

How? I want to ask, but I don't push it.

I sit back on the porch bench, examining the yard, the old barn, and her studio, with its chipping paint and lopsided hinges. "Speaking of studios, yours could use a coat of paint, you know. Maybe a new door."

My mom shrugs. "I like it this way. It feels like *itself.* Like it should be." She stares at it for a moment, as if lost in thought, and I wonder if she's lying. Or if she'd rather just accept it instead of wish for something she can't have. "Anyway, what are you doing up so early, besides learning about art and feminism and giving your mother a hard time?"

I close the book, checking the time on my phone. "I have to pick someone up before school."

"Reggie, that sweet kid who got bullied on the school bus?" She looks at her watch. "But he's just down the road. You'll be early if you leave now . . ."

I shake my head. "A new rider. I've added one more to the morning route." I don't want to tell my mom what happened, that I owe someone hundreds of dollars. She'd probably just tell me to call the insurance company and give up my whole plan.

My mom looks down at her coffee for a moment. "I worry you're burning the candle at both ends."

I inhale slowly through my nose, practicing some yoga breathing that Sydney taught me the other day to deal with stress. "I have to save my money. Now more than ever, since I might get to go to New Mexico."

My mom nods. "I just don't want you putting too much pressure on yourself, that's all. I know things around here aren't . . ." She pauses. "What you might want them to be. But I don't want you missing out on anything. Or burning out altogether. That's all I'm saying. When I was living in New York—"

I shake my head, standing up and grabbing my empty coffee mug. "I know, I know," I tell her. "It was the best time of your whole life, until you met Dad. Can we not have another story of all the things you left behind when you moved to this tiny town?"

My mom blinks. "I don't really see it like that. I just feel nostalgic sometimes." She comes over and puts a hand on my arm. "Certain parts of our lives aren't meant to be forever. But that doesn't mean that they don't shape who we are. Don't forget that. Okay?"

I swallow, feeling heat rising to my cheeks.

"Okay," I say. "I better go. I don't want to be late."

♥ ♥ ♥

A little while later I pull up outside Reggie's house. He is out the door before I've even put the car in park, hustling down the stone pathway, his oversize backpack swinging his small body to and fro. I don't know exactly what happened on the school bus last month, but I know it was bad enough that Reggie's parents are more than happy to buy a monthly ride package so he can come with me instead for the foreseeable future. His mother leans out the door, her arm extended in an eager wave. I wave back as Reggie throws his body into the back seat and heaves a dramatic sigh.

"I'm worried about Nathan," he says plainly as I pull away from the curb.

"Who?" I ask.

"Nathan. My tadpole? For months he hasn't grown any legs. But now he has grown legs, but those legs aren't growing fast enough. And don't even get me started on his nonexistent arms. The textbook says those should have grown in ages ago."

I tune out at this point, still stewing over the conversation with my mom. How does she not realize she's telling me two contradictory things? To slow down, appreciate what I have, and to not miss out on what matters? I can't do both.

"So anyway, maybe Nathan is just a bit of a late bloomer," Reggie is saying as we pull up outside of Andre's house. When I dropped Andre off here it was dark out, but now, in the morning light, I take it in. Unlike the rest of the houses on the street, with white picket fences and cream-colored shingles, the shingles on Andre's house are a deep, natural wood, with burnt-red trim. I think I can spot the edge of a fenced-in vegetable garden around the back. There's a coziness about the place, a way that it seems to welcome you home while also blending in seamlessly with the surrounding trees. "But I mean, so am I, so I can't really fault him for that," Reggie continues.

"What?" I ask, distracted.

"I'm a late bloomer," Reggie repeats. "Like Nathan." Irritation creeps into his voice. "Are you even listening?"

"Um, not really," I admit. "Sorry."

"Well, what's wrong?" Reggie asks.

"Look, Reggie," I say. "I don't get involved in the lives of my passengers, as much as I can help it, so you don't have to get involved in mine."

"Fine," Reggie mumbles, clearly hurt, and I cringe inwardly. I want to take it back.

It's at this moment that I see Andre step out his front door and stride down the path toward us. His mom, a friendly-looking woman with short, dark brown hair, is digging around in her garden out front. I wonder what he told his parents about this situation. If he made up some excuse, or if he told them the truth: some crazy chick rammed into him with her puke mobile, and now refuses to pay for it.

"Morning," I say as Andre ducks into the passenger seat of the car. His hair is still wet, and he smells like soap, and he's crunching on a granola bar with his mouth half open. He says nothing to me in response.

"Morning!" Reggie says. "I'm Reg." I make a face. *Reg?*

"Hey, dude." Andre cranes his head around toward the back seat, offering Reggie a hand. "I'm Andre. What's up?"

"I know who you are," Reggie says quickly, not embarrassed whatsoever. "And nothing much, just talking about tadpoles, I guess."

I try to suppress a snort as I pull away from Andre's house and take a right out on the main road heading toward school. Andre notices my expression, but instead of laughing, he turns back to Reggie.

"Cool, man. You're a freshman?" he asks.

I watch Reggie nod enthusiastically in the rearview mirror.

"Don't take this the wrong way, but you look kind of young, even for that. How old are you?"

I glance back at Reggie, wondering if he'll be offended by this. But instead, he looks proud.

"I skipped a grade."

"You *did*?" I say. "I didn't know that." It all makes so much sense. Why he's so innocent. My affection for him grows in this moment. How brave he is, going it alone.

"You never asked." Reggie shrugs.

"Wow. I'm lucky I *passed* eighth grade, and you straight-up skipped it?" Andre lays his head back against the seat. "What's your secret, Reg? What makes you tick?"

"He just told you he's technically in the eighth grade," I mutter. "How does he know what really makes him tick?"

Andre looks skeptical. "Reg, what do you have to say about that?"

Turns out Reggie has a great deal to say on this topic, what his pursuits and passions are, giving Andre the full rundown of the tadpole life cycle, what his hopes are for Nathan, and when he plans to release him into the wild.

But Andre doesn't stop there. He asks Reggie about everything. When is his birthday? What did he do this summer? Does he like sports? What movies has he seen lately that he would recommend? I have to admit it surprises me, and I can't decide if it's in a good or bad way. I mean, I knew Andre could charm anyone. I just didn't know he chose to. Especially freshmen most seniors wouldn't even know exist.

"Oh, that new one with Meryl Streep that just came out?" I try to add, but Andre ignores me, choosing only to interact with Reggie for the rest of the ride. My annoyance grows slowly until we pull up at school.

"So, is it going to be like this every time?" I ask, after Reggie gets out of the car and Andre has his door open.

"What?" he asks.

"You punishing me, or whatever?"

Andre looks back at me absently over one shoulder. "You

know what I really wanted to do when I woke up this morning, Charlie?"

I roll my eyes. "What."

"I wanted to take a shower, get in my car, and go grab a giant iced coffee in town, before moseying my way to school. But I can't do that anymore. Would you like to know why?"

I breathe slowly through my nose. "I have an idea."

"I'm sure you do," he says.

"I mean, I can *bring* you iced coffee, if that's what you want," I offer.

"What I want is to have my car back." He groans.

"You and me both!" I call out as he stands up, grabbing his bag. I feel relieved to have him finally out of my car. But before I can drive away, he sticks his head back in.

"See you at four," he says.

I balk. "Four? School gets out at two thirty!"

"And lacrosse practice gets out at four," Andre calmly replies.

"And what would we do without lacrosse?" I smile, through gritted teeth. Then seeing the look on Andre's face, I backtrack. "I guess I have a project I could work on for a few hours."

"That's the spirit," Andre says, giving the roof of the car a double tap. Then he strides off into school leaving me fuming.

I put my head on the steering wheel and groan. This is going to be harder than I thought.

Chapter 10

LATELY, I'VE BEEN THINKING A LOT ABOUT WHAT MAKES a place start to feel small. And I don't just mean a room, or a building. I mean a whole place. Like a high school, or a town, or a community. When it goes from the beauty of the familiar to something worse. When it goes from feeling like exhaling a deep breath to feeling like it's closing in on you. Like you're living in *Groundhog Day*. Like there's no room or possibility to grow.

I used to have all of these favorite things about Chester Falls. Like this one particular loopy, windy stretch of road that always made me feel like I was in a luxury car commercial. Or the old Victorian that someone recently repainted in sage green and removed all the shutters from, making it look unexpectedly modern. Or the field just past Tessa's farm that's filled with the most incredible variety of wildflowers, like somebody imagined it and then painted it there on the side of the road.

But now, sometimes when I'm driving through Chester Falls, it's like I can see two versions of it, two parallel universes, layered over each other. One of them is comforting, the other terrifying. Like if I'm not careful, I'll be looking at these things, and only these things, for the rest of my life.

I'm sitting in the cafeteria at lunch with Sydney, considering all of this, when Grant Chase walks by and takes my sketch pad right out of my hands, scooping it up with ease.

I take a deep breath and calmly stand. "Could I have that back?"

Grant turns. "What do you even *do* with this?" He flaps it around, before opening it up and spinning through the pages with his grubby fingers. Sketches of people, of landscapes, of imaginary buildings and real buildings alike, flash by. "Seriously."

"Why does it matter to you what I do with it?" I ask, feeling my blood start to boil. But with guys like Grant, freaking out is exactly what they want. You have to remain calm. If you get upset, it only eggs them on. If you do nothing, they get bored.

"I dunno," he says, scoffing, like he's searching the depths of his mind for any rational response. I imagine the inside of his brain, a hollowed-out space filled with cobwebs and internet porn. "It's just weird. Like, join the real world already. Or sit with the art kids. Pick a side."

I frown, and open my mouth to say something, like, *Oh, really? You think THIS is the real world?* when Sydney speaks out for me.

"Hey, Grant?" she says sweetly, twisting her hair around her finger.

Grant instantly softens. He comes and sits down at the edge of the bench next to her, and leans over his knees, looking at her adoringly. Sydney is without a doubt the most sought-after girl in our grade, maybe even our school. But she doesn't date. I've asked her about it, why she never goes for anyone, but she always just shrugs off my question, saying she hasn't met the right person.

"Could you do something for me?" Sydney is asking Grant in her sweetest tone.

"Anything for you, babe," Grant says.

Sydney tilts her head to one side, looking at him admiringly. "Could you stop being such a walking caricature of yourself, give Charlie her sketch pad back, and maybe *try* getting a life?"

It seems to take Grant a moment to register the words Sydney is actually saying, since her tone remained sickly sweet the entire time. Then he frowns, glares at me, and drops the sketchbook on the table with a loud *bang,* so loud that most of the other tables turn to look.

"Whatever." He shrugs. "Just imagine there's better stuff you could be doing with your time."

"Like what, making fart jokes in class and humping people in the hallway?" I ask.

"Have a nice day, ladies." Grant all but laughs in my face before returning to a table of hockey players. They high-five, for what, I have no idea.

"Oh, we will *now,*" Sydney says back, watching him walk away with an ice-cold look. I can't help but snicker at this.

"God, I can't wait to get away from assholes like that," I say.

Sydney shrugs. "At least here we can talk *back* any way we want. In the real world, someone like Grant ends up being your boss. At least in our little town we're all on the same playing field."

"I'm just over it," I tell her, shaking my head and putting my sketch pad back in my bag, where nobody can steal it away from me.

Sydney side-eyes me. "I can tell."

I look at her. "Meaning . . ."

Sydney shrugs. "Meaning, you're just giving off a general vibe these days. Like, you're okay being here, but you're not excited about it. Like you stopped giving this place a chance."

"What place?" I want to know.

Sydney sighs. "This town. Our *home*."

I take a deep breath. "I've lived here for seventeen years. I think I've given it a chance. Besides, maybe I don't want to get stuck here."

Sydney takes a sip from her drink. "You mean like your mom?"

"Like both of them," I mutter.

"It's so interesting. Because to *me,* your mom is just a super-chill lady with a great sense of color, enviable hair, and a vast handmade clog collection," Sydney says, while simultaneously tapping away on her phone.

I snort. "To me she is a woman who constantly wishes she was someplace else."

"She always *seems* happy," Sydney says, now examining her manicure, a unique, tiny ice cream cone perfectly painted on each nail.

"She's living in a house with a man she no longer loves, dreaming about all the fun she used to have in her life," I say.

"Well, maybe you don't know the full story," Sydney tries.

I'm considering this just as Andre walks by and gives me a look that neither acknowledges me nor ignores me altogether. I give it right back.

"And what, may I ask, was that?" Sydney watches me with wide eyes. I sigh, resting my head in my hand, before filling her in on what happened at Tessa's party, and my new reality with Andre Minasian.

"So now you have to, what, like drive him around all the time?" she asks.

I let out a groan. "Yup." Andre in my car, asking my passengers too many questions. Andre chewing loudly on a granola bar. Andre and his ever-confident, happy attitude, which he seems to want to use on anyone but *me*.

But when I look up to meet Sydney's eye again, she's smiling at me.

"What?" I ask.

Sydney shrugs, as though trying not to laugh. "It's just that Andre Minasian is hot. Everyone thinks so."

I frown, glancing over to where Andre has just sat down with a group of friends, mostly skiers and a few guys on the lacrosse team. There's an abundance of fleece, of microfiber half-zips and wool sweaters, happening at that table.

Sydney leans over, locking her eyes with mine. "Come *on*," she says. "Tell me you don't see it. Especially that jaw."

I look closer at Andre, who is holding a french fry in his hand as he gestures wildly while he talks. I take in his high cheekbones. His hair, nearly jet black, which is pushed away from his face.

"I guess he does have a nice neck," I say, observing the way it slopes into his sweatshirt. There's a super-thin gold chain just visible above his T-shirt that normally isn't my style, but on him, I like it.

"His *neck*?" Sydney says, so loudly I'm afraid everyone will hear. "How about his *abs*? How about his *shoulders*? He could carry you over a mountainside if you needed him to. Rescue you during an avalanche."

"Why all the mountain fantasies?" I ask.

"Because he's a skier, duh. That's not even getting into how gorgeous his eyes are. Like some honey-yellow thing happening?"

Now I am laughing, and I'm not even sure why. "If you like him so much, you should drive him."

Sydney rolls her eyes and dodges my question, like always. "Anyway, good luck being trapped in the car with that *babe*." She takes a deep sip of her water. She looks startled when we're joined at the table.

"Who is Charlie going to be trapped in a car with?" Tucker asks.

Sydney casts a look at me, then shrugs. "Oh, nobody, just now that Charlie's constantly driving, she gets all types. Like how about that weird girl you told me about, the one with the box?"

I feel a flush come over my cheeks as Sydney and Tucker look at me with interest. "She really isn't that weird. I mean, I don't know what she's up to, but that's no reason to judge her for it." I feel suddenly defensive over my sweet, private client. Why can't people be accepted for their eccentricities, instead of rejected for them?

"Seems weird," Sydney says, oblivious, as she takes another sip of seltzer.

Tucker turns to Sydney, putting an arm around her shoulders. "You're weird," he says.

He starts tickling her, and Sydney starts cracking up.

♥ ♥ ♥

Later that afternoon, after the hallways have cleared out and everyone has gone home, or off to practice, I stand in the art room and stare at three large, plain white sheets of paper laid out before me. I don't even know what I'm doing with them exactly. I just figured it I could visualize the space I need for a portfolio, maybe I'd have a better understanding of how to fill it.

The question is, what does Ava Adams want?

I pull up her social media feed, a grid of neutrals, creams, organic textures, and dark wood. I click on one of the videos, the opening image of a woman standing in the desert. Instantly, Ava's voice comes on, and the film begins.

"For our latest project, we partnered with OurLand, an organic olive oil farm out in Joshua Tree. After purchasing some old buildings that had once belonged to a ranch, they needed to spruce them up, and they needed it done on a budget, with limited resources. Watch and see what we did."

Next, the video is fast-forwarded as figures move on- and

off-screen, painting, patching, hauling wood, laying rock, and working with pipes. The end result is a beautiful, simple form of a building, with a tin roof and a modern bathtub outside made of poured concrete, surrounded by plants.

"My approach is never to start over," Ava says to the camera. "It is always to build off of what is there."

I rest my head on my forearms, and think. "What can I build off of?" I whisper aloud. Then I sit up, a light bulb going off in my head. Screw sketches and inspiration. What could I actually . . . build? Ava would never see that coming.

♡ ♡ ♡

At four p.m., my hands aching from holding a pencil so long, the tips of my fingers dyed in black charcoal, I make my way out of the studio building and find Andre sitting in front of the gym waiting for me, looking annoyed.

"You're late," he says.

"I am not! It's 4:05!"

"And what is 4:05?" he asks.

"Um, I don't know. What?" I say, my tone dripping with condescension.

"Not four p.m." He stands up and motions his head toward the car. "Let's go. I need a milkshake."

"I'm taking you home," I tell him.

"No, you are taking me to get a milkshake," he says, without stopping.

"You can get your own milkshake. I'm not your catering service."

"And I just burned about a thousand calories in the span of an hour, Charlie," Andre says. "Unless you want me to pass out in your car, let's go. I don't think you need another violation."

I wince. "You are so dramatic."

He tilts his head at me. "What if I'm buying?"

I hesitate. "Fine. But we're doing drive-through."

Andre grins. "Look at that. A beautiful compromise."

"I guess there is hope for us yet," I say.

♡ ♡ ♡

A little while later we're parked in the lot at Rick's Diner, milkshakes in hand. I'm ready to get this over and done with so I can go home and obsess over my portfolio, but I can feel Andre watching me out of the corner of my eye.

"What?" I ask him, without turning my head.

"I was just thinking about something," he says, offhand.

"Are you going to tell me, or stare at me?"

Andre snorts now. "Fine. I was thinking about how when you hit my car, you told me you had the highest safety rating in the county. And yet you were also one safety violation away from losing driving privileges."

He waits for me to respond. Eventually I do.

"I *did* have the highest safety rating."

Andre nods. "So . . . what happened *that* time?"

I fiddle with my straw wrapper. "You really wanna know?"

"No, I'm asking because I don't wanna know," he says, and I shove him. He grins, and it takes up half his face.

I breathe slowly through my nostrils. "You know Mateo Miller?"

Andre bites his straw. "Uh, yeah. He's our student council president."

I groan. "I am aware."

"What did you do to Mateo Miller?" Andre says now, looking both scared and intrigued.

I bite my lip as I relive the memory in my head. "I gave him a ride to school a few weeks ago."

Andre's eyes get a kind of mischievous sparkle. "Go on."

"Well, I had to swerve to avoid a deer . . ."

"Oh no . . ."

"And you know that dumb thermos he's always carrying around? Like he's commuting to work or something, or in between meetings?"

Andre laughs. "Yes. And that *briefcase*."

"Well, he had the thermos that morning. And he was just taking a sip when I swerved."

"Oh, *man*."

"And he may have spilled it into . . . his lap."

Andre leans forward now, his head resting on his forearms, and for a few minutes I'm not sure what he's doing. Then I realize he's convulsing.

He looks at me. "You burned Mateo Miller's crotch?"

My mouth falls open in horror. "NO!" Then I think. "I mean, I guess, yeah. Technically I did."

Andre looks delighted. "I wondered why he was walking funny at school."

"Stop!" I cry. "I already feel awful about it!"

Andre smiles devilishly. "In truth? I can't stand that guy. He acts like he's the president of the United States, not our tiny high school. And he talks to me like we're at some kind of cocktail party."

"Yeah, well, he also reported me for a safety violation to the app. And maybe because he has pull around here, he got it."

Now Andre frowns. "That's effed up. All the more reason he deserved coffee in his crotch."

"Can you stop saying *crotch,* please?" I burst out, and Andre starts cracking up again, looking at me out of the corner of his eye.

"What?" I throw my hands in the air.

"Can't believe *you* just said crotch," he says. Then I start laughing too.

We sit there next to each other in silence a little while longer, sipping our milkshakes.

Chapter 11

IT'S RAINING ON FRIDAY, NOT TOO HARD, BUT FALLING in the kind of heavy mist on the windshield where I have to put the wipers on high. I've always been a safe driver, and there's something I love about being in a warm car, beneath a roof of sloping tree branches, gliding around the curves and over the hills of Western Massachusetts on a stormy day. For all its shortcomings, the giant Prius has a front windshield with the visibility of a spaceship. I can see everything. Colors stand out in unexpected ways, and you notice things you might not have seen before, like an old house hidden behind a stone wall, or a glimpse of light over the top of a mountain through the clouds.

Driving for a ride-sharing service, eighty percent of your rides are nothing out of the ordinary. Sometimes you barely even speak to the person in the back seat, even if you kind of know them from school. They tap away on their phone or put in earbuds or film a video for their social media and you both just continue on with your days.

But roughly ten percent of riders could be described as anywhere from a little strange to outright bizarre, and you can never predict how a ride will go with someone new. I've had people pass out in my car, make out in my car, and get into arguments so bad one actually just got out and walked when we pulled up at a stop sign, even though we were still a ways away from their destination and the car hadn't fully stopped yet. I've helped people transport everything from snowboards to giant dollhouses to live animals. I've been privy to far too many people's personal details, as though we don't live in the same town and I couldn't just tell anyone I wanted to (although I never do). Long conversations by cell phone that I have no choice but to listen in on. One person actually handed me a piece of paper and asked if I could *fax* it for them, as though I had that kind of setup in the front seat of my aging Prius. And then there was the senior earlier this year who, sporting a backpack, black clothing, and a helmet with a strange contraption on top, had me drop him at the top of a mountainside, where he said he was hoping to have an "extraterrestrial experience."

But none of these passengers, it is safe to say, prepared me for what it would be like driving every day, to and from school, with Andre. He knows everyone, and if he doesn't know them, he wants to know all about them. And by Friday, I have just about had it. Not only has driving him added several miles onto my usual days, not only have I been forced to stay late at school and watch him put more food into his body than I thought humanly possible, but he truly never shuts up. He leaves no stone unturned—from finding out about Emma Sykes's mom's dental practice to Sarah Kelley's hopeful run for political office to where to find the best blueberries in Western Massachusetts.

But the real problem is that suddenly, all these people are in *my* brain, too, taking up space. Space I would much prefer to use on other things.

So, this is where we are, on Friday afternoon in the rain, driving Dennis Kim home from school.

"Why is your car so weirdly clean all the time?" Andre asks, looking around like he's trying to find just one piece of trash.

"Because it's part of driving for the app?" I give him an obvious look. "And because I like it this way." I watch Andre tuck his Power Bar wrapper in the side pocket of the door. "Not that you make it easy on me."

Andre rolls his eyes. "I'll grab it when I get out."

"Really? Did you also wanna go back in time and grab the other nine you've left in here?"

Andre squints at me. "You know, for someone so creative, you are truly uptight."

I open my mouth wide. He mocks my expression by opening his in return.

Dennis is silent, unusually silent from my experience of sitting next to him in English class, but I am fine with this. I could use the silence too. I have a lot on my mind. I want to get my portfolio to Ava as soon as possible, and I've barely started. Maybe Dennis has something like that going on too, and I'm happy to respect that.

Andre, however, is not.

"So, how was your week?" Andre asks, turning around to check Dennis out. "You're a junior, right?"

Dennis nods, then leans his head against the window, looking dejected. "It was all right."

Andre tosses some popcorn into the back of his mouth. "I get it. Junior year is the worst. So much pressure. So much studying. You feel like everyone is asking everything of you."

I glance at Andre. Is he speaking from the heart, or is he just trying to connect with Dennis?

Dennis sighs. "Thanks. It's not really that, though."

A silence falls over the car.

Just let it go, I think, and for a minute, Andre actually does. He turns back around in his seat and faces forward again, and we go about a mile in blissful peace.

But then Andre speaks.

"I give pretty good advice, if you wanted to talk about it."

I snort.

"Do you have something you'd like to say?" Andre asks me.

"Just let it go," I say. "Why are you pushing him?"

"I'm not pushing him!" Andre says. "I'm being friendly. I'm being helpful. Unlike you, who would be happy to remain a perfect stranger to your riders."

I frown and am just about to say something when I hear Dennis announce, "You know, you guys sound like a bickering old couple."

This makes my cheeks burn, and Andre says nothing. I swallow. "All I am saying is, maybe Dennis *doesn't* want to talk about it?"

Andre frowns. "Or maybe he does?"

"Well, maybe he's more comfortable keeping some of his thoughts private?"

"Well, maybe you should let him answer that for himself," Andre says. We lock eyes with each other at a stop sign, tension building between us, when we hear a sound from the back seat.

Dennis clears his throat. "No, it's okay, Charlie. It's just, it's kinda personal. I don't wanna make stuff weird, or whatever."

Dennis takes a breath. "So, I've been hanging out with this girl. And I kind of like her."

Andre's eyes slide over to me, and I try and ignore him. Relationship drama is his favorite topic. I dread it.

"But I'm pretty sure she just sees me as a friend."

Andre's thick eyebrows knit together in a quizzical expression. "What makes you say that?"

"I dunno. I guess because most girls just think of me as a friend?"

Andre peers around. "And what makes you say *that*?"

Dennis laughs now and scratches the back of his head. "Well, I mean, nobody's ever said they liked me before."

Andre whips back around. "Charlie, as an aforementioned girl . . ."

"Yes . . ." I roll my eyes.

"I'm just saying. Have you ever been into anyone before and not said so?"

I squint. "No."

Andre shakes his head. "Come on. You can't mean that."

"I mean, not *really*," I say. Because the truth is, I haven't liked enough people. "But, taking gender out of it, I think it is completely possible for someone to like someone else and not tell them."

Andre nods. "See, Dennis?"

Dennis moves his head around, like he kind of gets it. "Okay, but I am pretty sure this girl isn't into me."

"Why?" Andre asks, incredulous.

"I don't know!" Dennis throws his hands up in the air. "Because she, like, always talks about what good *friends* we are? How lucky she is that we are *friends*?"

Andre makes a low *mmm* sound, like he's the host of an advice talk show on the radio. "Okay, I hear you. It could go either way. Is that what's bugging you?"

Dennis lets out a groan, shaking his head. "That's the thing, man, I don't even know. Basically, we were in science class, and we had to choose partners, and this girl Annabelle asked me, and I said sure. And now this other girl, the girl who we shall not name . . ."

"She's pissed at you," Andre jumps in.

A beat.

"How did you know that?" Dennis asks.

"Yeah . . . how *did* you know that?" I want to know.

"Because girls always do this kind of thing!" Andre shrugs. "Pretend they don't care, and then they totally do, once you show interest in someone else."

"Oh, give me a break," I say. "Where'd you read that? Some how-to article from the fifties?"

"But I'm not even interested in this other girl!" Dennis says. "She's just nice, and she asked me."

"You need to make a move, dude," Andre says.

"I do?"

"He does?" I ask.

"Definitely," Andre says.

He looks at Dennis in the mirror. "Otherwise, how will you know? And you can't go on living like this, right?"

"I'm sure he will survive," I say.

"You're right. I definitely cannot go on living like this," Dennis mutters.

"I think you should do it now," Andre pushes.

"NOW?" Dennis asks.

"No time like the present. Text her and ask her what's up."

"I don't know if I can, dude!" Dennis whines.

"Yeah, honestly, this is even stressing me out," I say.

"Shhh, Charlie," Andre says. He turns to Dennis. "Do it, dude. Or at least just see if she wants to hang out."

There is silence from the back seat, and a tapping of fingers on glass.

Ding!

My heart seems to stop beating for a second, and Andre's eyes are wide in anticipation.

"She says she does!" Dennis says. "She wants to meet up tonight."

"And when you do . . ." Andre says.

"I'm going to tell her how I feel," Dennis agrees.

"That's my man," Andre says. He grins from ear to ear, bouncing around in his seat. And now, Dennis is laughing too, bouncing around in his.

"Hey, thanks a lot, you guys," Dennis says as he gets out of the car in front of the pharmacy where he works after school. "You really helped me out."

"No problem," Andre tells him, reaching out and giving him a pound. "Let us know how it goes."

We drive in silence for a moment, until I say: "Did you really have to do that?"

Andre frowns. "Do what? Help a guy out? Possibly change his entire high school experience and romantic trajectory?"

I blink. "This is still my car, you know."

"So?" he says.

"So, say you overstep one day. Go too far."

"How would I go *too far*." Andre makes quotation marks.

"People have boundaries, is all I am saying. I mean, maybe you don't, but–"

"Oh my god, Charlie, you need to chill out. We're talking about high school students. Have you ever been on Tik-Tok before?"

"Whatever, if you piss someone off, I'm the one who gets penalized. You get that, right?" I ask. "This is my job. I'm not doing it for fun."

In the silence that follows, my phone buzzes with an alert. Andre picks it up. "Well, Dennis just tipped you twenty bucks on a seven-dollar fare, so sorry to ruin your bizarre conviction that I'm destroying everything."

"He did *what?*" I try to grab the phone and almost swerve off the road.

"Watch it!" Andre says.

"I can't believe it," I say, staring ahead at the road. "I've never been tipped that much before."

"I told you. People like talking about their problems, Charlie." He gives me a smug look.

"I'm not giving you that twenty bucks, you know."

Andre makes a face like he could care less. "Fine. You can use some of it to buy road snacks tomorrow."

"Tomorrow is Saturday," I remind him. "And I—"

"And you have a lot to do, I know," Andre says, sounding bored. "The problem is, it's a long drive to Wilson. Don't blame me if you get hungry."

I laugh. "And why exactly would I be going there?" Wilson College is one of the most competitive liberal arts schools in the country. It's also located in the middle of nowhere, i.e., . . . an hour from where we live. The campus is beautiful, and the students are supposed to be really smart, but you'd have to hit me over the head with a frying pan and drag me there unconscious if you wanted me to attend a school that felt even smaller than the town I grew up in.

"Because that's where Jess is at school," Andre says, looking absently out the window. "Obviously."

I brake hard at a stop sign, and Andre's body nearly goes flying into the front dash. "Serious question. Are you trying to kill me today?" he asks calmly.

"Are you trying to kill *me*? You want me to drive you over an hour away?"

"Um, yeah," Andre says.

"That was not part of our deal!"

Andre makes a thoughtful face. "Funny, because I thought our deal was for you to drive me *anywhere* I need to go. Which, if I am not mistaken, includes Wilson. To see my girlfriend."

"What's next, you want me to drive you to Boston?" I ask. "How about Chicago?"

Andre makes a face, like he hadn't considered it.

"That was a *joke*. And how important can this relationship be if you've never even mentioned her to me before."

Andre looks at me quizzically. "Come on. Everyone knows about me and Jess. We've been together forever. And anyway, it'll be fun for you. You can go to MaCA on your way home. Do all your arty things."

I frown, just as we pull up outside of Andre's house. "Is this why you accepted my deal? Because you knew I'd drive you to Wilson every week, and you could save on the gas money?"

Andre grins as he hops out of the car. "See you tomorrow. Nine a.m. sharp. Don't be late."

"I'm gonna get you back for this, Andre," I call out the window, but all he does is wave goodbye.

CHARLIE'S BACKSEAT REVIEWS

★★★★★ Yo Charlie's the coolest. Reliable service, cares about her riders a lot. Maybe too much . . . ? —Dennis

Chapter 12

"YOU SERIOUSLY CAN'T COME?" SYDNEY WHISPERS TO me upside down early on Saturday morning, out of the side of her mouth, as we push and fold our bodies into downward dog. "It's going to be epic. My mom is even letting me take her new SUV. That thing drives like a sports car."

I shake my head. "Trust me, I really wish I could."

Sydney groans. "Such a bummer. I thought you'd enjoy being in the passenger seat for once."

I make a face, trying to communicate as silently as possible how much that means to me. Sydney, Tessa, and the rest of our friends are heading to the outlets in Lenox, and it would feel really great to just cut loose for a day. But unlike Sydney, nobody is going to pay me *not* to work, and unlike Tessa, I'm not inheriting my lifelong dream. And so unfortunately, I have other plans, driving a boy I hardly know and can barely stand to visit his girlfriend an hour away.

"Andre is such a *turd*," Tessa hisses. "Getting you to drive him around all over the place without warning you those rides would eat up hours of your time."

"I mean, to be fair, Charlie *did* hit his car and ask him not to report it," Sydney mutters. Tessa and I both turn to look at her as a voice comes from the front of the room.

"Ladies," Janice Millman says, her gray hair pushed back in a colorful headband, her arm muscles enviably toned for a sixty-year-old. "You know we love having you join us here, but please be respectful of your other classmates."

I glance around the room and am met with the annoyed stares of twelve septuagenarians in sweatpants. About a year ago, Tessa, Sydney, and I took a girls' trip with our moms to Vermont, where we attended our first yoga class. We loved it and made a pact to do it regularly when we got back to Chester Falls, but the only class we could find within my budget was at the senior center. Tessa pulled some strings, and offered to bring fresh flowers, so we go every Saturday morning now. It's not *exactly* the most rigorous workout of my life, more like light stretching, but it still feels great to be hanging with my dudes.

"Now, ease forward, and lower your body to the mat," Janice says in a soothing voice, and we follow her instructions to the sounds of light Tibetan wind music and possibly the sound of someone releasing gas.

"Confession. I've always thought Andre Minasian was *really* cute," Tessa whispers.

"That's what I said!!" Sydney whisper-shrieks, and a series of shushes go up across the room.

I refuse to participate.

"Charlie Owens, heart of stone," Tessa mutters.

"Just watch," Sydney says. "Maybe Andre Minasian will finally be the one to crack her hard candy shell."

Now, both Tessa and I make a face at Sydney.

"Sorry, I've been reading too many of my mom's romance novels." Sydney's voice is muffled by the mat.

"Well, considering the fact that Andre has a girlfriend, I think that might change our love story."

"No way," Tessa says. "That's why you're driving him to Wilson? He's still dating Jess Miller? Wow. I thought for sure they'd broken up when she went to college."

"So did I. He literally never talks about her." I happen to notice Sydney's face. She's smirking.

"You like him," she says.

"What?" I ask.

"You're not just pissed about the ride. You're pissed he didn't mention Jess. And the fact that he didn't mention Jess is one hundred percent suspicious. Maybe things aren't as serious as they used to be. You know this is the exact time when a couple like this grows apart."

I look back down, thinking. Does Sydney have a point?

Tessa groans as she stretches.

"Are you okay?" Sydney asks. "You sound like you're dying."

"I've been working overtime at the farm. My parents are short on cash right now," she says.

"Since when?" I say. "The farm is always in such good shape."

Tessa looks at me like I'm a cute but ignorant child. "Charlie. The only farmers who are rolling in dough are ones that made millions on Wall Street and are doing it for fun. If I want to keep this farm alive for the next generation, I have to get creative, or die trying."

"I had no idea," I whisper. "I'm sorry."

"Ladies!" Janice Millman says, exasperated. "If you want to be allowed back, you're going to have to—and please excuse my hostility—shut the hell up."

Sydney turns to me, eyes wide. "I thought yoga was supposed to be relaxing."

♡ ♡ ♡

After a shower and a fresh change of clothes, I've been sitting in the car outside Andre's house for a good fifteen minutes before I decide to knock on the door. He's not answering his texts, and I will die before I become one of those people who honks to let someone know they've arrived. Even if that someone is as much of a pain as Andre Minasian.

But as I approach the front door, afraid to disturb the household on a Saturday morning, I realize that the house is already most definitely awake. And the reason I know this is from the sound of loud Brazilian jazz music that is threatening to burst out the windows.

Tall and tan and young and lovely, the girl from Ipanema goes walking . . .

I try the bell, but nobody answers, so eventually I just push the door open and take a few careful steps into the hallway.

"Hello?" I call out, but I don't see anyone, so I follow the sound of the music into an open and airy kitchen, where I find Andre and his parents seated around the table, eating breakfast and laughing.

They turn to look at me, and we all just stare at each other for a moment, before his mother opens her arms wide. "Charlie!" she exclaims. Andre's dad beams, and Andre looks embarrassed as his mother gets up and embraces me tightly and his father leans over the table to give me a warm hand-shake.

"Welcome! Sorry about the music. Bossa nova is a great way to start the day, I think." Andre's mom motions to Andre, who gets up and turns it down on the stereo. "We didn't know you were coming so early." She turns to Andre. "You didn't tell us she was coming so early! Can we get you a bagel? Mark made them fresh."

I have a feeling Mrs. Minasian is not the kind of person you say no to. She is petite and fit, with short brown hair she wears closely cropped to her head. She's wearing a tight magenta zip-up top and running capris. I know immediately that this is where Andre must get his bold personality, his enthusiasm, his abrupt movements. His dad, who looks a lot like him, is calmer, more reserved, with a pleasant smile and Andre's dark eyebrows.

Before I can even answer her, Andre's dad starts throwing things onto a plate.

"Mom," Andre tries to say, coming over and putting his arm around his mother, a gesture that, against my will, I find heartwarming, "Charlie doesn't have time for a feast. We have to hit the road."

"It's so nice of you to drive Andre around, after what happened to his car the other day."

I swallow and glance at Andre, waiting for her to say it. That I am the girl who backed into her son's car, the one he worked so hard to pay for. So here we are.

But instead Mrs. Minasian says: "So disappointing that someone backed into you and then took off. We may *never* know who did this. Thank god you have such nice friends." She beams at me.

My eyes lock with Andre's, just for a second, and I feel more guilty than ever before. *Why didn't he just tell her I did it?* But then Mrs. Minasian leans in closely, as if whispering a secret everyone in the room can hear. "Although, let's be honest, that car was kind of a piece of crap."

A genuine laugh escapes me.

"Mom!" Andre moans. "What the hell!"

"Okay, let me just pack up a few things," she says, dismissing his anguish and getting back to business again. I try to protest, tell her not to go to the trouble, but Mrs. Minasian is already behind the counter, grabbing a plastic bag out of a drawer and putting a bagel inside it.

"You showed up," Andre says quietly to me. He looks pleased.

"We have a deal, don't we?" I say. Out of the corner of my eye, I'm distracted by an exchange happening between Mr. and Mrs. Minasian.

"I'm headed out too," he says. "Going to go grab some supplies so we can finally keep those bunnies out of your vegetable garden."

"You are my hero," Mrs. Minasian says. She leans up and gives her husband a kiss before turning back to us. "Have fun, sweetheart. And be safe, okay?"

"Oh, Charlie is always safe." Andre smiles. "She has a perfect safety record."

♡ ♡ ♡

"I can't believe those are your parents," I say to Andre as we buckle our seat belts.

"Why?" the genuine confusion on his face makes me snort a little. "Oh, I see. You think I was raised by wolves or something?"

"Not exactly. But the Brazilian jazz . . . the Saturday brunch . . . your mom is so . . . cool. And so . . . in control."

"And I am *not* cool?" Andre asks, in a way that almost makes me laugh out loud.

"So," he says as we take Route 2 out of Chester Falls and past fields, old houses, and bored-looking herds of cattle. "Excited for our adventure?"

"Thrilled," I reply, ignoring the constant texts popping up on my phone, my friends having a blast without me as they head off to the outlets. "This is the best day of my life. Thank you so much for this opportunity."

"I can tell," Andre mutters, making a face and reaching toward the stereo. "This music sounds like somebody died."

My mouth falls open as I look at him. "Excuse me, but I like them. I saw this band play in Northampton last year. They were awesome."

"I just bet they were," Andre says in a tone that in no way aligns with his words. "Were you at a funeral?"

"Fine, what do *you* like to listen to?" I ask, even though I don't care.

"May I?" Andre says, waving a hand toward the stereo like a magician.

I shrug. "Good luck. This car is too old for Bluetooth, and the aux jack is broken."

To my disappointment, Andre takes a CD out of his bag.

"I took note of the stereo situation. And these guys are my everything." He hits play.

As the soulful crooning washes over us, I stifle my laughter.

"Boyz II Men? Boyz II Men is your everything?"

Andre looks at me, his face serious. "The harmonies give me goose bumps."

"Don't get me wrong, they're amazing. I just wouldn't expect it from you."

Andre nods along as the music floats out of the speakers. "Nineties R&B gets me in the mood."

"Gross," I say.

"I didn't mean it like *that*. Get your mind out of the gutter, Owens," he says, frowning, but grinning too. There is something so contagious about Andre's enthusiasm, though I hate to admit it. I have to work hard to hide my own smile.

I think back to what I know about Jess Miller, a skier, like

Andre, who graduated last year. She was petite, with light brown hair that she always had in a high ponytail. She was nice, but she was also kind of intense.

"How long have you and Jess been together?"

"Since my freshman year," Andre says, placing the CD case in the console.

He turns then, looking surprised at the face I'm making. "What?"

I move my head around, deciding. "It's just such a long time, that's all. What makes you . . ." I struggle to find the words. "What makes you stay in something that long?"

Andre scoffs. "Um, because I love her? She's gorgeous, and smart, and she likes all the same things I do. Why *wouldn't* I want to stay with her?"

"Because you're only eighteen years old," I tell him. *And, I think to myself, because this is the first time you've ever talked about her that way.*

"What does age have to do with anything?" Andre asks.

"I mean, don't you want to get out there and live more of your life? How could you possibly know what you want right now?"

Andre looks at me like it's so simple. "Because my life is here."

I blink. "Okay . . ."

"I'm serious. My life is here. I'm gonna finish up strong this year, get off the wait list at Wilson, go to school with Jess, move home, and start living the rest of my life. What?" he asks, seeming more annoyed.

"Well, did you get in anywhere else?" I ask.

Andre nods, fidgeting, which I've noticed he does a lot. "I got into Tulane. But I'm not going there."

"New Orleans?!" I say. "You could go to school in New Orleans, and you'd rather be *here?*"

Again, Andre looks like something is wrong with me. "Obviously."

I sigh. "Have you ever even dated anyone else?"

Andre says nothing for a minute. "I mean, not in a real way, no."

"So how do you even know what you want? How are you so ready to be stuck with someone for the rest of your life when you don't even know what it's like to be with someone else?"

"I am not *stuck* with her," he says. "I *choose* to be with her." Then he mutters something under his breath.

"What was that?" I ask.

"I said, like you should really talk."

"Care to elaborate?"

"Have *you* ever dated anyone? How could you tell me anything about relationships?" he says. "I have found the perfect person for me. She's beautiful, smart—"

"You said that already."

"Athletic—"

"Scary," I add.

"What?" he asks, like I'm crazy.

"She can be kind of scary." I shrug.

"She is *not* scary," Andre says, his voice weird and high. I've gotten under his skin.

"Have you ever played kickball with her?" I ask. "I did, at summer camp in middle school. I feared for my life."

Andre looks at me. Then he starts laughing. "You're just a sore loser."

I raise my eyebrows. "Oh, I was sore all right. Sore from her slamming the ball into my skull every chance she got."

Andre rolls his eyes, the grin remaining on his face. "Keep your eyes on the road, Owens."

Chapter 13

AFTER THIRTY MORE MINUTES OF BICKERING AND switching the stereo back and forth between indie rock and soul tunes, and of Andre singing Boyz II Men so off pitch it sounds like a different genre of music altogether, we drive up and over a low hill and plunge down into the beautiful, lush, rolling college campus of Wilson College. Andre directs me down a quaint main street and to the back of a brick building, where he barely waits for me to stop the car before opening the door.

"Just confirming I do not need to pick you up, right?" I ask. "Jess is driving you home?"

"Correct." Andre smiles. "My gift to you. You're welcome." I'm about to ask him what exactly I'm thanking him for, when he keeps talking. "We're going to go on a hike, get lunch, and see her friend's band play tonight. Stop that," he adds, when he finally notices me laying my head back against the car's headrest and pretending to be asleep. "You're just jealous I have plans."

"Oh, I've got plans," I tell him.

"I'd ask, but I don't really care." Andre turns away from the car, giving one last wave behind him.

"Have fun!" I tell him sarcastically.

"Don't miss me too much on the drive back," he calls after me.

♡ ♡ ♡

After grabbing an iced coffee on campus, I head back on Route 2 and take the exit for New Winsor, a town that was once the bustling epicenter for a powerful electric company but was "deindustrialized" after the 1980s, meaning once other companies began making their products more cheaply overseas, the electric company was forced to close, and one quarter of the population lost their jobs. New Winsor has struggled to get back on its feet for the last fifty years, but it has no shortage of supporters, people from the nearby town of Wilson who want to see it survive, those who appreciate its history, and even a famous indie rockstar, Stephen Lagrange, who was born in New Winsor and has put much of his earnings back into the town.

I can feel my whole body releasing its tension as I pull off into the parking lot outside three large, historic warehouse buildings that, fifteen years ago, were purchased from the electric company and turned into one of the most important modern art museums on the East Coast: MaCA. The spaces don't just hold gorgeous, light-filled galleries, but plenty of outdoor public art space, several stage venues for a visiting summer series, and what I think is coolest, a series of programs and residencies dedicated to helping artists work on their craft.

I spend the first thirty minutes of my visit carrying out my usual routine, hitting up my old favorites: Sol LeWitt's murals, Louise Bourgeois's giant spider sculpture, and a series of portrait photographs from an emerging artist from West Texas.

Then I sit on the third floor of Building C, my favorite spot, a small space lined with windows and strung with an installation of light bulbs that gives me a perfect view of the rest of the complex and allows me to watch people move through the space.

I am always surprised by the way people walk through museums too quickly to take any of it in. In my mind, the point is not to have "seen it" but to be "in it." To feel it under your skin, to think critically about what it means. Otherwise, why come? Everyone always seems so eager to leave. Is it so hard to spend two hours of the day in a beautiful place?

I am just beginning to explore some of the newer exhibits when I pick up my phone to check the time and notice four missed calls from Andre. I am still debating whether to call him back when he calls a fifth time.

"Did you forget something?" I ask, without saying hello.

"You aren't home yet, are you?" he asks, and I can barely hear his voice, it's so low and quiet.

"Actually I'm . . . wait, why?" I try to imagine what could prompt him to call me in the midst of the love fest he was so eager to get to.

"Just tell me if you're home, Charlie," he says, his voice irritable and scratchy.

"No, I'm at MaCA."

I hear him breathe a sigh of relief into the phone. "Good. Can you come back?"

"I mean, not really, I just got here. Plus, they just opened up a new wing. I've been so busy I haven't seen it yet." I glance down the hallway where the new wing beckons, a literal light at the end of a tunnel.

"I really need you to come back, Charlie," he says, and his voice sounds anxious in a way I can't even imagine coming out of his mouth.

"Well, contrary to your belief, Andre, my life does not actually revolve around you. I can't just go chasing you around town all the time. If I'm going to waste my Saturday—"

"Charlie, just *come*. Okay?" Andre says, and his voice cracks. "I just . . . I really need to get out of here."

I swallow, already reaching into my bag for my car keys. "Andre?"

His voice comes out soft again, so low I can barely hear him. "Jess just broke up with me. I'm stranded. Can you come pick me up, or am I going to have to walk home?"

♥ ♥ ♥

I am not sure there has never been a sadder sight than Andre sitting, knees curled into his chest, on the edge of the curb outside his girlfriend's—now ex's—dorm, his shoulders slumped, his chin resting on his arms.

I roll up next to him and lower the window.

"Your chariot, my lord?" I'm trying to be funny, to lighten the mood, but Andre barely manages to lift his head. Eventually he pulls himself up, bags seemingly having formed beneath his eyes in the last hour, and drags himself into the car. Once seated, he crosses his arms over his chest and leans his head and shoulder into the window, as if he wishes he could curl into a tiny ball. As if the window is another dimension and he is trying to slip right into it, away from this existence.

I try to ask a question or two, to understand what happened, but he shakes his head before I can get more than a syllable out. So, instead, we drive. My sad indie music is more fitting than ever, in the worst possible way, and glancing over at Andre, I realize it's probably not the best choice for his current state. Quietly, without him noticing, I skip to the next CD in the player, and the low croons of Boyz II Men begin floating out of the speaker. After all, who better to make one feel seen about love and loss?

"Don't," Andre says.

"Okay," I say, shutting the music off altogether, so we just ride along in silence.

"I don't want to talk about it," he says, his head on the window, gazing into nothingness.

"Okay," I say again.

After a few more moments, though, he speaks. "She said we needed time apart."

I want to chime in, to say she's probably right, but I have a feeling that would be exactly the wrong thing to say at this moment in time, so instead I listen, nodding, and staring at the road as we make our way back to Chester Falls, as Andre continues in a low, apathetic tone. One I've never heard him use before. "She said maybe I won't understand right now, but one day I will." He sniffs.

"I'm really—" I start to say, intending to finish with "sorry," but Andre keeps going, lost in his own thoughts.

"Three years of dating, and it's over. Just like that."

"You don't know that it's *over*," I tell him. "People break up and get back together all the time."

"She said things had been weird with us for a while," Andre continues, his voice slowly growing higher, getting more worked up. "How can you love someone, make *plans* with someone, and then just . . ." He pauses, staring ahead. ". . . not?"

"Well, had they?" I ask.

Andre breaks out of his haze, turning to look at me for the first time during the whole ride, his brown eyes flashing. "Had they what."

"Had they been weird for a while?"

Andre snorts, like it's the dumbest question ever invented. "Of course things hadn't been great. I mean, we've barely seen each other. And we didn't have as much stuff to talk about as we used to. But we were figuring it out. It was never going to be easy. But we had a plan."

"Well, maybe Jess's plans changed?" I suggest.

When I happen to glance over at Andre, I find him glaring back at me. "I am painfully aware of that."

I shrug. "I'm just saying! How could either of you know what you really want yet? My mom says some experiences aren't meant to be forever, but that doesn't make them less special."

Andre's expression hardens further as he stares straight ahead out the windshield, his posture stiffening. "Okay. Whatever."

"I'm not trying to upset you. I just mean, when you talk about Jess, you talk about how she fits into your life. Your plans. You don't really talk about her. How can you grow together if you want to keep everything the way it's always been?"

Silence.

"Maybe instead of obsessing about every single tiny step of my future, I prefer to just embrace what I already have," Andre says.

"Well, maybe you should think bigger," I mutter.

"Stop the car," Andre says.

"What?" I ask, glancing down at my phone GPS. We're still on Route 2, nothing around but fields and an occasional house. We're a good twenty-minute drive from the outskirts of town, over an hour's walk.

"Stop the car. I wanna walk home."

I balk. "Because of what I said?"

Andre says nothing.

"Okay, how is this suddenly my fault?"

Silence.

"Andre, I'm not stopping on the highway to let you off on the side of the road. What if you get murdered?"

Andre rolls his eyes so big I think they might get stuck up there. "Just let me out, Charlie."

I look over at his serious face. "News flash, I want to be helping you deal with this breakup just about as badly as you want me to be helping you. But here we are. We are stuck together. And all I'm saying is, you're young, and maybe you got ahead of yourself, and maybe Jess has a point."

"Let. Me. Out. Charlie," Andre says to me, slowly, like I'm a child. "My girlfriend, excuse me, ex-girlfriend, just lit my heart on fire and then drop-kicked it into a trash can, and the last thing I want is to be stuck in this giant, stupid Prius with a person who doesn't even believe in love."

I scowl. "Oh my god, *fine.* I have to pick up something at the hardware store. If you still want to walk home by the time we get there, be my freaking guest."

Andre makes no reply, he just crosses his arms over his chest as we move speedily home.

"So dramatic," I say under my breath.

Chapter 14

I PULL INTO A SPOT IN FRONT OF JACOBSON'S HARDWARE, then get out and walk inside the sliding double doors without turning to see if Andre got out too. If he wants to walk home so badly, if being around me is that hard, he is more than welcome to do so. I do feel bad for him, of course. I know from watching Tessa go through it over and over that breakups are awful. But I also don't really know what to say, so maybe he'd be better off without me anyway.

When I was little, I used to love coming to Jacobson's with my dad. While he got his tools sharpened and talked shop, I'd browse the endless treasures that the old store seemed to offer. Like tiny flashlights and key chains, permanent markers in all the colors of the rainbow, and every kind of glass jar you could possibly imagine. And, my favorite, a small wall of penny candy in the far corner. Peppermint patties and

Hershey's bars and gum balls. My dad always let me pick out one.

Then, as my dad slowly stopped making sculptures, stopped going out to the carriage house, we stopped coming to Jacobson's. I almost never set foot in here anymore, but today I am determined to make some progress. And that progress is going to start with fixing the bathroom.

On instinct, and because I feel I deserve it, I grab a peppermint patty from the candy display. Then after a moment, I grab one for Andre, too.

I approach Bill Jacobson, who is standing behind the register reading the day's paper.

"Charlie Owens, is that you?" he asks with a warm smile. "Haven't seen you around here in a while."

I do my best to smile. "I'm here to buy a manual on toilets."

"What do you need that for?" he asks.

Good question, I think, *why am I, a seventeen-year-old girl, buying a manual on toilets, when I live with two adult humans who could do this themselves?* Instead, I shrug. "Got a broken toilet."

Bill studies me for a second, removing his glasses. "Follow me."

He takes me to an aisle in the back with manuals, pulls one out on toilets. "Think this will do you just fine," he says, then walks it back to the front with me. "How do you wanna pay, Charlie?"

"My parents still have a charge account here, right?" If I'm doing the work, they can certainly pay for it.

Bill clears his throat and makes a pained face. "Not really."

"Oh," I say, embarrassed.

"They had one, but your dad wasn't paying it. In fact, he still has a balance. So I'm afraid I can't add anything to it. Store policy."

I blush, looking down. "I'm sorry about that," I say. "He forgets. He's just not . . ." I trail off.

"It's okay. It's just, do you have another way to pay? Shops like ours aren't exactly thriving these days, what with Home Depot and everything else."

I nod, passing my own card across the counter, biting the inside of my cheek with my teeth. I need to remain calm. No need to make a scene. I put the candy back where I found it, having lost my appetite.

"Charlie," he says as I turn away. "I hate to do this, but when you see your dad, can you tell him he needs to pay his tab?" Bill asks. "I'd never make you pay for it. It's not your problem."

"Of course." I grab the bag and head for the door, trying to hold back my tears. Because the truth is, it very much is my problem.

And just before I reach the door, I see Andre standing over by the reusable water bottles, watching me with a weird expression on his face.

Great.

I walk back outside, my face feeling hot, and open the door to my car and get in, where I lean down and rest my head against the wheel, taking slow, deep breaths.

I hear the sound of the other door open. And, without lifting my head, out of the corner of my eye, I see Andre get back in the car. He gently places a peppermint patty on the armrest between us.

♥ ♥ ♥

"Do you want to talk about it?" Andre asks after a moment or two. His voice comes out sounding tired. He has barely moved a muscle. Not to look at his phone, not to eat some of the candy he bought for himself.

"Talk about what?" I ask feebly, my head still on the steering wheel.

"Come on, Charlie."

"I'd rather not."

"Well, I get that. But maybe if you *did,* you'd feel better."

"Fine," I say, sitting up and leaning my head back against the headrest. "My parents are just . . . so frustrating sometimes. Our house is basically falling apart around us, and they don't even seem to care. Not to mention the fact that they are living together, but not *really* together. And they keep acting like I'm overly sensitive, like I worry too much. They keep telling me to 'let them do the parenting.' And trust me, I would really like to! Except shit like this always happens. And now I feel like I'm going to be trapped here, too. Forever."

I realize my breath is coming faster, and I take a few big, deep breaths, my chest heaving, as Andre sits next to me in silence.

"Yikes," Andre finally says, and I cannot believe I just told him all that. "You're not going to be trapped, though." He moves his head side to side against the headrest.

I throw my hands up in the air in defeat. "It's not like I don't want to help. I just wish they had an actual plan."

Andre is silent for a while. "I'm sorry, Charlie."

"No, *I'm* sorry," I say, shaking my head. "You don't want to be hearing about this. You just got your heart lit on fire and drop-kicked into a trash can."

Andre snorts. "Right. For a minute there I forgot." I glance at Andre out of the corner of my eye, realizing that even though I've only known him a matter of days, we've had more real conversations than I've had with plenty of people in my life.

"Can I just ask, though," he says, turning his head slowly to gaze into my eyes. "What exactly is so terrible about Chester Falls?"

I shake my head. "That's not what I'm saying."

"Seems like it's part of what you're saying. You seem so desperate to leave. But you still have a whole other year here."

I stare out the windshield. "There are just things I want to do, and I can't do them here."

"But you're seventeen," Andre says. "You have plenty of time!"

"Well, you would say that, because apparently you don't want to be anywhere else!"

Andre sighs and runs a hand through his hair. "It's not that I think this town is the best place on earth." He clears his throat. I watch him, waiting for him to continue. "I've just seen how it can come together. How it can make a difference. That's all."

I shake my head. "I love this town. But I know what it has to offer me, and it's not what I want."

Andre squints. "Sounds like you don't know this town very well."

"Well, apparently I'm going to have all the time in the world to figure it out," I say.

I restart the car and drive Andre back to his house. When we pull up outside, he moves to get out of the car, but he looks exhausted, his movements slow and creaky.

"You should get some rest," I say. "I'll see you on Monday."

When he looks at me, I notice a twinkle in his eyes. "Actually, there *is* something I would like to do tomorrow," he says.

My shoulders slump. "Seriously?"

Andre snorts. "Promise you won't hate it."

I eye him suspiciously.

"How about this," he says. "If you do hate it, I'll start paying for my rides. Deal?"

This has my attention. "You will?"

He nods. "That's how confident I am that you'll enjoy yourself."

I tap my fingers on the wheel of the car a few times, and, though I have no idea why, I say: "Fine."

I'm watching Andre get out of the car and start walking toward his house when a strange feeling comes over me. It's so out of place, I almost don't recognize it at first. A kind of pang in my chest. A desperation. I realize, for the first time since I started driving Andre around . . . I don't want him to leave.

Chapter 15

THE NEXT DAY, AFTER DROPPING OFF LULU, I ARRIVE AT Andre's house, secretly looking forward to interrupting whatever happy family dynamic is going on inside. I liked Andre's mom, the way she seemed so prepared and in control of everything around her, whereas my parents often forget to go grocery shopping or pay the electric bill.

But I don't have a chance to go inside this time, because I find Andre leaning against his fence instead, a backpack slung loosely over one shoulder.

"Hi," he says after hopping in the car.

"Hello . . ." I cautiously reply. I want to ask him how he's doing. He has small bags under his eyes, and his hair is messy, like he didn't sleep well. But I'm also pretty sure he doesn't want to talk about it. I'm genuinely nervous about what his plans are for us today, but Andre *did* say he'd pay for all his future rides if I didn't have fun. And, okay, a part of me feels like if this excursion helps him forget about the fact that his girl-friend of over three years dumped him only twenty-four hours ago, maybe I'll allow it.

"So, where to?" I ask, hands gripping the steering wheel.

A mischievous smile comes over Andre's face. "Well, first things first. How would you feel about me driving?"

I lean away from him in alarm. "Uh, I would not feel good about it. Last thing we need is for both of us to be without a car."

Andre rolls his eyes. "You are the one who hit *me*. Of the two of us, statistically, I am the much safer bet."

I shrug. "Well, I'm not willing to take that chance." When Andre says nothing in reply, I glance back at him, only to find him gazing at me.

"What."

"I think you just like being in control," he states.

I gasp dramatically. "You've figured me out! Nobody has ever seen me so clearly!" I close my mouth and stare ahead. "And on that note, where are we going?"

Andre slumps back into his seat. "Parson's."

I make a face. "This is the *secret* thing you needed help with. Groceries?" I put the car into gear and pull out onto the road. Parson's is the town's general store. It's been around since Chester Falls' founding and has every kind of thing you can imagine. Basic grocery staples, penny candy, local soap, beer. Lately, it's started selling other items, too, like artisan flour, and small-batch coffee.

"Nope," he says. "We are getting you a Chester Fizz."

I squint. "A what?"

Andre smiles happily. "Exactly."

♡ ♡ ♡

At Parson's, Andre greets Dick, third-generation owner of the store, as we come in the door.

"Andre," Dick says. "Great to see you. How's your mom?" A look of concern flashes across his face, but Andre seems unfazed.

"She's doing great, thanks. Do you know Charlie Owens?" Andre nods his head in my direction.

"Hey," I say with a small wave.

"Sure, I think I know you," Dick says, leaning on the counter in a flannel shirt. "I always place pie orders from the shop through your dad. How is he doing?"

"Fine, thanks," I say, busying myself with sniffing some artisan beeswax candles.

"What brings you both in today?"

"We're here to remedy a dire situation, Dick. Brace yourself," Andre says, grinning. "Charlie has never had a Chester Fizz."

Dick's mouth curls into a smile. "You've never had a Chester Fizz?" he asks, enunciating each word like he can't believe what he's hearing.

"Will someone please just tell me what a Chester Fizz even is?" I exclaim, holding my hands up in surrender.

Dick lets out a laugh. Then, with a glance at Andre, he holds up a finger. "Hang on."

As Andre smirks at me, like, *just you wait,* Dick disappears into the back of the shop and returns a short time later with two to-go cups with straws. The liquid is a pale, purply pink. The first thing I think of is that I must get one of these for Theo. The color is beautiful. Something my mom would put on a canvas.

Dick hands one over to me, and I can tell from the look on his face that he's waiting for me to try it. Feeling his and Andre's eyes on me, I take a reluctant sip.

"Damn," I say, lifting the drink up to my eyeline to stare at its contents again. "That's *delicious.*"

Andre nods his head vigorously as he sips from his own straw.

"What's in this?" I ask.

Dick looks at Andre.

"Rhubarb, raspberry, mint, and seltzer," Andre says.

"I mean, really. I cannot believe you've never had one," Dick says again.

Andre goes to pay, but Dick won't hear of it. "Come back and buy some flowers for your mother," he tells Andre.

"Done," Andre replies. Then he puts a gentle hand on my back as he nudges me out of the store. It's a gesture that takes me by surprise but one, I realize to some amount of horror, I don't totally hate.

"Keep it moving," Andre says. "We have more things to do."

♡ ♡ ♡

"So, let me get this straight," I say a little while later. "The purpose of this day, of me taking time off of homework, and time away from my friends and family, was to get me a fizzy beverage and take me to a . . . Little League game?" We are sitting in the stands watching the Chester Falls Falcons face off against the Berwick Bears. I'm almost finished with my Chester Fizz, and I wish it wouldn't end. Next to us is a bag of fresh-baked granola that Andre also picked up on his way out. It's addictive. We alternate sipping from straws and crunching on handfuls.

"Not exactly," Andre says as a boy who I could lift with one arm gets struck out by the pitcher.

A man behind us gets up, screaming and red faced. "COME ON! YOU CALL THAT A BALL? THAT WAS A STRIKE IF I'VE EVER SEEN A STRIKE!"

"He looks a little old to be the father of one of the kids on the team," I whisper to Andre. In fact, most of the people in the stands, or in lawn chairs on the grass, I recognize from my senior center yoga class. "They can't *all* have grandchildren on the team, can they?"

"The Chester Falls Falcons have a deeply loyal following," Andre explains. "Many of the people in town have never missed a game in their entire lives."

I sit back, observing a tiny kid hit a grounder, to an absolute uproar. One man throws his popcorn.

"That's actually really cute."

"It's more than cute. It's beautiful. It's community." Andre rests his elbows on his thighs and studies the field. "How's your drink?" he asks, without looking my way.

"It's gone." I wiggle the empty cup in his face. "And I want another."

"I'm glad," Andre says. His tired look has diminished, and his cheeks are rosy in the sunshine.

"So, has everyone in town had a Chester Fizz but me?" I want to know.

Andre laughs. "Actually, I made it up." Then he takes in my look of confusion. "The Chester Fizz. I made it up when I was a kid. Now I order one whenever I go in there. Dick was just playing along."

I think this over. "Then why was it so important for me to have it?"

"I'm going to let you figure that one out," Andre tells me, studying the field.

"Okay." I frown, just as a kid's bat connects hard with the ball, and it goes flying. The crowd stands, shouting. When I notice Andre smiling at me, I realize I'm shouting along with them.

"This team is good," I admit.

"Told you," Andre says.

♡ ♡ ♡

After the game, we drive into the mountains, which are cut right through by a winding river. My mom calls this place her church, open space slicing through giant pieces of rock, light dappling the windshield. Then we take Route 2 up and up, until Andre tells me to stop on the side of the road, in the middle of nowhere.

"Don't be offended, but . . . have you taken me out here to kill me?" I ask.

Andre lays his head back against the car seat, shaking his head as he stifles a laugh. "Just get out, Charlie."

"Fine, but I just want to state for the record that this sounds *pretty* murdery to me." I unbuckle my seat belt. My fears aren't exactly eased as I watch Andre disappear through a series of bushes into what I can only assume is a steep drop-off, or total nothingness, or my imminent doom.

"Andre?" I call as I push through the leaves. "Seriously?!"

"Hurry up!" he calls back. "The sun is setting in forty-five minutes!"

"Just in time for the ritualistic sacrifice?" I shout back, but the end of the sentence catches in my throat as I reach the end of the path and it opens up into one of the most beautiful places I've ever seen.

There, just a few yards off the side of the road, hidden behind a grove of trees, with steep, rocky ledges and sunlight reflecting off crystal clear water, is a perfect, sparkling swimming hole.

"You've never been here?" Andre asks, standing a few yards away at the end of the rock as he pulls off his shirt, revealing toned arms and a lean stomach. I look down automatically, color rising to my cheeks.

"Nope."

"Well, you've been missing out. This is my favorite place on earth." And then, before I can say anything back, he jumps off the high rock surface and into the pond, letting out a loud whoop the whole way down.

I find it hard to take my eyes off him, caught up in his energy. He dips his head under, then comes up, shaking it and smiling wide. "Well, what are you waiting for?"

"I didn't bring a swimsuit," I call down.

"Oh." Andre looks momentarily uncomfortable, averting his eyes from me, as though I'm already undressing. But then he seems to shake it off. "Go in your underwear! I'll close my eyes while you get in." He turns around, treading water as he does. The light glints off the side of the rock, the trees dappling the light. I watch him, floating like that. I can't even hear the road from here.

"Are you coming or what?" Andre calls again.

Quickly, I pull off my clothes, down to my underwear.

"Come on, Charlie!" is the last thing I hear Andre say before I jump.

Chapter 16

EVERYTHING IN THE WORLD IS SILENT, SAVE FOR A FEW birds chirping in the trees above, and the rustling of leaves, and the thick gurgling of the stream as it falls over and around smooth rocks and pebbles and into the swimming hole. I lie on the edge of a flat rock surface, wrapped in a towel that Andre brought with him in his backpack, secretly saving the best part of the adventure for last. For the first time in weeks, everything feels clearer. Like my breath can leave my body more easily. Like so much of what has been happening these past couple of months, my parents, and the house, and my fears about the future, was all a part of something I got caught up in that kept catapulting me forward. And now I'm easing my way out of it, back into my body.

Faces from the day flash before my eyes. Dick Parson, grinning in his beautiful, crowded family-owned shop. Old men cheering for nine-year-old boys like they were watching the world series.

"I think I understand the point of the Chester Fizz," I tell Andre, my eyes still closed.

"Go on," Andre replies. His voice comes out kind of scratchy, and closer to my ear than I expected. I open one eye just a crack and realize he is lying down beside me, his eyes closed. His hair glints, still wet.

"It wasn't about showing me a side of the town I hadn't seen before, or something unexpected," I say.

"No?"

I shake my head, even though he can't see it. "It's about the fact that we live in a place where you can develop a relationship with a shop owner where he will literally let you design your own beverage, and order it whenever you want, and furthermore, not charge you for it."

I peek another look at Andre and see that he is smiling now, his eyes still closed. His lashes are heavy and thick, almost too perfect to be real. "Yeah, basically you're on the right track."

"Clever."

"Thank you," Andre replies.

"But there's one thing I'm still kind of confused about."

"What's that?" Andre asks.

"Why did you decide it was a worthy use of your time to take an entire Sunday and try and show me what's so great about this little town?"

Andre clears his throat, opening his eyes and staring up at the sky, as if waking up from a dream. He sits up. "First of all.

What's so great about this little town can absolutely not be re-vealed in one single day. And second of all, I kind of needed a distraction."

"Right," I say, feeling silly. "Of course." But Andre isn't done yet.

"Third of all, I guess just the idea that you might miss out on a huge part of this place, about what makes it special, about what makes it *yours,* was totally inconceivable and unaccept-able to me."

I sit up too, gazing out over the swimming hole.

"It's not that I don't understand that it's special," I tell him. "I just don't want this to be . . . it. I guess I'm just afraid that if I don't go now . . ." I look over to where Andre is studying me. "Maybe I never will."

Andre frowns. "You know, other places could stand to learn a lot from this town."

"What makes you say that?"

Andre looks down at his hands for a moment. "Because when my mom got sick four years ago, and we thought we might lose her, this town came together in a way you couldn't even imagine."

A vision of Andre's mom appears in my head. Her toothy smile, the way she gave Andre just a little bit of a hard time. What seemed like boundless energy radiating off of her and onto her son.

I shake my head. "I didn't know. She seems so . . . strong."

Andre smiles. "She *is* so strong. And she has come such a long way. She kicked cancer's ass. But a big part of that is be-cause of this place. When she was nauseous, or tired, or feeling too weak to get out of bed—and she was, for a very long time—this town was here for her. They brought food over nearly every night. They hosted a fundraiser to help pay for some experimental treatment. They made sure we weren't alone." Andre is gazing off into the distance and seems to snap out of it. He glances over at me. "I know this town can feel small. I know it can be gossipy, and isolated, and I know there is so much more beyond the boundaries of this place. But for me, having seen the genuine goodness here . . ." He stops, and says softly, as though to himself: "There's just nowhere else I'd rather be."

I nod, trying hard to see Chester Falls from Andre's perspective. That the nosiness, and the history, could be frustrating, but it could also add up to something really good. Why you might be afraid to let go of it.

"Maybe that's why you were clinging so tightly to Jess."

Andre's brows scrunch together quizzically. "Meaning . . ."

"Well, you went through something really hard. The whole town came together for you, and I assume she did too. When you said the other day that things were just getting back to normal . . . it must be hard to go through all of that with a person, depend on them in that way, and then not have them be a part of your life anymore. And maybe that's partly why you're here. You don't want to be alone."

Andre stands up. "Wow, you see me so clearly," he says, in the exact same kind of tone I've used with him. "Enough of the deep, soulful talk. That was not the point of today's journey." He holds out a hand to me. "One more jump?"

Smiling, I take his hand.

♡ ♡ ♡

"Where have you been all day?" my mom asks later that night, when I walk in the door a little after five p.m. The scents of onion, garlic, and carrot hit my nose, and my stomach growls. I haven't had anything to eat since a hot dog at the baseball game, granola, plus some cookies Andre's mom snuck in his backpack.

"Around." I take a seat at the table with my dad, who is studying me like a painting.

"Why is your hair . . . wet?" he wants to know.

I pop a baby carrot into my mouth.

"You're sunburned," my mom observes.

"I am?" I lean away from the table, trying to get a sense of my reflection in the side hallway mirror. Sure enough, the tops of my cheeks, forehead, and tip of my nose are all pink, and my hair looks like I went through a car wash.

"There's something else, too," my dad says.

I roll my eyes. "Oh my god, Dad. This isn't one of your detective shows." I hold my hands in the air. "I swear, I'm innocent."

My dad is undeterred. "Do you see it, Helen?" he asks, his eyes not leaving my face.

My mom tilts her head to the side, wielding a wooden spoon. "I do."

"She seems . . ."

"Happy?" My mother finishes his sentence.

"Happy." He nods in agreement.

I get up and start pulling down the plates for dinner. "I

had kind of a fun day, I guess. If it's such a big deal. I went to a swimming hole."

"That's fun!" my mom exclaims. "With Sydney and Tessa?"

"No, this kid Andre Minasian." I lay the plates down on the table one by one.

My mom turns back to the stove. "I didn't know you two were friends. His mom just recovered from cancer earlier this year. Nice family."

I head to the utensil drawer. "Well, we aren't exactly friends. I kind of backed into his car the other day, while I was driving, so I started giving him rides."

"And one of those rides involved taking you to a swimming hole?" My parents share a look.

I put a hand on my hip. "He wanted to show me his favorite spots in town. I guess he feels like I'm missing out on the magic of Chester Falls, or something. What?!" I finish, as my parents share another look. "Just say it."

"It's just, it's nice. Nice to see you doing something fun for a change."

"Youth is wasted on the young," my dad says wistfully. Then, he follows it with: "What makes the Minasian kid so special, by the way?"

I stop. "What do you mean?"

"Well, you haven't taken a single day off in the last six months. How'd *he* get you to do it?"

I pause. I didn't realize I hadn't. "I don't understand the question, and I won't answer it," I tell him, in my best Lucille Bluth impression.

My dad grins. We've always loved *Arrested Development*.

"You know," my mom says. "You should use this. This new perspective on Chester Falls. Bring it into what you're working on for Ava. After all, it's such a big part of you."

I make a face. "That's a matter of opinion."

My parents laugh.

"Sweetheart, you were born here. You grew up here. You ate the food that is grown here and traveled the roads that wind through here. Whether you like it or not, this place is a part of you," my mom says.

"That was poetic," my dad tells her.

"Thank you." My mom looks satisfied.

I look between them, trying to decipher their behavior. Is it me, or are they being weirdly nice to each other?

"But Ava Adams doesn't know anything about Chester Falls," I say.

My mom looks exasperated. "So what? Show her something she's never seen before."

As I watch my mother at the stove, my eyes trail past her, out the window, to her little studio in the dusky light, lopsided and in need of a good coat of paint.

Which is when I realize there is something I could work on, right here at home.

Chapter 17

I SPEND EVERY FREE MOMENT DURING THE NEXT WEEK hunched over my phone and computer, studying Ava Adams's Instagram—her photos, and all the projects she has worked on through the years. Her natural-wood finishes and reclaimed terra-cotta planters and imported textiles. I claw my way through our dusty, dangerous attic trying to find original floor plans for my mom's studio, then just end up measuring it myself and creating detailed before-and-after renderings of the interior and exterior. I'm obviously not a contractor, nor do I have the funds to hire one, so I'll have to stick to the basics. I'll keep the cubbyholes, the general layout, but I'll sand and paint. I'd also like to figure out how to make a sink using rain or hose water, nothing too crazy, just so she can rinse off her brushes without walking to and from the house.

I go to Jacobson's Hardware to pick up some extra paint samples that Bill saved for me, relieved at how small the square footage of the building is. For the interior I choose a crisp, warm white, to open the space up, and for the exterior, a dark slate color, which seems to be all the rage on the west coast right now, a way to turn something historic into something more modern and stylish.

"It's just so . . . dark," my mom observes, when I show her the renderings at the dinner table.

"That's the whole point," I say. "I'm making it contemporary! Chic. Right now, it's kind of a mess."

My mom fidgets. "Well, what if I like it being kind of a mess?"

I shake my head impatiently. "Mom, this is what people like Ava Adams are into. Eliminating some of the craziness and streamlining things. I promise, you are going to love it."

My mom sighs. "I'm all for it, but maybe you could just try something other than the slate. Like a dusty sage?"

I bite my lip. It is her house, after all. "Okay. I promise I won't go too far."

♡ ♡ ♡

Reggie went home early with a stomachache on Thursday, so Andre and I pick up two extra riders for the route home, which I am grateful for. One of them I've never seen before, and one is a girl I only vaguely recognize. I think maybe we had math together sophomore year. Shara. She approaches the car carrying a heavy guitar case. Andre hops out and, ever the gentleman, helps her put it in the giant Prius trunk, which opens like the door to an alien spaceship.

"Thanks," Shara says sweetly as she climbs into the back. Her friend climbs in with her.

"Ashley and Shara, right?" Andre says. He looks at Shara. "We had English together last year."

Does he really know everyone? I wonder.

"That's right." Shara smiles. "Mr. McDougal."

"That dude has style," Andre says, and I have no idea what he's talking about, but Shara lets out a high-pitched, shy giggle.

"He totally does!"

Andre whips his head back around, scrunching up his eyebrows. "Hey, by the way, I didn't know you played guitar."

Shara shrugs. "I don't. Not really."

"Really?" He shares a conspiratorial look with her friend. "Then why are you carrying one around."

Ashley looks meaningfully at Shara, who sighs. "I mean, I sort of do. But mostly just for myself. I take one lesson a week after school." She pauses, as though she isn't sure she wants to continue, then goes on. "I actually started writing some songs recently."

"They are *so* good," Ashley says. "I'm not just saying that to be nice, or whatever. Like I actually ask her to play all the time for me."

"Really?" I chime in. "That's awesome. I'd love to hear them sometime."

Andre makes a face at me like he's shocked.

"What?" I ask softly.

"You need to perform the songs, Shara," Andre announces.

"That is what I always tell her!" Ashley says.

Shara looks horrified. "Are you crazy?! No way."

"People would love it."

Shara is silent, but when I glance back in the mirror, I can see a small smile playing over her lips. "I dunno . . ." she says.

"Okay, here's what you're gonna do," Andre tells her, like everything is totally fine. "You're gonna think about it. You're gonna decide this is a great idea. Then, you're gonna stop into the Smokey Owl in town, when you're ready. The manager there is Gus. Tell him Andre sent you. He'll hook you up with a set."

"Wow, okay . . . thank you!" Shara whispers with excitement.

"Don't thank me yet," Andre says. "Thank me when everyone in town is going crazy over your music."

After we drop Shara off at her guitar lesson, Andre catches me watching him at a red light.

"What is it *now*?" he asks.

"What made you do that?"

"Do what?"

"Suggest she have a gig? You don't know her well. You've never heard her music."

Andre shrugs. "I could tell she just needed a little encouragement." He pauses. "Now, *you* on the other hand . . ."

I balk. "Me? What did I do?"

"I'd love to hear your songs sometime," Andre teases in a mocking, high-pitched voice.

"I was being nice!"

"I know," Andre says. "It was weird."

I knock him in the shoulder. He smiles at me, and my heart does a little fizz. *A Chester Fizz.* I smirk to myself. And then I feel dumb.

♥ ♥ ♥

"Let me just ask this question, and please do not get mad at me," Tessa starts the following Friday afternoon after school, her eyes roaming over the inside of my mom's studio, which bears no resemblance to its former self, or any functional building for that matter. Wood shavings line the floor, tools are strewn about, and paint swatches cover half the walls. "Is it possible that you have bitten off a bit more than you can chew?" Tessa, Sydney, Tucker, and Marcus all stopped by in person since I haven't been great about returning texts lately.

I groan, crouching back down to start sanding again. Turns out sanding takes a lot longer than I thought. Every muscle in me aches, but I don't have time to cry over it. I have to finish so I can get to painting.

"Couldn't you just sketch it out?" Sydney cuts in. She's seated on a bucket just outside the door of the chicken coop, refusing to come in, on account of the fact that she's allergic . . . to what, she didn't specify.

"Ava Adams is a doer," I tell them, looking up from the floorboards. "She's very hands-on. I have to show her I can come and do the work. That I can look at something and transform it on my own."

"You know what you need?" Tucker asks, running his hand along a windowsill and sending a stream of sawdust onto the floor. "Pizza. Pizza will make it all better."

"He's right," Tessa says. "It's never good to do work like this on an empty stomach. It'll fuel you up."

"How much more can you expect to get done tonight?" Marcus says. "Just start up tomorrow. I'll even come back and help you."

"You will?" I stop sanding and look at him.

"You *will*?" Tessa says.

Marcus shrugs. "I mean, maybe. Probably. We'll see."

Tessa shakes her head at him.

"Just go, you guys," I tell them. "It's no big deal." Sure, my hands are raw, and my eyes are red from sawdust, but I'll get this done. I always find a way.

I work a little longer, then sit back against the wall, exhausted. My phone buzzes. I expect it's Sydney, trying to lure me to the barn, or the movies, or whatever else they're doing tonight. But it's not. It's Andre.

ANDRE: Let's meet up. There's something I need to show you.

CHARLIE: Another swimming hole?

ANDRE: No. This is much, much better.

♡ ♡ ♡

"My experience with extraterrestrials began in my early twenties," Matilda Straus explains as we stand atop an old water tower at the back of her property, which sits on one side of a small mountain at the edge of town. It's no longer in operation, and Matilda has painted two words in black print high at the top. UFO'S WELCOME.

"How did I not know about this place?" I whisper to Andre.

"Just listen, for once," he mutters to me out of the corner of his mouth. Then he nudges me playfully with his hip.

"As I was saying." Matilda gives us a look. "Late one night I was driving home from the grocery store when I saw a round, disk-shaped light up in the sky. I thought it was a streetlamp, at first. But the longer I drove, the more I realized it was miles away. It blinked across the stars before speeding up. Then it stopped DEAD." She looks at me, her eyes wide. I swallow. "That's a clear giveaway. A dead stop. No man-made aircraft is capable of movement like that."

I have no way of knowing whether this is true, but Matilda, with her long single braid, simple linen dress, and giant, rose-colored eyeglasses, is convincing.

"Crazy," is all I can manage to say.

"Crazy indeed," Matilda replies. "So I realized, other people have to see this, too. I took a trip to Colorado with my husband, and Joshua Tree National Park, where there are more believers, and of course, Arizona. Around here, people just come for kicks. They don't really *believe* any of it. But you'd be surprised, a lot end up seeing the way. This high up, with an unobstructed view, the sky simply opens up to you. You see things you could never imagine."

"And how many sightings have there been up here, Matilda?"

Andre asks, his arms crossed, his brow furrowed in concentration. Always the conversationalist, even here, one hundred feet above the ground.

"Depends." Matilda scrunches up her lips in thought. "One hundred and eighty?"

I blink.

"Over one hundred alien sightings?" I ask.

Matilda continues. "I've seen about thirty personally, and my husband, Carl, has seen three." She leans against the creaky side of the water tower, and I'm tempted to reach out and grab her before she falls right over the side. "Of course, those are just the ones that have been documented by visitors. Who knows how many haven't been? We encourage you to report them, by the way." She looks between the two of us.

"On it," Andre says.

"You know, there have been a lot of documented alien sightings in the area since the 1700s. Not many people know this, but in 1969, at least five different people encountered the same alien spacecraft just outside Great Barrington. All of them described it the same way. It hovered, it was a bright light, and they each lost at least ten to fifteen minutes of time."

"How do you know this?" I ask.

"I know everything," Matilda says. "And also, it was on *Unsolved Mysteries.*"

I steal a glance at Andre.

Matilda goes on, gazing out at the treetops. "We have a delightful garden. I highly suggest you take a look before you leave. We've had over six psychics all tell us the same thing.

There's a vortex in the garden that creates a connection to another universe."

I bite my lip hard and want to laugh even more when I see the straight face Andre is still maintaining after all this time, listening to every word that comes out of Matilda's mouth.

"You must be very aware of your body in the garden. Ninety-nine percent of people feel the energy. But you must be open to it. Ask the guardians for assistance. Don't be surprised what happens."

"So many statistics," I whisper.

"You don't believe me, and that's fine," Matilda says. "But there have been truly miraculous occurrences."

"Don't knock it until you've tried it, Charlie," Andre says, his face serious. I scowl at him.

"I'm sorry," I say, feeling surprisingly ashamed. "I look forward to checking out the garden, Matilda. I promise to be open."

"The choice is yours, of course," she says. "Whether you are ready to change your life or not. Now, I'll leave you to it." Matilda pauses before climbing back down the ladder. "Please sign the guestbook."

Alone at the top of the tower, I turn to Andre. "This is insane," I say.

"Or is it?" Andre asks. "How are we to really know, if we've never experienced it?"

We sit down, letting our legs dangle over the edge of the tower.

"So, why exactly did you bring me here?" I ask.

"Thought maybe you needed a break," Andre says. "And anyway, it's not all about you, Charlie." He glances at me, smirking. "In truth, I needed a breather too. Jess has been hitting me up nonstop. She wants to talk. To make sure I'm okay, or whatever."

"Oh," I say, surprised by the disappointment I feel. So that's why he wanted to come here. "Well, I'm glad I can be a distraction then, too."

"We can be distractions for each other," Andre adds.

"Do you want to talk about it?" I ask, after a few moments of silence.

Andre shakes his head. "You think I took you out to an alien watchtower only to talk about my ex? No way."

I nod, secretly relieved.

CHARLIE'S BACKSEAT REVIEWS

★★★★★ So friendly and encouraging. Glad I had a ride with Charlie. —Shara

Chapter 18

I SPEND HALF OF MY SATURDAY SHUTTLING PEOPLE around Chester Falls, to sports games and hair appointments, study groups and dance practice, imagining a time very soon when I will be far away from here. The other half of the day I finish painting, plus installing the hose-connected sink made out of poured concrete, really just a little box with a drain hole in the bottom.

On Sunday morning, I wake up extra early and paint the interior of the chicken coop with primer. I want to get the primer in a position to set while I drive Lulu. This would be the perfect time to bail on her, but I never would. I know I've got a lot going on, but from what I know about architects, and from Ava's Instagram, this is what their lives are like. Racing against the clock, balancing multiple things at once, negotiating budgets and trying to get the best possible outcome with tons of conflicting opinions and logistics.

This time, on the drive from Lulu's house to the abandoned municipal building, I find it unusually difficult to silence all the questions I have for her in my head. I keep imagining what Andre would do if he were here in the passenger seat next to me. How he would respond to the briefcase she carries, her perplexing drop-off location. Would he coax the details out of her by sharing something about himself, or would he just out-right ask in his unassuming, charming tone? Either way, there's absolutely no chance he would let her get out of the car with-out revealing her life story.

Lulu catches me staring, but still says nothing. She just looks away.

"See you next week?" I ask once we pull up outside of the old building and she gets out of the car.

"See you next week," she says with a sweet wave.

I watch her set off across the parking lot toward the brick building, and for a brief moment, I think about following her. She wouldn't even have to know, but I'd finally have the an-swers I've been so curious about. I go so far as to put my hand on the car door handle before changing my mind.

"Stay out of her business, Charlie," I say to myself as I pull away. "You wouldn't want her meddling in yours."

♡ ♡ ♡

"This looks *incredible,* Charlie," Andre says on Monday as he sorts through the photos on my phone that I took of the fin-ished chicken coop. I tried to protest, but he snatched it from the cup holder and wouldn't stop bugging me for the code. And when Andre looks at you with his light brown eyes, a smile peeking through at the corner of his mouth, he can be really hard to say no to. I also notice he's jumpy today, more so than usual. I wonder if Jess is still on his mind, or something else. I wonder what it's like to have this energy coursing through your body at all times. "I can't believe you did all of this by yourself." A rush simmers up through me when he says this, swiping through the pics in wonder.

"It really does look good," Reggie says, leaning over from the back seat. "I've never seen a house that color before."

"Thanks, Reggie," I say, and I mean it. My body is tingling with energy from head to toe. I've never felt this proud of anything.

When I got back after driving Lulu yesterday, I started to paint the exterior of the chicken coop a pale green, but I kept imagining what Ava would think of it. Shabby chic. Pedestrian. Childish. After only a few strokes I dug around for the cans of slate I originally picked up and got to work. I know my mom asked me not to, but once she sees it, I'm confident she'll love it.

I strung up patio lights and added a wooden planked entrance for people to scrape off their shoes before entering the space. My mom is always getting her shoes covered in mud when it rains, and it pools there. This should take care of that.

Then I replaced all my mom's stuff, took photos, and left it for her to find this morning. I can't wait to see her reaction when I get home. I thought she might text me or something, to tell me what she thought when she saw it, but she's never been great with phones anyway. She's always forgetting her passcode.

All I keep thinking is, if I was able to do this, in such a short time span, what else can I do?

Andre hands the phone back to me. Our fingers touch for a moment. He smells good, and warm. My cheeks start to feel warm, too. *Remember, you're just a distraction, Charlie,* I think to myself.

"I can't wait to hear what Ava thinks," I say. "I'm pretty sure she wasn't expecting me to renovate an actual building when she asked to see my work."

"Definitely *not,*" Andre says, his eyes catching mine again. He runs a hand through his hair. "Well, I'll tell you what I think. You should be really proud. And you deserve to celebrate. We're going bowling."

♡ ♡ ♡

"I can't believe you didn't know about Lanes and Games," Andre says to me as we pull up in front of a nondescript, run-down building located at the edge of a strip mall two towns over. Reggie had to go meet his math tutor, and he was really disappointed not to join us. "It's the best place on earth."

The longer we're together in this car, the more agitated Andre appears. I tried to tell him I didn't know if I could take an afternoon off from work to go bowling, but he wouldn't take no for an answer. He just kept pushing it. So now, even though we're supposed to be here for me, I'm really here for him.

"Oh, I knew it was here," I say, my eyes taking in the dingy windows, the missing letters on the sign. "I just didn't know it was still in business."

Andre grins. "Just you wait."

Inside, Andre pays the shoe rental attendant and we sit down on a bench to pull on classic two-toned bowling shoes that reek of sole freshener. I am grateful I'm wearing extra-thick socks today, though they do make the shoes feel a little tighter.

"Have you ever bowled before?" Andre wants to know, his head tilted to the side as he bends over to tie his laces.

I think for a minute. "Once, a few years ago, when we visited my aunt in Boston. But we used the smaller bowling balls and little pins. Not the giant ones with finger holes you see on TV."

"Small pins are where it's *at,*" Andre says, always saying the thing to make you feel more comfortable. "They never get enough respect." He leads the way out and around the side of the shoe rental area, and the whole building opens up, revealing a space with bright lights, gleaming hardwood floors, and tons and tons of people.

"Wow. It's so . . . busy!" I exclaim as Andre sits down in a booth and starts inputting our names on a keyboard.

"It's Monday night," he says, like it's obvious. "Bowling league night."

I stare down at him. "How do you know so much about everything?"

He looks smug. "I'm smart, I guess. Also, it's written on the sign over there." He points to a placard next to a pinball machine.

I roll my eyes. "Okay, but I mean in this town in general. Seems like you know all the spots."

Andre looks down, his smile growing, and I could swear he's blushing. When he looks back up and meets my eyes, I feel suddenly self-conscious. "I guess I just pay attention."

I sit down next to him while he finishes putting our information into the computer and let my eyes roam the space more closely, noticing for the first time just how old everything is. The place we went in Boston was dark inside and had so many neon lights that you could barely see straight. Lanes and Games looks like it has barely been touched in sixty years, except maybe the bowling TVs atop every station. The walls are a pastel pink, the wood pins are covered in scratches, and it looks like the gutters are hand carved. A few steps up and over to the right there's an old-fashioned-looking pizza parlor and a large half-moon bar.

"This would be way more fun if we had White Russians right now," Andre says, his eyes darting around as he taps his foot.

"What's a White Russian?" I ask, wiggling my toes, trying to decide if they've gone completely numb or not. "And are you okay? You seem a little . . . off."

Andre stares at me blankly. *"The dude abides?"* he asks.

I blink. "Who is the dude?"

"The Big Lebowski!" Andre practically shouts, resting hands on top of his head like he can't believe what I'm saying. The people next to us turn and look, and he extends a hand in apology before continuing. "Only the greatest movie of all time! Tell me you've seen it."

I shake my head. "We didn't have a TV until I was thirteen . . ."

Andre rubs his eyes like even being around me is exhausting. "You say that like it's a valid excuse. *The Big Lebowski* should be seen by *everyone.*"

"Okay, well, what's it about?"

"Jeff Bridges plays this stoner who gets roughed up in a case of mistaken identity, has his rug peed on, and when he goes to find the man responsible for his exponentially shitty day, gets pulled into a crazy underworld of crime."

I make a face. "Sounds dark."

"It's actually a comedy," Andre explains.

"Oh. Well, then it sounds confusing."

Andre shakes his head. "It's awesome. He also drinks White Russians all day long and is in the finals of his club bowling league."

"No wonder you like this drink," I say, looking it up on my phone. "It's basically just a milkshake with alcohol."

Andre grins. "Exactly." Then he rotates toward the lanes. "Should we do this thing?"

Andre picks up a ball and throws it down the lane with more force than necessary. Then he steps back, moving from foot to foot. Like he is afraid to stop moving. Even when I bowl, he seems distracted, looking at his phone while he jiggles his leg, or chatting with nearby bowlers.

"Andre, seriously, are you okay?" I finally ask when I join him on the bench again.

He frowns, standing up. "Totally. I've just been having trouble sleeping, that's all." He avoids eye contact with me when he says this, which isn't like him. I wonder if Andre is completely willing to become engrossed in conversation as long as it has nothing to do with things that are really bothering him.

"You know, you can talk to me. I mean, you're always here for *me*."

Andre clears his throat. "It's nothing, it's just this thing with my parents," he says. "They told me they think I'm wasting my time waiting on Wilson. That I should go to Tulane." His eyes have become dark and angry.

"Why do you think they said that?" I ask delicately.

"They obviously know Wilson is a great school, but they said I should expand my horizons. That it would be good for me to get out of here for a little while."

I swallow. "Well, why did you apply to Tulane if you don't really want to go?"

Andre moves his head back and forth, thinking. "The lacrosse coach recruited me. And they have this famous social psychology program. My college counselor thought I might be interested."

"And were you?"

Andre shrugs. "I mean, yeah. But I'd rather be here."

As I watch Andre, slumped back in his seat, his arms folded over his chest, I realize something for the first time. He's not trying to stay close to home because he's so obsessed with it. He's trying to stay here because he's afraid to leave.

Andre interrupts my thoughts. "I know you're going to tell me to move on, in the Charlie Owens way. But I can't. Everyone keeps talking about next year, and right now I have no idea what next year is going to look like. I don't want to imagine."

I sigh. "I'm sorry, Andre," I say, and his expression softens.

"That's it? You aren't going to tell me I'm being dumb?"

I shake my head. "No."

A little while later, when Andre gets up to bowl his turn, I tell him he can bowl mine, too. Andre doesn't protest, and by the time my turn comes around again, I've returned with two creamy white cocktails.

"How did you do that?!" Andre asks. "Do you have a fake?"

"I told the bartender that my friend was having a tough week, and maybe he could do us a solid." We each take a sip. It tastes good, but it burns. Andre closes his eyes.

"Man, that is perfect," he exclaims. Then, before I know what he's doing, he hugs me. His skin is warm to the touch and his hair feels soft against my neck. I realize we've never done this before. Hugged. I also realize I really, really like it.

"Thanks, Charlie," he says pulling away. "This was really cool of you."

"Don't mention it," I manage, still regaining composure after the hug.

"Good, right?" Andre nods toward the drink.

"Good," I say.

"Thanks for coming with me today. This might be the best thing to happen to me all week."

I blush, and I open my mouth to tell him that he shouldn't be afraid, because honestly, a guy like him will do well anywhere he goes. But before I can get the words out, I feel a rough hand on my shoulder and look up into the angry eyes of a man with a Lanes and Games name tag on.

"Not again, Andre," he says.

Andre sighs. "Neil, I'm sorry. I didn't mean . . ."

"Enough of your excuses. You guys need to go."

Stifling our giggles, we gather our stuff, change out of our shoes, and leave.

♥ ♥ ♥

Once we're seated back in the car, Andre rolls his eyes, exasperated. "What a buzzkill that guy is," he says. "We were just having fun. Not like we're gonna get wasted off of one spiked milkshake in the afternoon."

"Yeah, but we were also drinking, underage, at his business," I offer. "Also . . . it kind of seemed like he's been down this road with you before." When Andre doesn't respond, I push him. "Andre."

"What? I mean, yeah, I got in trouble there a couple weeks ago with some guys from the team. I used a fake, the bartender doesn't care, Neil does."

"A couple weeks ago?! And you came back?" I lean back in my seat. "You really love to push the limits, don't you?" I breathe.

Andre turns his head toward mine, the smile gone from his face. "Can you just take me home?"

I swallow as I put the car in gear. "Yeah. Sure."

♥ ♥ ♥

When I get home from dropping Andre off in the late afternoon, I find my mom standing in the yard with her tea, her back to me, facing the new studio.

I walk up beside her, and she still says nothing, just stares at it.

"What do you think?" I ask.

"It's . . ." She blinks, hard, and shakes her head, as though trying to wake herself from a dream. She takes a step inside, and when a moment or two passes and she still hasn't said anything, I wonder if it's a good dream or a bad one.

"You don't like it . . ." I say, realizing it myself as I say it out loud.

My mom sighs. "I just . . . it's completely changed, Charlie. It's not even the same building anymore."

"And what's wrong with that?" I ask her. "What is wrong with one thing around here changing just a little bit? I wanted to make it feel modern."

"You can modernize a space without . . ." She struggles to find the words. "Without taking so much of it away."

I swallow. "You just don't get it."

I expect my mom to ask me what I mean, but instead she says: "What exactly did you think I'd say? It was my studio! And I told you I didn't like the color. You know . . ." She shakes her head.

Now I am the one pushing her. "What?"

"It's like you're so focused on what this Ava person will think, you're blowing off the things that should matter to you."

I look up at her. "I shouldn't be that surprised you have a problem with change, I guess." Then I storm off to my room.

Chapter 19

THE NEXT MORNING, I WAKE UP AND SCROLL OBSESSIVELY through the email I sent to Ava. The images, the description of the studio. I rewatch the video walk-through over and over until my eyes hurt. I know I should be more patient, but with each passing day, I'm only more confident that she will love what I sent her, mainly because it looks exactly like something *she* would do. Well, as close as a teen girl with minimal resources living in the middle of the mountains could get. I imagine her reaction when she sees it. Nodding in approval. Showing it to the rest of her studio team. Patting herself on the back for taking a chance on that girl from the ride share app in the Berkshires.

I'm feeling so confident that by the time my phone rings on Thursday night, I am in the middle of mapping out the route from Chester Falls to New Mexico and all the places I'll stop in between, like Philip Johnson's Glass House in Connecticut and Frank Lloyd Wright's Fallingwater in Pennsylvania. I want to go to the Arcosanti arcology in Arizona, and Spiral Jetty in Utah. Most of all, I want to visit the Chinati Foundation in Marfa, Texas. I hear there's a hotel there made entirely of vintage Airstreams. Maybe I can even take a detour out to California, see the Eames House in LA, and the Sea Ranch community and the Golden Gate Bridge in Northern California. Maybe on the way home I can go south, see Charleston and New Orleans. Or maybe I'll have to save that for a separate trip —

"Hello?" I answer, my voice coming out weird and strained, and my chest catching in my throat when I see Ava's name.

"Charlie? Hey, it's Ava."

My heartbeat picks up a mile a minute now as I greet Ava in return, only slightly eased by the friendliness in her voice.

"Oh, hey!"

"Hi hi. So listen, I got all your images. The work you did on the chicken-coop studio." There's a pause, and I hear her take a breath. My heart flips.

"It was great work, Charlie. It really was."

"That's so great—" I start to say, excited to tell her more about my process, ready to explain why I chose to do it the way that I did, but Ava cuts me off before I can speak, her tone smooth and direct.

"But ultimately, I have to say that I did find it a bit derivative."

I swallow, heading outside so I can hear her better. "Okay . . ."

"To be more to the point, it sort of looked like a lot of

what we are already doing. And a lot like what everyone else is doing. But the thing with design is, we are always, *always* trying to look to the future. We have to evolve. Do you know what I mean?"

My heart sinks as I try to muster the courage to speak, thinking of all the time I spent sanding the studio. All for nothing. "I think I do, yeah. I mean, looking into the future is like, all I think about." I laugh, but it sounds high pitched and hollow.

"Well, that's great. And I know you are young, don't get me wrong. But I found myself wondering, as I looked through the images, and watched the video: What is Charlie's actual perspective? What does she want to bring to the table?"

I take a deep breath. "I guess . . . I guess I thought I was still figuring that out?" I stutter. I want to tell her this is the first thing I've ever worked on. How proud I am of it. But I don't want her to know how green I truly am. "I'm sorry," I add.

There's a pause on the other end of the line, and Ava's voice comes out tinged with regret. "Do not apologize. Listen, when you get to architecture school, critiques, they are no joke. Architects love to tear each other down. It's all part of the process of getting better. I'm just giving you feedback here. The sooner you can grow a thicker skin, the better off you will be."

"Okay . . ."

"So, I want you to take another shot at this. Show me your perspective. Not mine. Don't just take a structure and change it into something that looks pretty. I want to know why you made those choices. What did you think about while creating this?"

I nod vigorously, even though she can't see me. "Okay, I can do that."

"Great!" she says brightly, and just like that, the critique is over. "Do you think you could have it to me in three weeks?" Her voice goes down to a whisper. "The truth is, my business partner has someone who is interested in the gig, but I really want to give you a good shot of getting it."

I nod again, swallowing, feeling a brief burst of confidence. "I won't let you down, Ava."

Ava laughs. "It's not about that. Really. Just show me who you are. Okay?"

"Okay. Thank you," I tell her.

"Anytime, girl. Talk soon."

I let the phone fall to my side and stare at the chicken coop. Suddenly everything that seemed so perfect about it, so sleek and smooth, its clean lines and overuse of plants, seems utterly ridiculous. A child's exercise.

What was I thinking?

Tears start forming, and I can't make them stop. She hated it.

I hear a shuffle behind me. "Was that the tiny house woman?" my dad asks.

I wipe my eyes. "Ava," I say. "She didn't like it. She called it your least favorite word. Derivative."

My dad's face contorts into a heavy frown. "Oh, come on. Most of what's out there is derivative. Give me a break!" He looks genuinely pissed on my behalf. "You're seventeen years old!"

"She said I need to show her more of my perspective. I'm standing in my freaking yard!" I say, and then the tears start coming.

"Come here," my dad says, putting his arm around me. "Come on, don't lose hope. You renovated a whole building! Do you know what you'll be doing in five years? Ten? Can you imagine?"

I wipe my tears away. "Mom hates it. She's mad."

My dad shakes his head. "She doesn't hate it. She just doesn't feel it's very . . . authentic."

"Her and Ava."

"Okay, well, let's talk about it," my dad says, guiding me over to the porch bench and sitting us both down. "You took something from your house, yes. But then you sort of just . . . washed over it."

I sniff. "I just wanted something to change. Anything." As soon as the words leave my mouth, I know I'm not really talking about the house, and I wonder if my dad knows it, too.

"Yes, but you also made it look like everything else," my dad says. "It's in your yard, but is it you?"

I shake my head. "I don't know."

"What if we help?" My dad squeezes my arm, but I shake him off. "Your mom and me. You know, I do have some experience with woodworking . . ."

"Thanks, Dad, but I need to do this on my own."

"Why?" my dad asks, and I don't know how to tell him that

I'm not sure I can really trust him to help. And I can't have him let me down right now.

I head upstairs to my room and pull my phone out of my back pocket, staring at it. My stomach dips a little bit when I realize there's really only one person I want to call right now, and it's Andre. After what happened yesterday, I'm not sure if I should. He seemed kind of pissed after the bowling alley. But right now, I don't care. Right now, I just need to hear him tell me that everything is going to be okay.

He answers on the first ring. "Hey."

"Hey." I steel myself. "Can we talk?"

"Yeah," he says, his voice softening. "Actually, could you come get me? I kind of need a ride . . ."

"It's like nine p.m. . . ." I frown. "Where are you?"

From the other end of the line, I hear the sound of Andre clearing his throat. "I'm at the police station."

My breath catches. "Andre, are you okay?"

"I'm okay. But I can't really talk. I'll explain when you get here."

♡ ♡ ♡

I move quickly when I hang up the phone, pulling a sweater on over my T-shirt and sweatpants and heading down the mountain, taking a right and then a left until I end up outside the Chester Falls police department. Andre is sitting there on the steps, looking like he did the day I picked him up outside of Jess's dorm. Except tonight he doesn't look sad, he looks exhausted.

Andre gets into the car, and suddenly I'm nervous.

"Thanks," he says, smiling at me in a way I haven't really seen him do before. It's sweet, and it's grateful. It's also adorable. "Sorry about this. But I couldn't call my parents, and when you called . . ."

"Andre, what happened?" I ask. "Are you hurt?" I want to reach out a hand to touch him, but I stop myself.

"I'm fine," he says. "Seriously. We didn't even mean for it to be a big deal. It was just a silly prank."

I straighten up. "A prank. You got . . . wait, you were *arrested*? I thought you'd been in an accident or something."

Andre shakes his head. "Nothing like that. It was all just some fun, I swear."

I frown. "What did you do?"

"We kind of tried to borrow some chickens from the Perrys' farm . . ."

"You stole the Perrys' chickens?" I ask.

Andre clears his throat "*No,* not stole! Borrowed! Everyone keeps using that word." He runs a hand through his hair. "We were just going to put them around the school so when everyone woke up, there would be chickens running around. It was harmless. A senior prank."

I stare at him. "You were going to steal someone else's property, and break in to a school. Do you know how much trouble you could have gotten in for that? What is wrong with you?"

Now, he laughs. "What is wrong with me? Charlie, this may come as a shock to you, but this is a thing high schoolers do. Stupid stuff. Make mistakes. We were just having a little fun."

"Yeah, this seems super fun," I say, gesturing toward the police station.

Andre's jaw juts out. "You're acting like my mother or something," he says, and I want to tell him that tracks, since he's acting like a child.

Instead, I stare at him. His leg is jiggling again, and he's gnawing on his lip. "I know you're scared," I say quietly.

Andre whips his head around and stares at me like I'm a movie in a foreign language that he can't understand. "What?"

"I know you're scared of what's next. Of leaving this place. After everything that happened with your mom . . ."

"Please," he says, shaking his head. "Don't."

"But you can't run away from it. You can't pretend it's not happening. You say you like to be in the present, not obsess over the future. But I don't think you're really in your present at all."

Andre stares at me, his face cold. "That's really what you think of me?"

I open my mouth to speak, then close it. Suddenly I wonder . . . what am I doing here? I was so worried about him, and he doesn't even get it. He's only thinking about himself. "I care about you, Andre. But I'm not going to let you string me along like you do everyone else, just because you don't have your shit together."

Andre nods, like he's digesting what I've said. "You've made that perfectly clear. Sorry to get in the way of all your important plans, Charlie. This was a mistake."

"You're right," I say, starting up the car. "This is something you need to talk about with your parents, anyway. I'll take you home."

"No, I mean this," Andre says. "This whole situation. Us riding together. It was a bad idea."

"Wait, what?"

"You think you've got me all figured out, Charlie," he says. "I liked it better when you wanted nothing to do with my life."

Before I can say another word, Andre gets out of the car. And he's gone.

Chapter 20

"WHERE IS ANDRE?" REGGIE ASKS ON TUESDAY AFTERNOON, when he climbs into the back of the car and finds the front passenger seat empty once again. I did my best to distract him the last couple of days, dodging his frequent questions. Instead, I decided to do what Andre would do. Ask him about himself. We covered Nathan's progress (promising), how school is going (very well), and if he's making any friends (long silence after this one, so I changed the subject). It was hard, listening so intently, not to mention coming up with follow-up questions, and it made me miss Andre's presence in an unexpected way. How easy he made it all look. How he seemed to always bring out the best in people.

Now, I'm out of distractions, unable to explain, to tell Reggie what really happened. Andre and I had a fight. Andre doesn't want to ride with us anymore. Or maybe it was me?

Was I the one who made him feel like he couldn't come? However you spin it, the one true fact is that Andre is getting to school some other way from here on out.

I texted him this morning, but still haven't gotten a response. I waited to see the simple ride alert pop up on my phone. To see him begrudgingly get into the car, even if he wasn't happy about it. But the alert never came, and I picked up Reggie, and only Reggie. And it's impossible for me to ignore the fact that Andre had become way more than just another passenger.

I did see Andre today at school, at a distance across the cafeteria, but this time, he didn't even lock eyes with me, in a way that seemed purposeful, instead engaging in some animated conversation at the table with his friends.

"Andre isn't coming," I tell Reggie finally.

"Why not?"

"He's just over it, I guess," I say, because really, that's the best I can do.

"Over us?" Reggie asks.

I turn around and look at him. "No. Not you. Me."

"Well, can't you fix it?" Reggie asks, and I find myself wondering the same thing when another alert pops up on my phone and, before I even have a chance to really look at it, a boy opens the door and pokes his head in. "Charlie?" he asks.

"That's me."

"Okay if I sit up front?" As the boy gets into the passenger seat, wearing a perfectly ironed button-down shirt and khaki pants, I notice a plastic box in his hands. It has clear sides and a perforated top. And inside is the distinct form of a—

"Is that a snake?!" I ask, my voice coming out in a squeak.

The boy looks sheepish. "I promise he's friendly. And besides, he can't get out. I swear."

"Okay." I swallow, trying to think if Backseat has any rules about this. But even if they do, am I really going to say no to this kid? He clearly needs a ride home.

Any other thoughts I have are blocked out by Reggie screaming.

"ARE YOU SERIOUS?" he exclaims, scooching up to the front of his seat and peering around the boy. "What kind is it?"

The boy's face lights up. "It's a California kingsnake."

"Cool," Reggie says admiringly, getting his face level with the box. "I read that those hunt rattlesnakes."

"Wait, they eat rattlesnakes?" I ask. "But aren't rattlesnakes already, like, really terrifying?"

The boys ignore me. The new rider, whose name I have now determined is Jasper, nods eagerly. "It's so cool."

"So badass," Reggie agrees.

"Did you know that in prehistoric times, snakes actually ate—"

"Baby dinosaurs?" Reggie squeals, practically jumping out of his seat at the same time Jasper says it, and they both laugh. I find myself laughing along too, despite how disturbing this is.

"Gross," I add, and the boys look at me like I'm insane.

"My mom won't let me have any snakes," Reggie laments. "So I have a tadpole. But he's well on his way to becoming a frog."

"Nice," Jasper says. "I'd love to see him."

"I'll bring him into school sometime," Reggie says happily.

I press my lips together, trying to remain cool. Reggie is finally making a friend.

Then my heart sinks, because all I want to do is tell Andre.

"I mean, you could hold him now, if you want?" Jasper says, looking up at me hopefully.

"DEFINITELY NOT," I say. "Now everyone put your seat belts on or I'm not going anywhere."

"You sound like my mom," Reggie says.

"Are far as you're concerned, right now, I am."

♡ ♡ ♡

"Is he going to come back?" Reggie asks after we drop Jasper off and once we pull up outside his house. He has one hand on the open door, one leg dangling out onto the road.

"Who?" I ask, even though I know who. Suddenly, I feel so tired.

Reggie raises an eyebrow at me. "You *know* who."

I sigh. "Probably not, if you want the truth."

Reggie scrunches his mouth together. I think he's going to push the issue again, but instead he just says: "Well, I miss him." He hops out (quite literally, as his legs are too short to reach the ground) and scoots up the front walk, where his mom waits by the open door. She gives me a wave. I wave back.

"Me too," I say out loud, even though there is nobody there to hear it.

♡ ♡ ♡

Later that night, I'm curled up on the sofa next to my dad's comfy chair watching two police detectives hot on the trail of a murderer who has left several victims dead in the span of a single month. They sit before the computer, waiting for DNA to turn up a hit, only to determine that the serial killer died three months before these women were murdered.

"Oh, come *on*," I exclaim.

My dad holds a hand up to silence me. "They'll figure it out," he says. "They always do."

I settle back in, unwilling to admit to anyone but myself that I'm actually enjoying this.

"So, what's up?" my dad asks, muting the TV during a commercial break.

"What do you mean, what's up?" I shove some popcorn in my mouth.

"Well, why aren't you out tonight, on one of your rides, or with your friends?"

"Not up for it," I say, mouth full. "Too much on my mind."

"Your portfolio?" my dad asks, and I nod, but in reality, it is so much more than that. Because the exact person I have come to count on in situations like these, when I'm feeling stuck, doesn't want to talk to me. "Don't lose hope, sweetheart," my dad says, and it takes me a second to realize who he's talking about. "Ava agreed to give you another chance because she is eager to see what you can do. You have to keep pushing."

I reach my hand in the bowl again. "Sometimes pushing things too hard can break them. Maybe you have the right idea."

My dad looks confused. "What?"

I study my hands. "I mean that you and Mom technically separated years ago. And now you're living together like everything's normal, but it's obviously not . . . and you haven't been in the barn in like, six years."

My dad leans forward. "I've definitely had some setbacks. And I know it must be hard to see that. You seem to think it's easy, just picking up and moving on. But it's hard for us. This place has a lot of memories. A lot of them very good. This whole town is a part of who we are." He looks over at me. "By the way, it's a part of who you are, too. You used to love it here. Hiking for wildflowers, going to the apple orchard, racing up and down that tiny mountain you can barely call a ski resort. Spending all your time at that run-down barn on Tessa's property, so I had to practically drag you home at night. You can't give up on a place. You can't just wipe it away and try and start over. You have to work with it. Make it suit *you*."

I stop chewing, thinking about what Ava said on the phone. About how the work I did on the studio didn't show my process. Didn't show who I was. But the barn is already a part of me. Maybe it's another chance.

I stand up, popcorn falling off my body.

"Where are you going?" My dad observes me closely.

"I think you just gave me an idea." The barn, the place I've always fantasized about renovating, about really using for something besides parties and bonfires. I can make it something special.

My dad watches me. "And you're not going to tell me what it is, are you?"

I shake my head. "Not until I figure out if it's possible."

I walk over to him and rest a hand on his shoulder. "But

Dad, if I'm going to figure out how to work with this town . . ."
I stop.

"What?" he says.

"Do you think you could try, too? Try to do the things that used to bring you joy?"

He clears his throat. "I can try." But I can tell he doesn't mean it.

As I head upstairs, I hear the TV turn back on.

CHARLIE'S BACKSEAT REVIEWS

★★★★★ Even when she's in a bad mood, Charlie always makes me feel welcome. Best part of my day, second only to bio class.
—Reggie

★★★★★ She was cool about my snake.
—Jasper

Chapter 21

"YOU WANT TO RENOVATE THE BARN?" TESSA ASKS, HER arms crossed in front of her chest. We're standing on her property, just below the big barn door, on which I've pinned up a series of plans, along with images I pulled from online and from the depths of my bedroom. Photos from our sleepovers. Old photographs of Tessa's relatives standing proudly in front of the barn when it was just built. Wildflowers, wool blankets, and locally made pottery for inspiration.

"Not renovate so much as . . . spruce up," I say as I admire the plans. I'm already seeing things I'd change, or things I'd like to add. It's fun to feel my mind working this way. Like it has a higher purpose.

"So, kind of like you did with the chicken coop?" Sydney has a hand on her hip, a look on her face that says she's trying to be supportive; she just isn't on the same page yet.

"Exactly. But this will be more intentional." I shove my

hands in my pockets. "The mistake I made on the chicken coop was that I tried to turn it into something it wasn't. I didn't pay attention to what it already *was*. Ava wants to understand my process and see *me* in the work. I want to work with the structure of the barn to make it a better version of itself. Something that straddles the old and the new."

Tessa frowns. "I mean, it's a great idea, but it's definitely a big project. Don't you need a contractor for something like this?"

"If we want to put a bathroom in, we do," I tell her. "But I looked up the property at the town hall, and we can get water and electricity out here if we want it. Or we can do a composting toilet and use the well for an outdoor shower."

Tessa looks impressed. "Wow. So this could actually . . . happen?"

"If we want to make it happen, we can," I tell her.

"I'll have to talk to my parents about it. They barely ever come back here, but it's still their land."

I pull out my phone, practically shaking with excitement. "That's by far the best part, Tess." I click on the Airbnb list I saved a couple of nights ago. "These are properties in nearby towns that people rent out for the weekend. Historic cottages and barns and apartments. Most of them aren't *half* as cool as what you've got."

Sydney takes the phone out of my grasp. "Holy shit, Tess, some of these run for over five hundred dollars a night!"

"And none of them are on this kind of land, with a pond, and views," I add. "City people love the country experience. A weekend on a working farm is just what they're looking for."

Now Tessa reaches out and grabs the phone. "This could be the extra income we need," she says, sounding breathless. "There are so many things we could put the money toward."

"You could drop off some of your fresh flowers and yogurt in the morning, your mom could bake some of those amazing scones, and guests could go and check out the alpaca while they sip their coffee. It would be such a hit."

"Damn, you make it sound like a place I'd even pay to stay at, and I *live* here." Tessa laughs, handing the phone back to me.

"That's what I was going for."

Tessa places her hands on her hips, surveying the land as though looking at it through new eyes. Slowly, she nods. "Okay," she says.

"Okay?" I ask.

"Let me talk to my parents."

I do a little dance. "This is going to be so fun."

"I'm really glad you're getting us involved this time, Charlie," Sydney says as she starts walking back to her car.

I pause my dance. "I didn't realize you guys wanted to help . . ."

Sydney and Tessa look at each other and shake their heads. "Of course we do. You just never ask."

♡ ♡ ♡

"What I am telling you is that you have given me a cursed product, and it has greatly affected my well-being and safety," Cindi Porter says. She is standing in the middle of Wild Oats, her cheeks flushed, beads dangling from her neck and wrists, her hair in a long French braid down her back. In her right hand is a bottle of tea tree oil. I came in to get a latte a few minutes earlier and found her telling Theo that the tree that the oil was harvested from is angry, and that the oil is now cursed.

"Mrs. Porter," Theo tells her, "I assure you, the tea tree oil is absolutely, one hundred percent *not* cursed."

"Well, I assure *you* that you are one hundred percent *wrong*," she says through gritted teeth. "Since I bought this oil, everything in my life has fallen apart." She leans in and whispers, "The tree has come for me."

I cross my arms, feeling unusually bold today. "Like what?"

She notices me. "What?"

"You're saying that everything in your life has fallen apart. So, what exactly has fallen apart?"

Mrs. Porter sniffs. "Well, if you must know. My car broke down on Mountain Road two days ago, all my peonies are dead, and I'm blind in my right eye."

I want to tell Cindi Porter that she broke down on Mountain Road because she drives a Volkswagen van that has to be jump-started at least once a week, and her peonies are dead, just like everything else in her yard, because she never waters them, and she's not blind in her right eye, her glasses are cracked. But there's no point. Some people just need something to be upset about. You learn that quickly when you work in a service job.

Theo shakes her head. "I would be more than happy to return the oil for you in exchange for a full refund."

Cindi shoves the bottle at her. "Just take it. I can have no further business in this store."

Theo closes her eyes hard and takes a deep breath.

"She's one of our best customers," she laments after Cindi leaves. "I'm just glad Roger and Kit weren't here to see that."

"You did good," I tell her, and she gives me an appreciative smile and walks off.

The door jingles again, and I prepare myself for Mrs. Porter to come back with another thing she wants to complain about, but instead I hear an odd sort of cough, and when I turn around, I'm looking right at Andre.

"Oh, hi," I say in an awkwardly and irrationally pleasant way, but he doesn't smile back. Instead, he looks down, then walks up to the counter. It's empty though, and Theo is nowhere in sight.

"I'm just here to pick something up," he says. "A carrot cake for my mom. I called it in earlier." He stuffs his hands in his pockets. "I didn't know you would be here."

My heart sinks. "Oh. Well, sorry . . . I am."

Now Andre is the one to close his eyes. "That's not what I meant. I just . . ." He stuffs his hands in his pockets and looks down.

"One carrot cake!" Theo says, appearing out of nowhere, setting it down on the table. "That'll be nineteen dollars."

Andre fishes some cash out of his pocket and hands it to Theo. "Keep the change."

"So, how have you been getting around?" I shift my latte between my hands.

Andre shrugs. "Different ways. My parents, mostly. My car should be ready in a couple weeks," he adds.

"That's great!" I say, and then we stare at each other for a moment. "Listen . . ." I start, but then the door bangs open again and a bunch of members of the volleyball team storm in, ponytails swinging like weapons, girls laughing loudly.

"Oh boy," Theo mutters under her breath. "Nine spinach-banana smoothies with whipped cream coming right up, as though that choice makes any sense." She rolls her eyes and walks off to get the ingredients.

My eyes dart between Andre and the incoming crowd. "Um . . ."

Andre holds the cake bag up in a gesture. "I'll see you around."

♡ ♡ ♡

A little while later, after the volleyball team has left in a sea of laughter, I'm just about to gather my things and head out when someone sets a pale green foamy beverage down next to me.

"It has chamomile," Theo says as she sits down across from me. "And pea milk."

"Neither of those elements explain why it's so *green*," I tell her.

She purses her lips. "Just drink it. It's soothing."

I raise an eyebrow suspiciously. "What makes you think I need soothing?"

Theo makes a face like she shouldn't have to explain herself.

I sigh, then pick the cup up and bring it to my lips, taking a sip and swallowing it down. "You're right. Also, it's freaking delicious."

Theo pumps her fist in the air in victory, then settles down.

"So, do you want to tell me what that was all about? With the handsome cake boy?"

I frown at her. "We never get into the nitty-gritty of our lives."

Theo shrugs. "Maybe that's because I never had anything very interesting to talk about. But clearly, you do." She glances pointedly back in the direction of the door.

I shake my head. "I may have screwed up."

Theo's eyebrows go up. "Charlie Owens? Who always has everything so under control?"

"Yeah. Not this . . ." I grimace.

"I'm listening . . ."

"He started out as one of my riders," I say. "But somehow, he became this big part of my life. The problem is, he also drives me crazy. He's constantly pushing the limits, and acting out, but it's obvious he's just scared of moving on from here. And me, all I *want* to do is move on from here. And he doesn't get that either."

Theo watches me intently, now sipping on what was supposed to be my latte.

"Sounds like you really care about him."

I watch her out of the corner of my eye. "What about our massive fight and total differences gives you the impression that we care about each other?"

Theo rolls her eyes. "Because if you didn't, then you wouldn't be so pissed off about what the other is doing with their life. And you wouldn't be so sensitive." She adds: "Trust me. This happens on *Riverdale* all the time."

I sigh. "I didn't mean for it to get this out of hand."

Theo shrugs. "So apologize," she says.

"Well, why can't he?" I ask.

"You're only asking that question because you like him, and you're scared of getting hurt," she mutters, and I know she's right.

Chapter 22

ON FRIDAY I SIT IN THE ART STUDIO LONG AFTER SCHOOL is over, working on my plans and periodically turning to look up inspiration on the internet or in some of the books I took out from the town library. I research the early farmers of the area, the way that buildings were designed so they could fit into their land. Nothing ostentatious, but everything designed around working, cooking, and family. Then I pull out old photos of our sleepovers from when we were kids, the way we used the top loft to sleep, and how we were able to fix the old hay trolley to lift all our snacks through the floors instead of having to try and balance them as we climbed the tall ladders.

But something doesn't feel right. There are so many possibilities, but I can't focus on one. I feel listless. It isn't enough to just look at these spaces from the outside. I need to be inside one of them. To feel what it's like to take something from the past and bring it into the future.

As my eyes roam over my digital inspiration board, I come across an image of my favorite room at MaCA: the atrium in Building C. I glance at my watch, noticing that I have two hours until closing. It's a little crazy, but it's just enough time to get there and walk around and try and spark something.

I hop into the car and make the fifty-minute drive to MaCA, and before heading to Building C, I take care to explore the exterior grounds, noticing what has changed and what has been deliberately left. The way they stripped down the industrial buildings to their bricks, but left the patterns of the paint, rust, and wear. The way they embrace how the buildings connect to each other, creating courtyards so people can appreciate the structures from every angle.

I finally head inside, where I walk the whole place from top to bottom and finish up in Building C. I watch the light come in across the courtyard and through the windows, I look at the way the corners have been brought together with new design to create a totally different space. Then I sit and jot down some ideas. It's not like I can do an actual renovation on the barn, but I can make little changes to it, here and there, like sanding and varnishing the old wood floor, putting in a new wooden ladder, and making use of the different levels within the barn for sleeping, socializing, and reading. Isn't that all anyone really wants out of a vacation, anyway?

After a while my arm is aching from sketching so much, and my stomach begins to rumble, so I pack up my bag and head back out the way I came in. On my way, I notice a familiar figure standing in front of a large colorful canvas, her red curly hair sticking out at all angles.

"This is amazing," I say as I walk up beside my mom, admiring the work.

"I told you that you'd like Rothko," she says with only a slight look to the side. Things have definitely been weird between us since the chicken-coop-painting incident. I apologized, but it was half-hearted, and so was her forgiveness.

"His colors are unexpected but still beautiful."

"I know," my mom says.

"They remind me of yours."

My mom doesn't turn, but she wraps an arm around my shoulders and squeezes me tight.

"So, what are you doing here?" she asks.

"This really smart person I know told me that when I'm stuck, I should go seeking inspiration from things I love. I think it's working." When I glance at my mom, I see she is smiling.

She nudges me with her hip. "You're welcome."

We're almost to the main set of doors in the now-empty entrance hall when I hear a voice.

"Hey, Charlie!"

The last time I saw Nicole Meyers she was being carried off over the shoulder of a football player at Tessa's party. Now she's standing in a chic industrial apron behind the counter of the gift shop.

"I'll meet you at home," my mom says, before kissing me on the cheek and walking out.

"Hey . . ." I say as I approach Nicole. This feels like some bizarre kind of dream where a person from one part of your life appears in another, like sitting next to your dentist in chemistry class. "You work here?"

"Just started." Nicole grins. "I'm doing an internship. I start in the gift shop, then go to the head office, and eventually I can help out with curatorial operations."

"I didn't know they had interns our age."

"They are open to high school students in the summer, when the college students leave. I started a little early because someone broke their foot playing Ultimate Frisbee." She smiles, seeing the look on my face. "You're surprised I'm doing this, right? You thought I was just a jock or something?"

I can feel the color rising to my cheeks. "No!" I stutter. Then my eyes find Nicole's, and I smile apologetically. "I mean, not really. I guess I just figured . . . aren't a lot of your friends lifeguarding?"

Nicole shrugs. "Who cares? I want to do this. I want to go into the arts when I get to college, I'm just not sure what. I'm hoping this internship will help me figure it out."

"That's really cool," I tell her.

Nicole leans on the counter, putting her chin in her hand. "So, what are you doing here on a Friday evening?"

Before I know it, I'm telling her all about Ava, about my project on Tessa's barn.

"That is *so* awesome." she says. "Hey, let me know if you need any help, okay? Actually, if the internship with the architect doesn't work out, I bet the museum is looking for more interns. They have this program for visiting artists and designers. I heard they need people to help out with that on the administrative level. I'm sure they would love to have someone like you around. You're so creative."

"I was planning to get out of Chester Falls, but that's good to know about," I say. Andre was right, I think. Maybe there are more possibilities for me around here than I realized.

Nicole nods. "I get it. I do too." She pauses. "But I also know that once I'm gone, it won't be as easy to come back. So I'm hanging on to it a bit longer."

"What do you mean, it won't be as easy to come back?" I ask. "I mean, they'll let us in, right?" I laugh.

Nicole laughs, too. "I mean physically, sure, I can come whenever I want, depending on where I go to school and what kind of job I have. But it's never going to feel the same. It's never going to feel this much like home."

♡ ♡ ♡

On Monday afternoon I'm sitting in my car in the school parking lot, examining the inspiration board on my phone and waiting for Reggie, when Andre comes sidling out. I fight the urge to duck lower in my seat. He obviously knows what my car looks like by now, but he hasn't seen me yet. I watch him fiddle with his phone and wonder who he's texting, or how he's going to get home today.

Not your problem anymore, Charlie, I think to myself, and then look down in horror when I see an alert pop up on my app.

Andre Minasian needs a ride.

I glance up just in time to see him frown at his own phone and then look up slowly in the direction of my car. My urge to duck is stronger than ever, but it would be even more useless at this point, since he's looking right at me.

Before I can figure out what to do, Reggie comes walking out the front doors behind Andre. "You're back!" he exclaims, loudly enough so I can hear it from where I'm parked. Andre looks from Reggie to me, his gaze piercing. I feel a pit grow in my stomach. Why am I so nervous right now?

As Andre and Reggie walk toward the car, I straighten my posture and absently clear any spare wrappers from around the front seat.

"Andre is back!" Reggie says.

I attempt a smile. "So I see."

Andre goes to open his mouth and hesitates. He holds up the phone apologetically. "Sorry. Think it was just bad timing . . ."

I swallow. "No worries."

Andre gets in the passenger seat, and we both sit stiffly. I wait for Reggie to get inside. But he's still standing there to the right of the car door, staring at us.

"Why are you guys being weird?" Reggie asks.

"We're not being weird," I say.

Reggie frowns. "You are."

"It's cool, little man," Andre tells him. "Just hop in and we'll hit the road." *And this will be over soon enough,* I know he's thinking.

"Oh, actually, I'm not coming today," Reggie says, which makes the pit in my stomach grow exponentially. Andre looks up sharply, too. Fifteen minutes alone in the car together, when the last time he was here he told me he'd rather do anything than get in a car with me again? Great.

"Where are you going?" I ask, and it comes out in a squeak, possibly even higher than Reggie's regular speaking voice.

Reggie looks around hopefully before his eyes lock onto something and he gives an enthusiastic wave, and I see Jasper, with the snake, wave beside a station wagon.

"See you guys!" Reggie waves with his whole arm as he walks off toward the wagon. "Andre, I'll see you tomorrow. We have so much to catch up on."

"Wait, who is that?" Andre asks, nodding to Jasper, as Reggie reaches the station wagon and climbs in the back.

"You missed a lot," I say as I put the car into drive.

♡ ♡ ♡

"I cannot believe Reggie finally made a friend, and I wasn't here to witness it," Andre says, his head back against the headrest in exasperation as we pull onto his street.

I can't help but smile. "It *was* pretty great."

"Was it *super* dorky?"

"There were reptiles involved."

Andre laughs then, pushing his head back even further, and something wells up inside me. I stare a moment longer than I should, just happy to be around him again, like a balloon has inflated in my chest. His eyes catch mine, and I feel a pang in my stomach.

"Hey," he says. "Look. About what happened . . ."

The air between us is so quiet, it's almost audible. I start feeling a little shaky.

"Yeah," I start. "About that."

Andre rests his palms on his knees and glances at me sideways. "I was hoping you were going to go first."

My mouth twists into a small smile. "You're the one who got out of my car, so . . ."

Andre nods, clearly uncomfortable.

"You were right," he finally says. "I *am* afraid of what's coming next. I think . . ." He sighs. "Stuff with my mom . . . stuff was just getting back to normal. What if . . ."

I lean closer. "What?"

When Andre turns and looks at me, it doesn't just feel like we're the only two people in this car, it feels like we're the only two people in the world. "What if I leave, and she gets sick again?"

My heart hurts for him. "Andre," I say. "You can't live every day worrying about that. And she would never want you to. Your mom? She'd kill you if she knew."

Andre sighs. "You're right."

I wipe some dust off the dash of the car. "You know, at first, I was angry at you. And I thought it was just because you were being an idiot. But really, it was because I never worry about anyone like that. And I did not like it." I clear my throat. "It was distracting."

Andre's gaze doesn't leave my face. "You were worried about me?"

"I just said that," I say, exasperated.

Andre's mouth curves into his signature dazzling grin. "You worry about me . . ."

I go to shove him, and he reaches up and grips my wrist.

We stare at each other for a moment. Andre's expression softens, and I notice his eyes trailing down my face.

"Speaking of," I say, taking my hand back. "Why didn't your mom pick you up today? I thought you said your parents were giving you rides."

Andre groans. "They were. But then my mom found out I wasn't riding with you because of our fight, and . . ." He chuckles. "She refused to drive me anymore. Said we had to work it out."

"What a woman," I say wistfully.

"Yeah so, usually I'd just wait until I saw you leave the parking lot to call a ride, to make sure we wouldn't end up stuck together."

This hurts.

"But," he adds, as though sensing my disappointment, "it's not going very well. Yesterday I caught a ride home with Isaac Russell, and I don't know if you are aware of this, but his car smells exclusively of gym socks. I'm lucky I made it home without barfing." He casts a sly look my way.

"Sounds like a genuine hardship," I tell him. "You're lucky you survived."

"I really am," he says, playing along. "And I'm not sure it's safe to risk it again. So . . ." He fiddles with something on the dash. "Do you think maybe I could come back?"

I shift in my seat. "Like, come back to ride with me?"

Andre nods slowly.

"I mean, if it would be helpful to you, then yeah, totally. I mean, I still owe you."

"Okay." Andre looks down, and the air in the car crackles. Why does this feel like we are talking about more than just Backseat?

"You missed a lot, though," I joke, trying to cut the tension. "Alison Kanter's brother just got home from college with a new girlfriend, and Jake Toth's father got a job in Seattle . . ."

Andre looks at me, his gaze penetrating, and he doesn't laugh. "How about you?"

"Me?"

"Yeah, what's been up with you?"

I fiddle with the AC. "Well, Ava didn't like the chicken coop. So that was a whole thing."

"What?!" Andre says, suddenly and loudly, and I reach up with one hand and jokingly plug my ear. "Sorry. But that's crazy. What you did was amazing." A ripple of something runs through my chest and I wonder why, whenever Andre has my back, I always believe him more than anyone else.

I shrug. "It's okay, because she offered to give me another shot, and I came up with a new plan."

Andre's eyes go wide with interest, and he leans across the armrest. "Well? What genius has Charlie produced now?"

I smirk. "I'm going to fix up Tessa's old barn."

Andre thinks about this for a minute. Then he nods, a smile coming over his face. "I totally see it. Can I help?"

"Frankly, I need all the help I can get, but what do you know about renovating?"

Andre makes a face. "I actually know a little bit. But my dad knows a lot more."

"Your dad?"

Andre looks at me and laughs. "Of course you wouldn't

know. Charlie, my dad is like one of the busiest contractors in Chester Falls."

My mouth drops open. "No way."

"Yeah way," Andre says, picking up his phone. He smiles at me as it rings.

Chapter 23

ON THURSDAY AFTER SCHOOL I HEAD OVER TO THE barn and pull one of the old tables into a corner. On the wall I pin up some new inspirational images, plans, my current list of to-dos and accomplished tasks, and on the table, I lay out copies of the budget.

I'm just sweeping a few last specks of dust out of the first floor when a shiny black truck pulls down Tessa's parents' side road and in front of the barn. I straighten my top and tuck my hair behind my ear as the most successful contractor in the county comes around the front of his car.

"Hey Charlie," Mr. Minasian says.

"Mr. Minasian, thank you so much for meeting with me," I tell him, putting out a hand for a businesslike handshake.

Andre's dad looks down at my hand, laughs, and shakes it anyway. "Andre was going to come with me, but I wouldn't let him. I figured if he came, he'd do all the talking for both of us."

I nod. "Probably for the best. We have a lot of ground to cover."

Mr. Minasian nods in agreement. "When Andre told me you were doing this, I thought it sounded like a great idea. Shows a lot of initiative, too. So why don't you walk me through the project."

I take Andre's dad through my whole thought process. Wanting to bring life back into a historic structure, but one that also has personal meaning for me, and would, ideally, give Tessa's family an extra source of income. Then he takes a walk around the place on his own, examining the boards, holding the plans up to reorient himself.

"Well, you've got electrical, but not a lot. We can put a few sockets in for lamps, and a coffee maker if you need it, but I don't suggest more than that. It's a fire hazard."

I pull a notebook out of my back pocket and start taking notes.

"And water will be tough," he continues. "That's a much bigger project than you're setting out to do. More expensive. I'd move that to second tier, for when they've earned some income off of the rental, and they can decide if they want to invest in it."

"I was thinking that too," I say, still jotting. "I found a composting toilet that comes really highly rated online."

"Smart," he says. "What are you thinking for a shower?"

"Well, there are these showers used on boats, where you can fill a bag up with water . . ." I start, but notice Mr. Minasian shaking his head.

"Nobody is going to pay much to stay someplace where

they have to fill a bag up with water," he says. "They might as well pay a lot less to go camping."

He thinks for a minute, walking outside, and I follow him. He turns on his heels and studies the exterior of the structure. "We can set a medium-sized tank up out here, with a nozzle," he says. "The Walkers can fill it up before each guest to make sure there is plenty of water for showers, coffee, etc. More work for them, but probably worth it. And if the guests need extra, they can get it from the pond."

"I love that idea! But what about in the winter?"

Mr. Minasian laughs. "Right now, this place has no insulation, Charlie. Nobody can stay here in winter. This is what you'd call a three-season cabin. Spring and summer for sure, and early fall."

"Okay, so another thing for second tier?" I ask him.

"Good thinking."

I jot a few more things down in the notebook.

"I'll assist you myself with the shower, and the sockets. I'll get a few guys over here to mend a couple of the broken boards and make sure the roof is in good shape. Our company will cover the cost, if we can put it on our website. Historic renovations like this diversify our clientele. How does that sound to you?"

I think. "Will you list me as the designer?"

Mr. Minasian runs his hand over his chin and smiles. "I wouldn't have it any other way, Charlie."

I feel a wash of gratitude run through me. "Thank you so much, Mr. Minasian. This is making my whole year."

He brushes it off. "It's only an afternoon or two. We're

happy to do it. We try to do a couple projects a year that help out in the community. We've got a site going on over in Northboro that people are pretty excited about. A small community of tiny homes."

My ears perk up. Tiny homes, in the Berkshires? "Is it a hotel?"

Andre's dad shakes his head. "No, it's affordable housing. It's not easy to come by in the Berkshires these days, since COVID-19 hit and people started buying up more land. And, of course, the smaller the house, the easier it is to cool and heat, which is a big issue out here."

"The architect I'm hoping to work with this summer makes tiny homes," I tell him.

Mr. Minasian nods. "Then you should let me know if you want to go check them out. Sounds like they are right up your alley. Now, how about we talk about the interiors?"

After we finalize the schedule and make a deadline in two weeks, I walk Mr. Minasian back out to his car, thanking him profusely.

Mr. Minasian pauses. "Andre has been different since you started coming around. He's talking about his future differently. It's not just about parties and having fun." He chuckles. "He talks about you a lot, Charlie."

I make a pattern in the dirt with my boot.

Mr. Minasian leans against his truck. "You know, when his mom got sick, it was really hard on Andre. I think he felt like he always had to keep this brave face on. Make everyone happy. And he still does."

I think about this for a moment. "I just want him to be himself."

Mr. Minasian looks surprised. "He's really lucky to call you a friend." Before he gets back in his truck, he says: "You know not all building and designing is on things you love, right, Charlie? Sometimes you have to take jobs you could care less about, just to make ends meet. I had to do a lot of office buildings and parking structures before I started doing restaurants, hotels, and residential."

"I understand that," I say. "But my hope would be to work long and hard enough that one day I can choose what I work on."

"You're going to have to work very hard," he says, and I appreciate that Mr. Minasian isn't bullshitting me. He's treating me like an adult.

"I'm up for the challenge."

Mr. Minasian smiles. "I believe in you. Who knows? Maybe one day we'll be working together."

As he drives away, though, all I can think about is what he said about Andre. About how much he's always doing for everyone else but himself. It's high time I did something for him.

Chapter 24

THE FOLLOWING WEEKEND, A VOLKSWAGEN BEETLE lumbers down the road to Tessa's barn in a color that can only be described as Barbie pink. I almost drop the broom I'm holding when Andre hops out.

"Okay, I'm here," he says. "What did you want to show me?"

"Turned the Saab in for something more suitable?" I ask him.

Andre grins. "It's my mom's."

I walk over and run my hand along the bright pink car, complete with convertible top. It's the car of a person who is ready to have a new lease on life. "I should've known. I really cannot think of a better ride for her."

Andre's eyes are bright and shining, and they linger on mine for a second too long. Then he gestures toward the barn. "Making progress?" From this angle I see what he sees: an abundance of trash bags and rusting barn gear. And then there's me, covered in dirt and wood shavings.

"I sense sarcasm, but actually, yes," I tell him. "And now that you're here, we're going to move even faster." I hand him the broom.

An hour later Andre has cleaned out the rest of the barn, and I have a list of to-dos and things I need to pick up from the hardware store. Covered in dirt and sweat, we decide to run into the pond to wash the grime off our bodies. I have a bathing suit on hand for exactly this purpose, and it turns out Andre brought one, too, with the hope of coaxing me to the swimming hole.

We float there for a bit, watching each other. I can't believe that only a few months ago, I barely knew this person at all.

As if reading my mind, Andre speaks. "Can you believe this is where it all went down?" He turns in the direction of the woods, and I know what he's looking at. The spot my car rammed into his.

"It's funny to think about that," I say. "What I thought of you before that day, and what I think of you now."

Andre inches closer in the water. "What do you think of me now?"

I watch him for a moment, drawing him in, before splashing water in his face.

"Oh wow, you are so dead." He starts swimming after me, and I run out of the water squealing.

"Okay, okay! Truce!" I shriek, reaching for my towel. "Time to go do something fun?"

"Charlie Owens wants to stop work and do something fun?" Andre asks.

I rub a towel through my hair. "Stranger things have happened. But this time, I'm running the show."

Andre's brown eyes widen, but he can't hide his adorable smile as he wipes off his legs, his wet hair falling in his face. I feel a little shiver run through me. "You're going to show me what you love about Chester Falls?"

I wiggle my eyebrows. "No, I'm going to show you what I love so much *outside* Chester Falls."

Andre takes this in. "Seems fair," he finally says. "On one condition."

"And what's that?"

Andre gestures toward the hot pink Beetle. "I'm driving this time."

♥ ♥ ♥

The first stop I direct Andre to is an old record store in New Winsor that is known for its genuine relics. People come up from New York City all the time to try and score rare, cheap vinyl. It's owned by two old hippies who discovered a whole bin of Grateful Dead tapes in a barn a couple of decades back, sold half of them for thousands of dollars, and used the proceeds to buy the shop. But these days it's mostly staffed by college kids, so it always has a good mix of quality records, old and new.

I explain all of this to Andre, adding that he probably won't find anything he's heard of, but I can help him find something he might like. Then, of course, the first thing he sees when he walks in the door is an old Boyz II Men album, which delights him beyond belief.

"I told you they were cool," he says triumphantly, holding it above his head like an Olympic trophy.

Andre rotates his body, holding up the album to the depressed-looking twentysomething behind the register across the room. "Name your price, good sir!"

"Do you even have a record player?" I whisper.

"Details, details," he says as he strides toward the cash register.

♡ ♡ ♡

Next, I have Andre drive to Overbrook House, a massive Federal-style mansion in Stockbridge that was built and lived in by a famous female author, and her suspected female partner, until the end of both of their days. Tall trees stretch down a long road, bringing us to the mansion's doorstep. Behind it is a carriage house big and beautiful enough for several families to live in.

"Isn't it so incredible?" I ask Andre as we stand on the great lawn and admire the house.

"It's gigantic," he says. "Can you imagine how much it would cost to heat that?"

"*That's* your takeaway?" I say, shoving him a little.

"I am my father's son." He shakes his head. "I can't believe this is so close to where we live."

"There are plenty of cool things in the Berkshires," I tell him.

"What's that?" Andre says.

I stop. "What?"

He cups his ear, leaning closer to me. "Can you repeat what you just said?"

I roll my eyes. "I said, there are plenty of cool things in the Berkshires."

Andre's mouth falls open. "I never thought I'd see the day. Hang on, can I pull out my phone so I can record this?"

"Shut up," I say, shoving him again, and this time he catches both my forearms, pulling me forward a bit. Our eyes lock. I dare myself to keep it there, to fight whatever feeling is happening in my bones. But the feeling never goes away.

Andre clears his throat, and I pull away finally, heading back toward the car. "We have one more stop."

"Please tell me that stop includes food?" Andre grumbles as he trails after me.

♥ ♥ ♥

I decided to save the best stop for last, and soon we find ourselves on the lawn outside MaCA. The sun is setting and the summer concert series is just beginning. We grab slices of wood-fired pizza from a local food truck and sit down in the grass to devour them. I didn't realize how hungry I was. It's primal, like each piece of cheesy dough is filling a deep hole in my gut.

"This is fun," Andre says. "Getting out of town."

"This is one of the best art museums in the country. I've been coming here since I was little."

"So, how did you get into it?" Andre asks. "Buildings, I mean. Design and architecture."

I pick up a few flowers from the grass next to me and start turning them into a daisy chain.

"I know it's not, like, unusual to have a thing for old houses, but I can't explain it . . . I just feel like my love for them is part of who I am. It has as much to do with their physical beauty as it does what they represent: a time when people took pride in the small stuff, instead of just buying it all from some place and throwing it out three years later. When they built something with the hopes that it would be around forever. Something to maintain some kind of legacy." I twist a flower around in my fingers, admiring it. "I love old houses because each one I look at has known so many people, families, and stories. It's like each room is a scene in a movie. Each window is the lens into someone's life." I look up, suddenly feeling embarrassed. "Sorry. Am I talking too much?"

Andre is studying me with an expression I can't decipher. He shakes his head. "Not at all. I like the way you see things."

I sigh. "The one problem with something really old, of course, is that it is only a matter of time before it breaks. In old houses, there are too many broken things to choose from. A busted pipe, or a nonfunctioning furnace. So you have to get creative. But our house is really the reason I want to become an architect."

"Doesn't sound like it was the house," Andre says after swallowing a bite of pizza.

I shake my head. "What do you mean?"

Andre pushes a lock of hair out of his face. "You grew up with these people who were so creative in everything they did.

They thought deeply about things. How could that not have affected the way you see the everyday world?"

I blink and stare down at the small daisy chain in my hands. "I'm not sure why I didn't realize that before."

"I think you did realize it," Andre says. "But maybe you've been too angry at them to really accept it."

As soon as he says the words, I know he's right. "I just feel like they gave up or something. They had these full lives and did all this really cool stuff. And now they just . . . are. They exist in this space together, without going after what they really want."

"It kind of sounds like you're putting all your hopes and dreams onto them." Andre bites his lip. "But maybe you don't really know what they want. Maybe what they want would surprise you."

I nod. "Well, shit. How much do I owe you for this therapy session?"

Andre laughs. "Call it even. You think I don't know what you were up to today?"

I put on my best frown. "What do you mean?"

"Showing me all these cool places I'd never been to, expanding my horizons or whatever. You're trying to show me what's out there."

I shrug. "Maybe."

"Well . . . it's working," he says.

I pick a few more flowers. "Yeah?"

"Yeah. But it wasn't really the trip. It was you. Listening to you talk about the things you love. That it's not enough for you to just love them. You have to understand them. I think it's cool. It makes me want to do that too."

I'm afraid to look back up at him when he says this, so I'm focusing on my daisy chain when I hear him say, "Maybe we could do this again next weekend?" Again, I feel a faint flutter of something in my chest. Is he asking me out on a date? Or is it just friends? It's becoming hard to tell.

"Is it possible you're becoming more adventurous? Andre Minasian, willing to set foot once again outside Chester Falls?"

I expect Andre to laugh, but instead he just thinks for a second. "You know, I've begun to realize that, after what happened with my mom, I was putting my need for stability onto other people. Like, I needed so badly to keep everything the same, and consistent, in order to live my life." He looks into my eyes now. "But I see now that's not the case. I need to be able to grow. To be my own person, outside of what I already know."

"I guess you've come to the right place," I say, leaning back in the grass and putting my weight in my hands. I give him my most obnoxious grin.

"I know I have," Andre says, his gaze serious. And then, to my astonishment, he moves his hand ever so slightly, so his fingers are entangled with mine. I stare down at our hands together, not sure of what to do. But I'm sure that my cheeks have started burning up.

"Charlie . . ." Andre starts to say.

Our moment is interrupted by a text on Andre's phone and

mine. He pulls his out first, then looks up at me with a mischievous expression.

"You want to go to a party?" he asks.

"Sure," I say. And when he gets up and offers me a hand, I let out a long breath.

Chapter 25

THE IDEA OF SHOWING UP AT TUCKER'S HOUSE PARTY together definitely didn't *seem* weird when we decided to go. But when we walk through the front doors of the house and every one of my friends turns and stares at us for what feels like an unnecessarily prolonged period of time, I realize maybe we should've given it more thought.

"Hi!" Tessa says, breaking away from Marcus's embrace and coming up to give me a hug.

"Hi?" I say back, trying to communicate with her through telepathy with a look that simply says: *Why is everyone being so weird?*

"I see some of my friends." Andre gives me a nudge. "Can I get you anything?" As I shake my head, he reaches and gently grazes my back, and his hand lingers there for a moment. We smile at each other and then my gaze follows him as he makes his way through the party. Tessa notices it. Sydney notices it. I notice them noticing it. As Andre walks off, we all lock eyes at the same time.

"Bathroom. Now." Sydney says.

♡ ♡ ♡

Tucker's parents' bathroom suite is something out of a mid-century dream. Big windows that look out on tall trees, and sleek lines of wood with large cabinets. Gorgeous, heavy-bottomed sinks. Every piece of space is used perfectly, with nothing going to waste, and I am positively in love with it.

"I honestly think I could live in here," I say, running my hand over the wood.

Tessa plops down in the modern tub, and Sydney joins her. They scrutinize me.

"Enough about the bathroom. Tell us what is going on."

"What do you mean, *what is going on?*" I ask, leaning against the sink, folding my arms over my chest, and avoiding their gaze.

They roll their eyes at each other like a pair of creepy cats.

"You and Andre!" Sydney says. "Something is *happening*! You are spending like *all* your time with him."

I open my mouth to say something sassy and coy but struggle to get the words out. "You do know that guys and girls can be just friends, right?" I manage to say, but from the looks on Tessa and Sydney's faces, they don't believe my bullshit any more than I do.

"They most certainly *can*." Tessa nods enthusiastically, eyebrows raised. "But it is quite difficult for them to be friends if they both have the hots for each other, which obviously both of you do"

I open a bottle of expensive room spray on the counter and sniff it. It reminds me of the way Andre smells. Warm, and sometimes kind of spicy, which I assume is his deodorant. But then I start to wonder if it's just part of him. If that's even humanly possible to —

"You're thinking about him right now, aren't you?!" I hear Tessa exclaim, and I blink to find them watching me from the tub with smirks on their faces.

I bite my lip. "Okay, fine," I say quickly, ignoring the squeals of Tessa and Sydney. I turn away from them and face the mirror, examining my reflection. My cheeks are pink, my eyes are shining. There's a looseness to my frame. I look . . . happy. Is this what my parents were talking about a few weeks ago, when I came home from the swimming hole? "There is something happening between us. I just don't know what to do."

"Uh, how about you *go for it,*" Tessa says, like it's the most obvious thing in the world.

"But why hasn't *he* gone for it?" I ask a little desperately. Then I notice the weird looks on Tessa's and Sydney's faces. Half shock, half delight. "What?" I ask.

"Nothing," Tessa says. "It's just that I've never seen you so wigged out over a boy before. It's kind of amazing."

I groan. "I am not wigged out. And besides, it wouldn't be anything serious, as, with any luck, I'm about to leave for two months."

"She's thinking about the future," Tessa says to Sydney. "About the long term. She is so into him."

"She's textbook afraid of vulnerability. She'd rather focus on the things she can control than risk being set off track by the things she can't," Sydney says back.

"You guys!!" I exclaim.

"What?!" They both say at the same time.

"Could we stop psychoanalyzing me for a moment and just help me figure out what to do?"

Sydney sighs dramatically, and Tessa rolls her eyes.

"Just keep spending time with him," Tessa says. "That's all you need to do."

"And don't be weird about it," Sydney adds.

"Great, thanks," I tell them as they open the bathroom door and march out.

♡ ♡ ♡

We head back out into the party, where I'm trying not to obviously look for Andre when I see him from across the room, and can tell that he is looking around, too. His gaze eventually shifts over to me, and he smiles. I smile back as he motions me over, holding up a beer.

"Go," Tessa whispers in my ear.

"Don't push me," I say out of the corner of my mouth.

"Maybe you need to be pushed," she says, and then she does, hard.

"I was looking for you," Andre says, after I stumble a few steps, regain my balance, glare at Tessa, and make it over to him.

"You were?" I try to ask casually. All of this is so weird. Me and Andre. Flirting. In public. I don't feel like me. I feel like I've body-snatched some other girl and her life. But I also kind of like it.

"I *was*." He turns to his friends, guys from the lacrosse and ski teams. "You guys know Charlie?"

They nod, and a chorus of "whattups" reaches my ears.

"We ready to play?" asks Andre's friend Devon.

I look between them. "Play what?"

"Beer pong," Devon says. "Minasian, you wanna partner with Ty?"

"Actually." Andre takes a step closer to me. "I'm gonna play with Charlie."

I point to my chest. "Me? I've hardly ever played before."

"I'll help you," Andre says. "Plus, I need someone to drink my beers, since I'm driving."

"Can we make a decision?" Devon says impatiently.

Just then, a ride alert comes up on my phone. I feel it buzz in my pocket and, on instinct, take a look. It's a decent fare and would earn me at least twenty-five bucks.

"Charlie?" I hear Andre ask. "You in?"

I stare at my phone, hesitating. Then I shove it back in my pocket.

"Okay." I look up and meet Andre's smile with my own. "I'm in."

♥ ♥ ♥

Turns out beer pong is actually a lot of fun. It also turns out I don't have to drink very much, because I'm really good at it, and so is Andre. I also can't help but notice the fact that each time we land a cup our interaction escalates, from high fives to double high fives to full-on embraces, which seem to last longer and longer. We take on four other teams and beat every one. I can tell Andre is proud. The more people we beat, the more I can feel his arm linger around my waist after each win.

Eventually I decide I've had enough and go to look for Tessa and Sydney. I find Tessa munching on some popcorn, sitting with her butt on the railing.

"Having fun?" she asks, a knowing smile on her face.

"If you must know, I am." I take some popcorn out of the bag and drop it into my mouth.

She grins. "Good."

"Where's Syd?"

I ask the question while Tessa is taking a swig of beer, and she clears her throat like she's choked, a weird look on her face.

"Oh, she's not around?" she asks. She looks pointedly back and forth around the party.

I shake my head. "Not that I've seen. Did she go home? Is she okay?"

Tessa laughs awkwardly. "You know her, she's probably hovering by the chips and dip. That girl loves a Cheeto."

"Why are you being weird?" I ask. "Are you drunk?" But just then, Tessa's face morphs into something even weirder, and I feel a hand on my shoulder.

"You wanna head out?" Andre asks.

A tingle moves up my spine. I examine Andre's face, turning the question over and over in my head. *You wanna head out?*

Is it just me, or does it have one million possible meanings? I always assumed I'd be better at this stuff, the dating stuff, once I actually cared about it. Apparently I was wrong.

"Yeah . . ." I say finally, a little breathless.

Andre's eyes linger on mine. "Awesome."

"Awesome!" Tessa calls, hopping off the banister. "Have fun, you two!" She walks away giggling to herself, and I cringe. But if Andre notices, he pretends not to.

We slowly make our way down the trail beside Tucker's parents' place to the street, where Andre's mom's car is parked and waiting. Before I get in, though, Andre turns to me.

"What were you and Tessa talking about?" he asks.

I swallow and shrug. "Oh, nothing. Just, you know."

Andre narrows his eyes at me. "Sure."

In spite of myself, I can't help but smile, and he smiles back.

I open my mouth to say something. *What are we doing? Are we going to kiss? Should we?* But then I decide, screw it. I decide to stop asking questions and just be.

Which is when a little voice comes out of nowhere. "Nice! I'm not too late!"

We turn to see Reggie scrambling out of the party, running to catch up with us.

"Can I get a ride home?" he asks. "Please?"

I look at Andre, who looks at me, and we both look at Reggie.

"Well?" Reggie asks.

"Um, sure?" Andre answers, and my heart sinks.

"Great," Reggie says. "We can take Charlie first, and drop me after."

Chapter 26

I CANNOT STOP THINKING ABOUT ANDRE MINASIAN. I think about him the entire ride home from the party, even though he's in the seat next to me. I think about him as soon as he drops me off, as I shuffle up the front walk of my house in a kind of daze, up the stairs, and fall into bed. I think about him until I fall asleep, and as soon as I wake up the next morning. I think about him when I pick him up outside his house and he offers me a bite of his granola bar, and after I watch him walk to his first class. Slowly, he has gone from the guy disrupting my life to the guy I want to be around all the time.

Obviously, and in the cold light of day, I have very little intention of doing anything about these thoughts. Especially when he gets in the car on Monday afternoon, his eyes bright, his smile warm, freshly showered from practice, wearing a green T-shirt that looks like it was designed for his skin tone. Tessa and Sydney may think it's a smart idea for me to start something with him, but now that the haze of the weekend is over, and with my deadline with Ava looming on the horizon, it will make things a lot more complicated than they should be.

"Hi," Andre says.

"Hi," I say, trying to keep my tone even. If I can just keep things as normal as possible, this doesn't have to be a big deal. After all, I remind myself, there *was* a period of time when the mere sight of him was totally infuriating to me. I frown to myself, realizing that's not true. Andre may have pissed me off time and time again, but the sight of him never bothered me. I always thought he was cute.

Damn it.

"What's up?" he asks, looking over at me lazily from the passenger seat.

"What do you mean?"

"You're gripping the steering wheel like we're driving through a snowstorm when it's late May and we haven't even left the parking lot."

"Oh." I loosen my grip. Then open my mouth to say something, when an alert pops up on my phone.

"Just need to wait for one more," I tell him, and Andre frowns, but I'm not sure what it means. And I would like to go back to a time when I wasn't wondering what all of his actions meant.

Moments later, Dennis hops in the back seat of the car.

"What's up, dudes," he says, buckling his seat belt and leaning back, a smile on his face.

"You look like you're in a good mood," I say to Dennis.

In response, Dennis just shrugs, but in the rearview mirror I notice a distinct gleam in his eye.

Andre leans back, fixing Dennis with a stare. "Would this have anything to do with your . . . friend?" he says pointedly.

Dennis blushes. "I mean, maybe."

"So, you told her how you feel?" I ask, and Andre shoots me a look, eyebrows raised.

What? I say silently back.

"Just surprised you're getting involved, that's all."

"I can be interested in people's lives." I shrug.

"I mean, yes, it's just that you rarely are."

"Weren't we talking about me?" Dennis wants to know.

"Right. Yes." Andre turns back to Dennis. "So, you told her how you feel?"

Dennis's face darkens. "Not really."

Andre pauses. "So, you're still friends?"

Dennis shrugs. "Kind of. Maybe?"

"What does *maybe* mean?" I want to know.

Dennis shakes his head, sighing. "It means we spend all our time together, and I really like her, and I'm pretty sure she likes me, but neither of us have exactly done anything about it."

"That makes sense," I say, at the exact same time as Andre says, "that's bullshit."

Now I'm the one to shoot him a look.

Andre ignores my gaze. "Do you want to be more than friends, Dennis?"

Dennis blushes again.

"That's a yes," Andre says. "Why haven't you just told her?"

"I . . ." Dennis starts.

"Well, maybe he's afraid?" I interrupt.

Andre frowns. "Of what?"

I shrug. "Maybe she won't like him back, duh!"

Andre rolls his eyes. "Were we listening to the same story? They spend all their time together. She got jealous of another girl. There's clearly a vibe here. Why waste his time wondering?"

"Well . . ." Dennis starts.

"Well, maybe he's just afraid of saying the words! Maybe he's afraid that things might change."

"That's ridiculous." Andre shakes his head. "The point is for things to change. If he wants to do something about it, he should."

This sends a pang through my heart. I frown. "So why can't *she*?"

"What?" Andre asks.

"Why can't she say something? Why is it up to poor Dennis?" I ask, motioning behind me.

"Well, actually . . ." Dennis starts.

"I mean, here we are *harassing* Dennis to make the move, and I think he's doing great. I think he's doing his best. You're doing awesome, Dennis. Okay?"

"Uh, thanks?"

Andre is frowning at me now. "What are you *talking* about?"

"Can we get back to me, though?" Dennis tries again. "Because this was actually helpful last time."

"We are!" Andre and I say at the same time.

"I'm just saying you act like the weight of their entire future rests on Dennis's shoulders. Like if he isn't the one who says something she's going to abruptly choose someone else one day and that'll be it for them forever . . ."

"Jesus, I'll talk to her!" Dennis practically yells, and when he does that, we quiet down. We ride in awkward silence for the rest of the ten-minute trip. I'm too afraid to look over at Andre, and dreading the moment Dennis gets out, leaving the two of us alone.

I'm just about to pull away from the curb when Dennis turns back and hunches down in Andre's open window. He looks annoyed.

"You know, whatever is going on between you two, you should just figure it out."

I make a face like he just said something deeply offensive.

"What?" Andre asks, in a similar tone.

Dennis rolls his eyes. "Obviously there is something weird here. And you just spent the whole car ride talking about yourselves instead of me. Yeah, it was obvious. You aren't going to see anything clearly until you deal with whatever this is." He waves a hand between the two of us.

I watch Dennis walk away, my heart starting to pound. I swallow, avoiding Andre's gaze. Then I pull away from the curb without saying a word.

♡ ♡ ♡

"We should probably talk about it," Andre says a few minutes later at a stop sign. Which only makes my heart beat faster.

"Talk about what?" I say lightly, even though my palms are sweating.

"Charlie."

I start taking the left onto Andre's street.

"Wait," he says. "Can't we go somewhere?"

Absolutely not. "I would, but I have, like, a million things to do."

"Like what?"

"Like . . ." I scramble, looking around the car console, which is mostly spotless as usual. Then I spot one speck of dirt on the windshield. "Like the car wash."

Andre's brows go up. "The thing you have to do so desperately is the car wash?"

I open and close my mouth repeatedly, searching for the right words. "Andre, this is my job. If the car isn't clean, my ratings suffer, not to mention my tips. I provide a full service. So yes, I need to go to the car wash." I finally stop, flustered, and wonder why I'm so annoyed, and I half expect him to call me out on it. Ask why I'm being so weird, ask what I'm so mad about.

Instead, when I finally turn to look at him, I find him narrowing his eyes at me, which gives me a strange noodly feeling in my bones.

"Great," he says. "I'll go with you."

"What?" I squeak.

He leans back in his seat calmly. "If you have to go to the car wash so badly, then I will go with you."

I grip the steering wheel once again, feeling like I might throw up. "Cool."

♡ ♡ ♡

I spend the first part of the car wash removing every possible spec of dirt from the car seats like some kind of CSI detective, turning the vacuum on extra loud to get behind the cushions, avoiding Andre the whole time, even though I feel his eyes on me. Truthfully, I could feel his presence with my eyes closed. But eventually, when there is nothing to pretend to clean anymore, I have no choice but to get back in the driver's seat and start easing us into the drive-through exterior wash. We're directed to put the car in neutral, and now I'm really stuck.

Andre and I sit in silence for a bit.

"So," he says.

I tap my hands on the steering wheel, looking everywhere but at him. "So?"

"About what Dennis said."

I roll my eyes and attempt a laugh. "I know. Kind of crazy."

"Right," Andre says, looking away from me for a moment. But then he looks back. "Was it?"

"What?"

"Was what Dennis said crazy?"

I realize my leg is jiggling and stop it before I accidentally hit the accelerator while we're on the tracks. I picture us careening through the glass window into the car wash office, next to some guy drinking a cup of coffee. Then I remember I'm in neutral. "Can't this thing go any faster?"

Andre sighs, slumping back into the seat. "Fine, forget I even brought it up."

"So now you're pissed?" I ask.

I can hear his breath rising and falling. I can feel his presence there. It does something weird to my heart, makes it fluttery but also makes it feel like a hand is holding on to it and could squeeze it at any moment.

"Maybe not," I admit.

"What?" he says, low, like I've surprised him, caught him midthought.

"I'm saying . . . maybe it wasn't so crazy. What Dennis said."

I finally look over at Andre and find his eyes are starting to smile, even if his mouth hasn't caught up yet.

"So you're saying there's something happening here."

"Well, are you?" I ask.

"I asked you first."

"But I'm not the one who just broke up with someone only a few months ago," I say.

Andre's look has gone serious again. "Wait, is *that* what you're worried about?"

I shrug. "I don't know." I shake my head. "I wasn't really expecting this. Like, at all."

Andre tilts his head to one side. "I wasn't either."

"I just . . ." I struggle. "I've never been in a relationship before . . . making time for someone. Prioritizing them in that way. What if I'm bad at it?"

Andre starts laughing.

"WHAT?"

"Well, you have been making time for it."

I frown. "No, that's not the same."

"We spend almost every day together already. How is that different?"

"Whatever." I shake my head. "Ugh, see? I *am* bad at this."

Andre leans closer to me, and my heart starts going a mile a minute. "Charlie . . . I like you. I wasn't expecting this either. But I like you, and I want to see where this goes. I don't want us to be in the friend zone anymore."

I like you. The way he says it. So open. So honest.

Why can't I just say it back?

I fiddle with a piece of loose plastic on the console.

"Charlie."

I can feel his face leaning in close to me right now, and I think really, my heart is going to pop out of my chest and hit the windshield and then we will have to go back out and clean the interior all over again.

"I like you, even though you trashed my car and refused to pay me back, and even if you make me talk to fourteen-year olds every morning before I've finished my coffee. I like you. Do you like me?"

Finally, I look up at him. There's a lock of hair falling into his face, and it makes him all the more adorable, especially because he has absolutely no idea. I want to reach up and push it out of his eye. But I don't, not yet.

"Yes," I admit. "I do like you."

His face erupts in a warm grin. "Good," he says. And then he leans in and kisses me. It's soft, but deliberate. His hand cups my chin. He pulls back, his eyes examining my face, and I feel suddenly drunk. I lean my forehead against his. Then I grab his shirt and pull him back toward me, kissing him hard. The weight of his body presses against me, and his hands run through my hair while mine roam his body. Andre's hair and

Andre's shoulders. Andre's smooth skin all right here in my grasp.

Only when someone bangs on the window do I realize we have made it out the other side of the car wash, and a bunch of people are staring at us.

I roll down the window to hand them a tip.

"Thank you so much!" I squeak before pulling out of the parking lot, both of us laughing the whole way.

Chapter 27

A FEW DAYS AFTER THE CAR WASH, I'M PUTTING SOME stuff in my locker after first period and trying not to look like I'm waiting around for Andre, even though I definitely am. He had a doctor's appointment before school, so his mom gave him a ride, and I was reminded, for the first time in a while, what it's like when he's not around.

As dumb as it feels to admit it to myself, the world does look a little different since the car wash. Warmer, and more sparkly. I feel it in my bones. Andre and I are together, which is exciting, but also scary. It's strange to be tied to another human being like this. I'm not sure how I feel about it.

I shut the locker and then I jump as Michaela Sullivan's face appears beside me.

"Hi," she says, leaning against the locker next to mine, her books tucked into her chest.

"Hi . . ." I say warily, since I can count on one hand the times we've ever spoken at school.

She smirks. "I heard."

"About . . ."

"Andre. It's true, right?"

I place my hands on my hips, stunned. "How can you possibly have already heard, when we've barely told anyone?"

Michaela rolls her eyes. "It's a small town, Charlie. Come on. And also, you were making out in Ben Cookfair's family's car wash. What did you think would happen? You know he's a gossip."

I shut my locker, having very little interest in responding, but Michaela is still watching me. "Yes?" I ask.

"I just think it's brave of you, that's all."

I roll my eyes. "Why." *And why does this feel like a trap?*

"Dating someone like Andre so soon after his breakup with Jess. They were really in love, you know."

The tiny thing at the pit of my stomach blooms into something else now, something that isn't sparkly or warm. It's hollow.

"I know that," I tell her. "And, while I also know it might be hard for you to understand, Michaela, some people actually are capable of moving on from one phase of their life to another."

Michaela scowls at me. "Wow. Okay. Don't come crying to me when she takes him back. Charlie finally breaks her dumb rules only to have her heart stomped into toothpaste."

I open my mouth to tell her that there isn't a chance in hell

I would ever come crying to her, but that her imagery is poetic. Then, at the end of the hall, I see Andre around the corner. His eyes land on me, and he smiles, and all the tension releases from my muscles.

"Hello," he says, coming up to me in front of Michaela and wrapping his arms around my waist.

"Hi," I say, sickened at the sound of my own swoony voice.

Michaela is still standing there watching us.

"Something we can help you with, Michaela?" Andre asks.

Michaela looks flustered all of a sudden, so I chime in for her. "Michaela was just grilling me about our relationship," I tell him. "How serious we are, et cetera."

Andre frowns, his face close to mine. "Are we serious? I thought this was just a casual fling." He smirks, and I want to kiss him in front of all these people.

"That's what I was trying to tell her."

"Whatever, you two are weird," Michaela says, and stalks off.

Andre puts an arm around my shoulders, and I feel them tense as we walk down the hall.

"What?" he says, stopping to turn and look at me.

"It's just, people are looking."

"So what?" he says. "They're bored out of their minds. Let's give them something to talk about."

Before I can do anything, he leans in and kisses me, right there in front of everyone. At first, I melt into it, because I can't help myself. But then I hear a noise, a giggle, and I stiffen. I push away from him, blushing.

"Maybe we need a no-PDA-at-school rule."

"Whatever you want." Andre shrugs. "I gotta run to math. See you at lunch?"

I clear my throat. "Oh, well . . . I usually sit with the girls at lunch."

Andre gives me a look. "I wasn't saying we had to sit together, I was just saying I would *see you at lunch.* Is that all right?"

I laugh, embarrassed. "Oh! Yeah, okay."

Andre takes a step closer, leaning in. "I'm not trying to marry you, Charlie," Andre says. "I'm just trying to date you." Then he quickly kisses me on the cheek. "Sorry, I broke the rule."

My mouth falls open, and his falls open in return, mocking me, like that was the most scandalous thing ever.

I walk off to class giggling to myself, but unable to shake the feeling of happiness in my bones. Screw Michaela Sullivan.

♥ ♥ ♥

That afternoon after school, Andre and I drop Reggie at his house, then stop by my place to pick up some materials for the barn. But before we head out again, my mom comes wandering out of her studio.

"Is this the famous Andre?" she asks, and I cringe inwardly. My mom has a weird look on her face, a kind of permanent bright smile, her brows pushing up against the top of her forehead. I don't love it.

"Nice to meet you, Mrs. Owens," Andre says, extending a

hand, and my mom waves it off, gesturing to the paint on her hands like a mime. "I've heard a lot about you. I can't believe it's taken us this long to meet."

"Well, you know Charlie . . ." my mom says.

They both laugh. I do not.

"I know!" she says, like a light bulb has just gone off in her head. "Why don't you come over tonight for dinner?"

I hope she will notice my expression of panic, but she doesn't. We never have anyone over for dinner. Not anymore. I have a strong instinct to object to this. Isn't it too soon for that? We haven't even been out on a real date! Andre hasn't even been inside our house. But I don't have much time to act, because Andre has already said yes, with a big grin.

♡ ♡ ♡

Later that night, after we put a coat of varnish inside the barn, I have a truly unique experience of bringing a boy home for dinner. I find myself seated at the table next to Andre, my parents across from us. My mother has put out her favorite linen tablecloth and is using the plates she bought from a ceramic artist she loves in Pittsfield.

"Sorry dinner is a little blah," she says as she serves up some veggie stew bowls. "If I'd planned ahead, I might've roasted a chicken or something."

"Mrs. Owens, this smells so good I could pour it directly into my mouth," Andre says. "Thank you for having me over."

My mom looks pleased as she takes a seat. "So, Andre, Charlie says your dad is a big contractor in town. It's nice of him to help with the renovation."

Andre shakes his head. "Charlie barely needs any help. And he was glad to do it."

I smile at Andre and nudge him with my shoulder.

"Have your parents been in the area long?" My dad asks.

"My dad's family has. They had a factory in New Winsor for a long time, until the about the 1970s, then got into construction. My mom met my dad playing club soccer in college."

"Really?" I ask, delighted. "I love that."

Andre grins back at me. "So, Mr. and Mrs. Owens, how long have you been in Chester Falls?"

My mom frowns, thinking. "Twenty or so years?" My dad nods in agreement.

"And what brought you both out here?"

"Well, my dad was born here," I tell Andre before taking a bite of stew.

My mom finishes a sip of wine. "But that's not why we came back."

I frown. "Yes, it is. Dad wanted to move home, and you came with him."

My mom shakes her head. "Sorry, sweetheart, but you weren't there. That is not what happened."

I sit back, folding my hands in my lap. But it's Andre who speaks.

"Sounds like a story," he says. "What *did* happen?"

My dad clears his throat. "Charlie's mom came home with me for Thanksgiving one year, and she fell in love with the place. She said she didn't want to go home." My dad turns to Andre. "Back then, Chester Falls was really something. It had a huge literary scene, tons of artists. People were thinking about the future, and how they wanted to shape the world, from their own little utopias here."

"In the city we were so burdened by just trying to survive day to day, pay our rent, stay in the hustle. Out here we could take a step back and focus on what mattered to us. We could make art, but we could also build something," my mom adds.

I stare at my water, stunned. "I always thought you followed Dad back here."

My dad laughs. "If anything, I followed her."

I sit there, unable to take a bite of food. So many things I thought about my parents aren't true. I'm debating what to do or say when Andre speaks.

"Do you have any pictures?" he asks. "Of Chester Falls back then?"

My mom grins. "Of course!"

Andre smiles back as he finishes chewing a bite. "I'd love to see them."

♡ ♡ ♡

After dinner, my mom pours some tea and we sit around the living room, where my parents produce an old album. In it, they are young and happy. Standing next to an old Volvo wagon packed to the brim with stuff, outside a brick building on a city street. Sitting with friends in a field, a bottle of wine between them, as the sun sets. My dad leaning against the wall of an old barn, arms crossed, proudly displaying one of his sculptures.

"Is this yours, Mr. Owens?" Andre asks, pointing to the massive structure that is at once unrecognizable but also in a way familiar, part of its genius.

My dad studies the photo for a while, then nods.

"It's beautiful," Andre says.

"He doesn't make them anymore," I say. I don't mean for it to come out as loaded as it sounds, but it does, and there's a pause.

Andre wraps an arm around my shoulders. "You're not working on anything now, Mr. Owens?"

My dad clears his throat. "Not yet," he says, like he's going to follow it up with more information, but he just leaves it at that.

"Well, I'd love to see what future work you do," Andre says. "When you're feeling up to it." He looks at me and smiles.

After dinner, Andre and I do the dishes, and "Girl from Ipanema" blasts over the speakers. As I watch Andre dance around the kitchen with my mother, I can't help but laugh. I also can't shake this weird feeling like he's always been here. That's how well he fits in. But then a tiny voice inside my head pipes up. Does he fit in *too* well? Where can this go from here? I look over at my dad, admiring my mom from where he's seated at the table. What does it mean to let someone into your life so completely? And am I ready for it?

Chapter 28

THE MORNING AFTER DINNER WITH ANDRE I'M UP EARLY, unable to fall back asleep. My brain feels stuffed with too many things. There's the barn, sitting over on Tessa's property, waiting to be finished. There's Ava, waiting for my portfolio in New Orleans.

And then there's Andre.

I take out my phone and send a text:

> **CHARLIE:** Are you walking today?

> **SYDNEY:** I'm already heading there. Want me to pick you up?

At six thirty a.m. Sydney and I do some light stretching next to her mom's SUV at the base of Honeycomb Ridge and set off up a trail speckled with early sunshine and lined with low trees and bushes. Sydney's been doing this at least three days a week for most of high school, which would surprise a lot of people. Yes, she's married to her phone and is the first one to shop the annual sale at Sephora, but she also has pretty bad anxiety, and a couple of years ago her dad, a doctor, recommended she try and work off some of the nervous energy in the morning. Some days it's walking Honeycomb Ridge, other days it's meditating, but she seems a lot happier for it.

"So, what's up?" she asks as we huff and puff up a steep incline.

"Does something have to be up for me to be here?"

"For you to join me on a morning walk, when you could be planning your day or how you're going to conquer the world? Kind of."

I swallow a sip from my water bottle. "Damn, you got me."

"Spill it," she says between breaths.

"It's Andre. I feel weird about it. Now that we're . . . whatever."

Sydney starts laughing, shaking her head.

"What's so funny?" I ask.

"You. You're so uncomfortable with the idea of dating, you can barely say it out loud."

I groan. "I *know*."

"But you *do* like him, right?"

I take a few more steps. An image of Andre sitting across from me in the car wash, gazing at me, his mouth in that perfect, perpetual smirk, flashes in my mind, and I feel my heart flutter. I think about the way he laughs, throwing his head back. The way his hair seems to have a life of its own, but it always looks so good. How ridiculous he looks when he cranes his neck around at ungodly angles in order to look people in the eye and engage with them directly when they're in the back seat. The way he puts people before himself. And how, if I'm being honest with myself, I often have a really hard time looking away from him. "Yeah, I really do."

When Sydney says nothing, I look over at her to find her smiling to herself as she walks.

"Oh, and something is funny about that, too?" I ask.

"No, I'm happy for you," she says.

"Well, what about you? Are you happy?"

Sydney exhales and takes a sip of water. She looks like she's going to say something, then shakes her head. "Never mind about me. Can I just give you one piece of advice, from a girl who also has minimal dating experience?"

"Okay . . ."

"Just relax. It doesn't have to be a big deal. Don't psych yourself out of this before you even get started. You're just getting to know each other. That's it."

I nod, just as we reach the top of the trail, and a beautiful vista spreads out before us. Nothing but green as far as the eye can see, the trees vivid and three dimensional against the rising sun. I always feel relieved when I come up here. Like, yes, the world may be burning down, but we've still got trees. "Thanks. I think I needed to hear that."

Sydney wraps an arm around my waist and leans a sweaty head on my shoulder. "I know you did."

We're standing there admiring the view when I get a ride alert on my phone and realize I forgot to turn my app off. When I open it up, I accidentally hit the Recent Rides tab, which tells you histories of riders you know, like how Venmo shows you money your friends have sent.

And that's when I see that Andre has just taken a ride. I open it up, curious why he wouldn't have asked me.

And then I see why he *didn't* ask me. Because I see where he's going. And my heart plummets into my stomach.

Wilson College.

♡ ♡ ♡

"Okay, let's not overreact," Tessa says as we roam through the swap shed at the junkyard later that afternoon. The swap shed is a hidden gem of Chester Falls, one my dad and I have been going to for years. It's a little building with shelves of things people are giving away: vases, jars, fishing rods, books and DVDs. But what I love most about it is that it's always neat and organized. Because people care about it. On Saturdays a group of senior citizens often gather, play a little music, and grill bacon-and-egg sandwiches for people coming to browse.

Sydney sits on an old vacuum cleaner in the corner, refusing to touch anything and pointing out objects that might be useful, like an old mirror and a frying pan. "He might have a perfectly good reason for being at Wilson."

"I was thinking maybe they were doing one of those breakup exchanges, you know, where they have to give all their stuff back?" I try, examining a beautiful old rocking chair with a slat missing.

"Totally!" Tessa says. "Or he could have any other good reason to be there. I mean, isn't he going there next year?"

"He's still on the wait list, but yeah, probably."

"Or, they could be getting back together, and in that case, screw him," Sydney mutters, then looks up from her phone. "What?" she says, noticing our expressions. "I thought we were reviewing all the options?"

"I think I'm going to be sick," I say, sitting down in the rocking chair, which is actually really comfortable. But it does little to ease the pit in my stomach, which has been there since I saw the alert on my phone and stayed with me all day.

"Just talk to him," Tessa offers. "Ask him what's up."

I groan. "This is exactly what I wanted to avoid."

"What?"

"Drama. Complications. I have enough stuff to worry about."

"But babe, this is what relationships *are*," Tessa says.

"It's true," Sydney adds. "I heard this sociologist talking about it on a podcast. Love is just two flawed human beings engaging in a courageous act by trying to live their lives together." She looks up from her phone again, seeing our horrified faces. "WHAT?" she says again, exasperated.

♡ ♡ ♡

I'm at home on Saturday night, feeling exhausted and reviewing the budget for the barn, when I get a text from Andre. I picked him up on Friday morning, but made an excuse about not being able to take him home.

> **ANDRE:** Yo

> **CHARLIE:** Yo!

> **ANDRE:** You haven't been answering my texts. Are you avoiding me?

I pause, shutting my eyes tightly for a second. *Yes, I am definitely avoiding you.*

> **CHARLIE:** No, sorry, I was at the barn.

> **ANDRE:** You were? I stopped by. There's something I want to tell you.

I feel a pit in my stomach. *Let me guess. "I'm getting back together with my ex-girlfriend"?*

> **CHARLIE:** We must have just missed each other.

> **ANDRE:** Well, how's it going over there? Looked good from what I could see.

> **CHARLIE:** Going pretty well.

> **ANDRE:** K.

> **ANDRE:** So. Davis is having a party tonight. You wanna go? I can pick you up. I got my car back!

I swallow, my heart hurting. *Maybe you do have the wrong idea, Charlie,* I think to myself. *Just talk to him!* But then I shake my head. This isn't going to go anywhere good.

> **CHARLIE:** Woohooo! But I can't go, I have to keep working on this.

> **CHARLIE:** Sorry!

> **ANDRE:** No worries. I'll prob stay in too. Talk later.

> **CHARLIE:** Sounds good. xx

As I close out of my texts with Andre, I see the Backseat app staring at me, beckoning me from my home screen. *Come on,* it seems to say to me. *Check me.* I know Andre went to Wilson the other day; I just don't know when he came home. Reluctantly, I click on it, then check his name.

> Andre Minasian: Rode with Jacob from Chester Falls, MA, to Wilson, MA, at 9:00 a.m. on the 22nd

> Andre Minasian: Rode with Margaret from

Wilson, MA, to Chester Falls, MA, at 7:57 a.m. on the 23rd.

I shake my head. He didn't just go to Wilson.
He spent the night.

♡ ♡ ♡

A few hours later I'm watching how-to videos from *This Old House* on YouTube when I get a call from Tessa. Instead of her voice, all I hear is yelling and laughter.

"What are you doing?" she shouts.

"Nothing?" I say.

"Come to Davis's party!"

"Can't," I tell her, flopping back onto my bed.

"Why?" she pushes.

"I . . . can't tell you?"

"You're working, aren't you?"

"No."

"Charlie Owens, you get your butt to this party or I will come and get you myself. And you know your parents will let me drag you out of the house. They want you to be a normal teenager just as much as I do."

I roll my neck, stretch my limbs above my head. I have been working a lot. I'm sleepy, but also antsy. If I don't get out and be around people, I might start forgetting how.

"I guess it could be good to blow off some steam," I say.

"YESSSSS!" Tessa half yells, half screams.

♡ ♡ ♡

Davis McAfferty's parents own a big family camp on the side of a mountain that only gets used in the summer, and for the occasional corporate retreat during the year. When I arrive at the party it's already in full swing, with people spilling out of different cabins and onto the porches outside. I find Tessa and Sydney on one of the porches, laughing, their faces framed in lamplight.

"There she is," Tessa says, her arms open wide.

"Is she drunk?" I ask Sydney as Tessa wraps her arms around me, planting multiple kisses on my cheeks.

Sydney makes a face. "Marcus got a ride with Angela Allen," she says.

"Just a ride?"

Sydney rolls her eyes as Tessa cuts in. "It's not important that he got a ride with her, it's important that he can't explain where they were together, before this.

"Yikes."

"Will you watch her for a second?" Sydney asks, her tone sounding weird. "There's something I have to do."

"Of course." I lean on the side rail next to Tessa.

"I'm so stupid," she says.

"You're not stupid," I tell her. "You just love him."

"I do love him." She nods. "But Charlotte?"

"Yeah, Tess?"

"I don't want it to always be like this."

"Like what?"

"All the drama. Blah blah blah. I'm so tired of it. I just want to live my life."

"I hear you," I say. After all, Andre and I only just started dating, and I'm already in over my head.

I sit her down on a chair, and she leans her body against one of the porch posts. "I'm going to go get you some water, okay? Don't go anywhere."

I head around the back of the building with a Solo cup, where I know I've seen a freshwater pump in the past, and stop dead when I see Tucker wrapped in someone's arms.

"Oops!" I exclaim, not knowing where to look. "Don't mind me, I was just looking for—" but the last of my words disappear inside my mouth as Tucker breaks away from the embrace and I see that the girl he is kissing is Sydney.

"Oh my god," Sydney says, looking embarrassed.

"Oh! Okay . . ." I say, the plastic cup hanging at my side.

"Charlie," Tucker starts, but I put my hands up.

"Don't let me intrude! I'll see you guys in a bit." I turn on my heels and do something between a walk and a jog back around the corner of the house. Sydney and Tucker are hooking up? How? And When? These are the thoughts running through my mind when I run smack into Andre.

He blinks at me, looking surprised, then knits his brows together.

"Oh, hi . . ." I say.

"Hey," he says. "I thought you weren't coming?"

I swallow. "Sorry. I wasn't originally, but then Tessa called." As I say the words, I realize how stupid they sound.

Andre nods. "Then Tessa called and invited you, but you didn't want to let me know."

259

I feel a flush come into my cheeks. "I . . . I'm sorry. I didn't think it would be that big a deal," I lie. Or didn't I? What am I really doing here? The truth is I didn't expect to get caught.

"Okay . . ."

I shift from one foot to the other. "Why are you making this such a big thing?" I ask.

Andre looks confused. "Am I?"

I shake my head. "I have to go find Tessa. She's super drunk."

"Wait. Charlie." Andre holds out a hand and grabs mine, pulling me back.

"What?" I ask, stiff.

Andre squints. "What is going on? You're barely responding to my texts, and now you're ignoring me?"

"It's not a big deal," I say.

"If you didn't want to date me, you should've just said so," Andre says.

I can't stop myself from snorting. "Right. *I'm* the one who started this."

Andre's frown is deep. "What are you talking about?"

People are looking now. And now I wonder how I became the one involved in the party drama, when I used to be able to stay out of all of it.

"Can we not do this now?" I ask.

Andre's mouth smiles, but his eyes don't. "No problem." He brushes past me, headed toward the cars. "Have a good night."

I watch Andre walk away and feel the tears welling up. I

want to go after him. Tell him he has the wrong idea. That it's not that I don't want to date him, I'm just afraid to. But I don't.

Instead, I think about it the whole way home, down the mountain roads alone and into my driveway. Where I see my parents making out in the light of the kitchen, through the window.

Chapter 29

THE WEEK AFTER THE PARTY WE HAVE NO SCHOOL, which is a relief. I spend the whole time with my head down, working on the barn, avoiding everyone. Like Sydney and Tucker, who I had no idea were hooking up. I'm not mad about it, not in the slightest, but they must have had a reason to keep it to themselves, and I'd rather them come to me on their own time. Or my parents, who are claiming to be one thing but are another thing entirely.

And of course, Andre. I don't even know what to say to him. And he's nowhere to be found.

I'm grateful to the barn, which has always felt like a safe haven, but now feels more important than ever. This I can make sense of. This I can change.

I keep the wood natural, and only paint the floor of the second level a dusty green, and the inside and outside of the barn door and window frames the same shade. Mostly, I sand and varnish and move furniture around. Tessa stops by to help, as does Nicole Meyers, and Theo swings by with refreshments once in a while. Mr. Minasian installs the light fixtures and makes sure the roof is patched well. Things are starting to look good, but there is still a ways to go. I need to decide where to place the art, put out all the textiles, sheets and curtains, and fill the cupboards. There are so many little things to be done in a process like this. Just when you think you are close to finished, you realize a whole other set of things you forgot about, like all the little knobs for the dresser that come separately.

On Thursday night, Sydney comes to drop off a set of vintage tin plates and mugs that her parents used to take camping. We've barely spoken. I want to leave it up to her to talk to me about it, but a small voice inside me knows that isn't right. It also knows it isn't what Andre would do.

As Sydney is admiring the shelving and helping me stack some cups, I swallow my nerves and decide to broach the topic.

"So . . ." I lean over the counter and looking at her intently. "When do you want to talk about Tucker?"

Sydney is silent, placing a stack of plates on the wall. "I'm sorry I didn't tell you," she finally says.

I scrape at a price tag that got stuck to the countertop. "Why didn't you?"

She shakes her head, straightening some placemats. "I don't know! You haven't been around very much, and then it just happened . . . and I felt weird about it. I knew you wouldn't approve."

"Well, I mean, he's Tucker!" I start laughing, until I realize Sydney isn't.

"What does that mean?" she asks pointedly.

I falter. "I mean, we've known him forever! Since he used to gel his hair, and when he went through that phase where he wanted to be a musician, but didn't know what genre to focus on, so he tried rap, alternative rock, and electronic synth all in the same month . . ." I giggle to myself. "And his wardrobe kept changing along with it!"

Finally, Sydney starts laughing, too. "Oh my god, that was so ridiculous," she groans. Then she stops. "But people change, Charlie. You know? We don't all have to be stuck this way. Sometimes it seems like you think this is how it's always going to be." She shrugs. "And besides, I've liked him for a long time. Gelled hair and all."

My mouth all but drops open. "This whole time I've been waiting for you to tell me who you like, and it was always just Tucker." I swallow, remembering our kiss. "If I'd known, Syd . . ."

Sydney holds a hand up to stop me. "Please. I know. Also, at a certain point I have to face the fact that maybe I just wasn't ready. I had my own stuff going on. If I'd really wanted to go for it, I would have brought it up."

I realize something. "That's what he kept trying to talk to me about," I say.

Sydney frowns. "Who?"

"Tucker. He kept wanting to hang out, and I kept making excuses. I thought he wanted to talk about *us,* when actually he wanted to talk to me about *you.*" I shake my head, feeling stupid. Then a smile creeps over my mouth. "Sounds like he didn't need me in the end."

Sydney grins. "You know, it was seeing you and Andre that pushed me to do something about it. The way you two became so close, when you thought you were so different. You learned all these things you never expected. It made me more open to what me and Tucker could have, I guess."

At the mention of Andre's name, I go back to unpacking the mugs and plates. "The more I think about it, the more I see you are obviously so great together," I tell Sydney, who beams.

"Thanks," she says. Then she gets a funny look on her face. "Did you know he plays the piano? Like, really well. Jazz stuff."

"Tucker?!" I ask. "So he really was good at music after all! He just kept choosing the wrong things." We both start cracking up again. Sydney's phone starts to buzz.

"Is that him?" I ask.

She nods. "I should take this."

"By all means," I say, noticing a series of texts on my phone, all from Ava.

> **AVA:** Hey. I know I said to get the portfolio to me on the 20th, but do you think I could have it tomorrow? My business partner is eager to decide, and I don't want you to lose this opportunity!

Tomorrow? I look around the barn, my heart racing. The paint is done, the roof is in, but only half the appliances and furniture are installed. I have at least two days' worth of stuff left to do.

I look back down at the text. This is my one shot. I have to make this work.

> **CHARLIE:** I'll have it to you by tomorrow.

> **AVA:** You're truly amazing. Can't wait to see it!

As Sydney walks back in, I'm just opening my mouth to ask her if she can stay and help when she speaks first.

"Tucker wants to take me to dinner!" She squeaks. "I've never been on a date before." Her face is lit up in a way I have never seen it. I see how happy she is and know I have to support her.

"Go," I tell her.

"You'll be okay here?" she asks.

I nod, already running my list of to-dos in my head. "For sure."

She looks around before she goes. "It's really coming together, Charlie. I'm proud of you."

♡ ♡ ♡

As soon as Sydney leaves, I allow myself exactly five minutes of panic. Five minutes for my mind to go blank, for me to wonder how the hell I'm going to pull all this off in the next eighteen hours, and then I jump into high gear.

The first thing I do is run to Home Depot to pick up curtain rods and a few other essentials.

Then I stop at my house and grab some of my mom's paintings, plus a few of my own, some extra sheets, and the coffee maker.

"Where are you going?" my mom asks, coming out of the house just as I shut the trunk on my car. She's followed closely by my dad. "Are you moving out already?" she jokes.

I shake my head. "I don't have time to talk about it right now," I say. "But I promise I will put it all back tomorrow."

"Charlie, it's nine p.m.," she says.

"Let her go, Helen. She's going to do what she's going to do."

My mom gives my dad a long look. "I am her mother, Hank. If I want to know what she is doing late at night, I will ask her. Charlie, can't it wait?"

I look between them. And now it starts again. They're good for a while, and then they kiss in the kitchen, and then they start being weird with each other. And eventually, that weirdness will lead to bickering. And we are back to square one. I throw my hands up in the air. "No, Mom, it cannot *wait*. I have one chance to get this done, to get it right. I'm not going to let my life just" — I wave to the house — "pass me by!"

"Charlie . . ." my mom says, struck.

"I saw you guys in the kitchen," I say. "The other night. And you may be content to . . . to just sit here and live in this state of ambiguity forever, but I won't. I refuse to. I'm getting out of here."

Then, without waiting for her response, I get into the car and drive off. I think for a moment that she's going to follow me, but she doesn't. Of course.

I spend the next couple of hours making up the beds, laying down some carpets I got secondhand, and hanging curtains, and I'm nearly done, aside from hanging the artwork and putting things away. It's late, and a cozy bed beckons me. I'm just feeling so . . . tired. I lie down on one of the made beds. If I just close my eyes for one second, I'll have more energy to finish.

When I open them, the light is shining through the slats, and it's morning. I sit up and look at my watch. Seven thirty?

"Oh shit," I say, pulling myself up, before realizing I'm not alone. I hear noise coming from downstairs. As I descend the ladder, I find my parents fixing up the last of the barn.

"What are you guys doing here?"

"We're helping, honey," my mom says. "You never give us a chance to help. But we're helping, whether you want us to or not."

My dad offers me a mug of coffee. "Also, you took the coffee maker. Which was a problem. Care for a mug?"

"Yes, thank you." I drink it down gratefully and admire what they've done, hanging the artwork and cleaning up all the mess. They also placed the art better than I ever would have.

"I can't believe you did all this," I whisper. Maybe they don't care about fixing the bathroom or killing the weeds by the front door, but they came here and helped me put this place back together. They came through here because, I realize suddenly . . . they were doing it for me. "You saved me."

"You kind of needed saving," my mom says. "Now finish your coffee and film your video. You have a deadline to make.

And then we are going to talk about the things you said to us last night."

$$\heartsuit \; \heartsuit \; \heartsuit$$

Later that morning, after I've gone home, written my synopsis for Ava, and sent her my video, where I walk through the space, explain the materials and details I used and where I drew inspiration, I head to breakfast with my parents. It feels funny to be in the way back seat of the car while they drive, like a child again. They're silent, and I know they're waiting for my apology.

"I'm sorry about what I said last night," I say finally, staring out the window at the road. "I just . . . it's hard. Living with you guys like this. Being unsure day to day of how your relationship has changed."

"But it's not your relationship, it's ours," my dad says firmly.

"But I'm your *daughter*," I say. "Which you sometimes seem to forget, when I'm the one fixing the lock on the front door and making sure your cars are registered. Don't you think I'm allowed to know if my parents, the parents I am living with, are *together* or not?"

"I hate that we've put you in that position, Charlie," my mom says. "We didn't mean for it to affect you this way. And that's not okay. Your dad and I have a lot to work out. But we'll be better about filling you in on what, exactly, that is."

I nod, but she's not finished. "And, as far as the house, I'm sorry that you feel frustrated with us, like we can't take care of things. But that's who we are. You act like we're wasting away here. But this is the life we chose. We want it this way. And, sure, maybe we could be better about fixing things, or keeping things painted. But that's not where our priorities are. As you go on with your life, you'll have the opportunity to make those choices for yourself. But you have to let your dad and me be who we are, too."

My dad is silent. "So let's just be clear, though. Is this about the house, or is this about us?"

"It's *both*," I say. "And I know I need to let you live your lives. But I also want more for you. Dad, I know you miss going into the carriage house and making things. And Mom, Elaine is asking you to show your work, and you won't even try. I'm sorry," I all but whisper. "But I guess I don't understand why you don't . . . want more."

"Charlie," my dad says. "This is our more. Prioritizing the way of life we want . . . this is our more."

"Okay," I tell him, leaning my head back against the seat, and open the email I sent to Ava. I'm so busy staring at the video of the barn on my phone over and over again that before I realize it, we're pulling into Rick's Diner.

"What are you doing?" I ask, panicking.

"Celebrating?" my mom says in the rearview mirror. "I thought you loved this place!"

"Um, can we go somewhere else?" I plead.

"Why?" my mom asks. "What is going on?"

"I can't explain it, we just need to go," I say.

"Hey, isn't that Andre?" My dad points. He waves. "Didn't he say he's the hamster?"

"Oh shit," I say, ducking low in my seat.

"Hate to break it to you, sweetheart, but he's already seen us," my dad says. "He just waved back."

"We have to go," I say.

"Why?"

"Please? I just need to go," I cry.

"Fine, fine," my parents say, pulling a U-turn in the parking lot and taking a left back on the main road. As I look out the back window, I see the hamster staring after us, his arms hanging at his sides.

Chapter 30

BY SUNDAY MIDDAY, I STILL HAVEN'T HEARD FROM AVA, and the confidence I felt after finishing the barn on Saturday morning is starting to wane. What if it was too similar to what I already sent her? What if it wasn't similar, but still a disappointment? After dropping Lulu at her usual spot, I have too much nervous energy to go home, so I accept a ride from a new client I've never met. His profile says he's a senior, and he's into filmmaking, eighties music, and vintage Nike sneakers. He comes outside a blue-shingled house looking nervous and leans an arm above the window, like somebody's dad.

"Um, hi," he says.

"Hi there." I smile. "Jeremy?"

"That's me." Jeremy keeps looking down at the ground. I can't tell if this is how he is regularly, or if he's just very, very nervous. "So, this is awkward," he says, "but I have something rather large I need to move. Is that okay with you?" He taps his fingers on the window frame of the car as he waits for my reply.

I shrug. "Well, it's probably fine, but can I ask what it is first?"

Jeremy pauses. "It's a teddy bear."

"Oh! No biggie! Just grab it." How big could a teddy bear be?

"It's a very *large* teddy bear . . ." he continues.

I narrow my eyes, trying to paint a picture in my head. "How large a teddy bear are we talking, exactly, Jeremy?"

Jeremy swallows and scratches the back of his head. "Probably better if I just show you."

♡ ♡ ♡

A few minutes later I'm driving a teddy bear the size of a person in the passenger seat next to me, because, for whatever reason, Jeremy decided he wanted to ride in the back. I have no idea where we are going, I don't recognize the address, and I'm just beginning to wonder if maybe this teddy bear is actually Jeremy's imaginary friend when we pull up outside a house and my app tells me we've arrived.

"Just wait here," Jeremy says, having remained silent the entire ride. "Would you? I have no idea how this will go." He runs a hand through his hair.

I nod, as reassuringly as possible. *Of course I am not leaving,* I think to myself. *This is far too interesting.*

Jeremy gets out of the car, opens the passenger door, and with some effort, pulls the giant bear out and lugs it up the front walk over one shoulder. He plops it down on the front stoop and rings the doorbell, tapping his fingers against his side while he waits. A girl around our age answers the door. Before she can open her mouth, Jeremy speaks. And, lucky for me, I can just barely make it out.

"I know I screwed up," Jeremy says to the girl. "The truth is, I'm just not very good at communicating. But I saw this bear, and I thought of you."

The girl looks at the bear. She looks at Jeremy.

"This is a ridiculously large bear," she says.

"I know."

"Like, obscenely so."

"I know," he says again.

"I don't even know where I will put it."

Jeremy nods.

Then she does something that takes both me and Jeremy by surprise. She pushes the bear aside, leaps into Jeremy's arms, and kisses him hard on the mouth.

My own mouth falls open and a flutter runs through my chest as I watch their Disney kiss. Then the girl pulls away and frowns at me over Jeremy's shoulder. Jeremy turns, too.

YOU CAN GO, he mouths urgently.

I make a thumbs-up and drive off, and I've gone about three minutes before I wipe my eye and realize I was tearing up. I pull over to the side of the road, and before I know what I'm doing, I put on Boyz II Men. And then I really start crying.

I'm caught off guard by the sound of my phone ringing, and I don't bother to look at who it is before answering.

"Yup?"

"Hey Charlie, it's Ava!"

"Oh, hey," I say, bracing myself.

"Are you okay? You sound a little weird."

I sniff. "No no! I'm fine." I think fast. "Really bad allergies up here this time of year."

Ava makes a sympathetic noise. "I've been there. Luckily for both of us, there isn't a whole lot of pollen in New Mexico . . ."

The words hang there, daring me. I swallow. "What did you say?"

Ava sounds like she's smiling on the other end of the phone. "I got your video. I'll put it simply: you've blown me away, Charlie. Also, you certainly have no shortage of historic buildings in Chester Falls, do you?"

I hold my breath. Is that a good thing or a bad thing?

"Sort of what we're known for," I admit.

"I know," Ava says. "And I love that. Unlike the chicken coop, I saw a lot of you in this project. It really made me happy and gave me confidence that you aren't just good at taking feedback, but that you will be able to grow as a designer." She pauses. "Charlie, we've decided to offer you the internship this summer."

Suddenly, I feel like I can't breathe. "Will you excuse me for just a sec?" I ask Ava.

"Sure, babe."

I mute the phone and scream at the top of my lungs. It was worth it. It was all worth it. And in a matter of weeks, I'm going to be driving to New Mexico to work with my idol for the summer. And with any luck, after that, I'll be heading to Cornell.

"Charlie?"

I unmute the phone, bringing it back to my ear. "Thank you so, so, so much," I gush. "I accept."

"Thank *you*," Ava says. "Now, I have another call in a few minutes, so on to business. I'm going to be back in Hudson next week. Is that too far for you to meet?"

"Not at all." A few hours, but who is counting?

"My schedule is tight, but let's get a coffee. Talk more about the project?"

"I cannot wait," I breathe.

♡ ♡ ♡

I spend the whole drive home thinking about the road trip, the places I'll stop, the photos I'll take, how big and beautiful my sketchbook will be by the time I return, until I pull into my driveway to find a familiar brown Saab waiting there, and a cute, serious-looking boy leaning on the driver's side door.

"Hey," I say, reluctantly getting out of the car.

Andre runs a hand through his hair. "Hi."

"Let me guess, you're here to hang out with my parents?" I joke, and Andre smiles, but it's a sad one.

"I'm here to talk."

I lead Andre out to the backyard, where we sit on the grass between the old carriage house and the chicken coop.

"So the car is finally fixed!"

"Better than ever," he says, offhand, and it's clear his mind isn't on his car. "I guess, I'm just confused," Andre says. "I know this, whatever this is, wasn't what we planned. But it happened. And it felt . . . really good. At least, it did to me."

I bite my lip and nod.

"So, what's going on?" he asks.

I take a deep breath. "I know that you saw Jess the other day."

Andre looks confused. "What?"

"I saw it on my app. It was an accident. I wasn't trying to snoop. I saw that you went to Wilson the other day, and didn't tell me. Were you visiting her?"

Andre closes his eyes and shakes his head. "You thought I was seeing her in secret?"

I close my eyes tightly. Even hearing him say the words makes me feel like I'm going to puke.

Andre leans forward. "Charlie. I wasn't there to see Jess. I was there to meet with the lacrosse coach. They let me off the wait list. I had a recruiting overnight with one of the guys on the team."

I blink. "Wow! That's . . . . that's good. Right?" But as the words come out of my mouth, I'm also imagining the worst. I'm happy for Andre, but what will this mean for him and Jess? Will they just start dating again when he gets there? I search his face. "Or maybe not, since you were only going there for . . . her . . ." I trail off, my mind starting to whirl all over again. "Unless . . . you're back together?"

"I have no idea if it's good or not," he says briskly. "I'm not even sure what I'm going to do yet. But one thing I *do* know is that you should've talked to me when you saw that ride. You shouldn't have just ignored me."

"I wasn't ignoring you!" I lie. "I was just working. I have a plan, Andre, and it's not going to come together by itself."

Andre leans back, hurt.

"You're so busy moving from one thing to the next, planning for a future version of your life, you can't sit for one second in the present."

"That is not true," I say. "I *am* living my life. And following this plan will help me keep doing that. Your identity is so caught up in this town you just can't even imagine a future outside of it."

Andre looks stung. "Have you ever thought about the fact that even when you leave, you still won't know who you are?"

My voice catches in my throat. "That is not true," I finally say.

Andre looks down at his hands. "I'm so stupid. When you said you were afraid of things changing when we got together, you didn't mean with us, or with our friendship. You meant with your life. Because it's always about you."

I frown. "Always about me? You're the one who dragged me all over town, spent time with me, when you weren't doing it for me, you were just doing it to distract yourself. To slow time down, before you have to go on to the boring life you've laid out for yourself because you're too scared to leave!"

"Well, if that's how you feel, I'm not really sure what we're still doing sitting here."

I feel a quick, involuntary intake of breath. "I'm not either," I say finally, even though a knife is going through my chest. But if it hurts like this now, think how much it would hurt later? Better to get it over with before things get too serious.

"After all this time, you still do not get me at all," Andre says.

"Then I guess you should go," I tell him.

"Happy to," Andre replies, and walks off. "Nice knowing you."

I watch Andre round the side of the house and hear his car engine start, and then I sink down on the bench on the back porch. I close my eyes and listen to the trees above, until I hear the sound of the back door slowly opening, and my dad walks out.

"You okay, sweetheart?" he asks. "That didn't sound too good."

I turn and face him, wiping a tear from my eyes. "I'm fine. It's no big deal. Plenty of other stuff to worry about."

My dad listens to me as he wraps an arm around my shoulders. "You don't have to do that," he says. "You can just let it out. It's me."

Then I melt into his arms and cry.

CHARLIE'S BACKSEAT REVIEWS

★★★★★ Helped me get back together with my girlfriend. I owe you, Charlie! —Jeremy

Chapter 31

THE NEXT SATURDAY, INSTEAD OF DOING MY USUAL rounds for the app, I drive the hour and a half southwest to meet Ava in Hudson, New York. I tell Theo about the café we're going to when I stop by to grab a latte before I go.

"I've seen that place on Instagram," she says wistfully. "Their drinks look next level. Get something delicious for me, okay?"

"One day, that'll be you," I tell her. "Once you're ready to step out on your own."

Theo thinks about it. "I do have a new concoction. I'm calling it Summer in the Fields. It has honey, lavender, and oat milk."

"Yum," I say, half sarcastically. "Sounds like soap."

"It *does* sort of sound like soap," she admits. "But it tastes like heaven."

On my way out of town I drive past Parson's, the Little League field, Matilda's UFO garden, and the spot along the route where you can park for the swimming hole, and I feel a hollowness in the pit of my stomach that I've been feeling more and more lately, except this time it makes me think I might be sick.

I focus instead on the drive ahead, through little towns, over picturesque vistas. I drink my latte, eat my snacks, put on my best road trip music, and then I just zone out, focusing on what's ahead, both literally and figuratively.

Hudson is a beautiful town on the east side of the Hudson River, located one hundred-plus miles north of New York City, and its easy proximity by train has made it a popular destination spot for weekenders and those ready to escape city life permanently. Those weekenders and city expats, along with artists and creatives, are partially responsible for turning Hudson into what it is today. After over a century of ups and downs of various industries, it's become a place with amazing restaurants, trendy hotels, and beautiful renovations on its historic buildings: a mix of Federal, Victorian, and Queen Anne–style architecture.

Everywhere you look in Hudson, old factories and banks have been turned into shops and apartments, and, my favorite, there are so many colors and textures to behold: moldings, shutters, patterned shingles, stained glass windows. I love that one tiny city can encapsulate so much, and still remain consistently beautiful. It's no wonder Ava likes it here. I knew we understood each other.

I park my car at a meter and walk a few blocks to the coffee shop, a sleek spot with slate-gray walls and gorgeous light and plenty of giant windows. I find Ava already seated at a table, an avocado toast and large mug set out in front of her in addition to her laptop, which she is furiously thwacking away on. She glances up toward the door, notices me, and waves brightly before getting up to give me a big hug, and I take note of how amazing she smells. Intoxicating and natural all at the same time. I can't believe I just hugged Ava Adams. Ava Adams is going to be my boss. Maybe even my mentor. Maybe even my . . . friend. She has on another cute outfit of high-waisted wide-leg jeans and a gray T-shirt with several gold chains around her neck, and I wonder if there's ever a time when she doesn't look absolutely perfect.

"Charlie, hooray!" she says after we pull apart, and she offers me a chair. "This is just so exciting. I can't believe how serendipitous this has all been."

"Me neither," I tell her. "You've basically saved my life."

Ava waves me off with a laugh as she takes a sip of tea. "Have you ever been to Hudson before?" she asks.

"A few times," I tell her. "My mom loves the galleries here."

"*Great* gallery scene," Ava agrees. "So many emerging talents. And the cutest interiors shops, too!" She glances around conspiratorially. "The architecture is kind of all over the place, though."

A nervous laugh escapes me. "Oh, yeah, totally," I lie.

"I mean, I love the newer stuff, like this place, for example." She waves around at the interior of the café, which looks like something she would design herself. The building has had its bricks painted white and the windowsills painted black. There's a long bar made of light-colored wood and minimal art on the wall. In the corner is a giant green fern.

"But you wouldn't want *everything* to look like this, right?" I ask after ordering my own toast and tea.

Ava shakes her head furiously. "Of course not! No way." Then she smiles. "It's just so beautiful! And simple. I prefer not to overcomplicate things."

I nod. "No, totally, it is gorgeous, but if everything looked like it . . ." I trail off, hoping she will get my point, but she still looks at me blankly. "Well, wouldn't that be kind of . . . boring?"

Ava shakes her head, laughing, and I realize she doesn't even think my comment is worth a response. "So should we start talking about the summer? We'll want you to come out as soon as possible. As soon as you can get away from school. We have accommodations at the camp, nothing fancy, but it'll do, and we do group meals together. So everything is paid for, you just need to get yourself there and back." She frowns. "Can you do that?"

I nod enthusiastically. "Absolutely. I've been saving for something like this for like two years."

She shakes her head in disbelief. "God, when I was your age, I was sunbathing on my parents' roof and reading romance novels."

I poke nervously at my avocado toast. "I have been told that I can be a little intense." I pause, thinking of something. "Speaking of, I did some research on the cabins you're working on, and I hope it's okay, but I took the liberty of jotting down some ideas and making some sketches. I know you've already done a lot of this, but I just wanted to show you I was taking it seriously."

I hand Ava my sketchbook and open to a page that includes sketches, layouts, and inspirational images I've taped to the page. She goes silent as she sifts through.

"Wow, Charlie, these are really awesome," she says in a tone I can't quite decipher. Then she puts the book down next to her.

"Listen," she says. "I am so impressed by your enthusiasm, and I really hope this summer will be a stepping-stone for you on your path to becoming an architect." She pauses and taps her fingers on the table. "But I don't want to give you the wrong idea of what this experience is going to entail."

"Okay . . ."

She takes a deep breath. "We love our interns. We do anything for them, really. For example, we write them great recommendations." She looks at me pointedly. "But their purpose is really to help *us* out."

"But that's what I was trying to—" I say, and Ava puts a hand up.

"I mean by keeping things running. Our interns answer a lot of emails, they run our social media, shoot photos, and frankly, they do a lot of cleaning and get a lot of coffee." She leans forward, a sympathetic look on her face. "Is that okay with you?"

I nod. "Of course! I'm no stranger to hard work. It's just . . ." I bite my lip. "If I was just going to be getting coffee, why did you ask to see my portfolio?"

Ava looks surprised. "To show us you were serious, of course. And to show us you have talent."

I nod in understanding. But all I can think, is, *Why does my talent matter, if I can't use it?*

"So," she says, pulling her avocado toast in front of her and cutting off a large chunk. "Should we move on?" she asks before putting the bite in her mouth.

♡ ♡ ♡

A little while later, I'm driving Ava to the airport. Dark clouds loom overhead and it's just starting to rain. She is talking nonstop about her studio, the people I'll meet this summer, and how much I'm going to love New Mexico. But I'm not hearing a lot of it, because something just feels . . . wrong. I've just spent weeks working with my hands, creating things I'm proud of. And now I'm going to leave it all behind and follow a woman to New Mexico just to . . . answer her emails?

The architecture is kind of all over the place, though, Ava had said of the architecture in Hudson, and that felt wrong too, deep down in my bones. You can't just make everything the same. Everything comes from somewhere. Everything has its own story. I look over at Ava, who is gesticulating with her hands, and then I grip the steering wheel a little tighter.

Everything deserves to have its story told. Like the countertop in our kitchen that my parents had renovated with a half circle cut out so my mom could stand with her pregnant belly closer to the counter while she poured coffee and made toast. Like the burn on the floor of our family room when the Christmas tree caught fire and we spent Christmas morning at Rick's Diner in our pajamas instead of in front of the fire, which turned out to be the best Christmas morning ever.

Like the colors of my mom's old studio, I realize, cringing to myself, before I tried to turn it into something it was never meant to be.

I have my whole life ahead of me, and I can't wait to see what I do with it, but I don't need to wash it over with something else and try to make it perfect in order for it to be worth something.

And then, as I turn that idea over in my mind, I realize I've made a terrible mistake.

Everything has a story, and maybe I'm not done telling mine.

"You okay, Charlie?" Ava asks suddenly.

"Actually, no, I'm not," I say.

And then I tell Ava that I'm not taking the internship.

Chapter 32

LATER THAT DAY, I HAVE JUST FINISHED COAXING SALLY into her pen and am feeding her some stalks of grass when Tessa comes around the corner of the barn, looking excited.

"Guess what?" she asks.

"What?" I say, running a hand over Sally's fluffy hide. Sally whips her head around and nudges me with her soft nose.

"We have our first guests!" Tessa shrieks, and then I am shrieking too.

"This is so huge, Charlie. My parents are psyched. The listing has only been live for a few days!"

"Well, it *does* look kind of awesome," I say.

"So awesome that Airbnb featured it on their main page," Tessa says. She takes both my hands in hers. "Thank you. With this income, we'll be able to do a lot of stuff for the farm, and for the family."

I drop Tessa's hands and bring her into a hug. "Thank *you*," I say. "For believing in me. This meant a lot."

"Well, I know it didn't prove as useful in the end as you thought it would." She looks sad. "Since you turned down the internship."

I shake my head. "That is not what we should be focusing on right now. And besides, I'll be fine. I always am. When do the guests arrive?"

"Tonight." Tessa looks at her watch. "Late check-in, around eight. We are totally ready to go, we just need to do one more thing."

"What?"

She reaches down to a spot next to the door of the barn and picks up two wicker baskets with open sides, handing one to me.

"Time to pick the wildflowers."

♡ ♡ ♡

Tessa and I have been picking wildflowers on a hillside on her property since we were little, and we've come up with quite a few rules over the years. For example, we always leave a wild space looking like nothing was taken. We use clippers, so things can grow back, and we only take what we need. We like to use creative and unconventional things in our bouquet. Berries. Grass. Vegetables, seed pods and buds. And we never fuss too much over the bundles. Wildflowers are supposed to be just that: as wild as the place from which they came. That is their beauty. Off-kilter stems, chomped leaves from a bug, you name it, it's all good.

"So, what are you going to do now?" Tessa asks as she leans down to pick some leaves. "This summer, I mean."

"I'm not really sure," I say. "Keep driving for Backseat, I guess. I definitely won't get into Cornell, but there are other programs out there. Other things I can do."

Tessa gives me a weird look. "No offense, but that is the least 'you' thing that I have ever heard come out of your mouth. You have a plan for everything."

I sigh. "Maybe it's not as important as I thought." Of course, this only reminds me of Andre. And then I miss him more than ever.

Tessa sighs. "Charlie, look what you've done. With the help of this town, and this place, and your memories. You don't need Ava Adams or Cornell. You don't need something like that to tell you who you are. Only you can do that."

I stare down at the basket of flowers in my hands. So much beauty that I found right here in this field, in my hometown. "I know there's a lot to be proud of here, Tess," I say. "I'm just sorry I didn't realize it sooner."

"Sounds like you're not just talking about the town . . ." Tessa hints.

I clear my throat, dodging the subject. "What's the latest with Marcus?"

"I've been waiting for you to ask me that all day," Tessa says.

"Sorry, I know, I've been pretty focused on myself lately."

"I broke up with him," Tessa says.

I almost drop my basket. "You did not."

Tessa grins. "I did."

"And . . . how do you feel?"

"You know what's weird," she says, standing up and gazing out over the fields. "I feel good. He was so important to me for so long, don't get me wrong, but I'm over his drama. I don't know if it was even him that I was in love with anymore, or if I was just afraid to be alone. We both deserve better, you know?"

I nod, still letting the reality sink in. People really can change, if you let them. "You certainly do. I don't know about him."

At this, Tessa throws her head back and laughs.

When we get back, we place the flowers in a few arrangements and leave them scattered throughout the house. Then we tidy it up and prepare it for the guests to come.

"You should be really proud of yourself, Charlie," Tessa says as we survey the barn, in all its imperfect coziness. "You've done something really amazing here."

♡ ♡ ♡

On Sunday morning I'm up early, standing in the yard and staring at my mom's studio with a cup of coffee, when my parents come out and join me.

"You doing okay?" my mom asks, walking up by my side, as my dad takes a seat on the wooden bench on the porch.

"I'm going to put it back," I tell her. "The studio. At the very least, I'll paint the interior to the color you loved so much before. I can't take the shingles back to their original state, but I can paint them white, or any another color you might like. I can use some of the money I'd planned to use to get to New Mexico." I turn to my mom now. "I shouldn't have done it. Taken its charm away. I see that now, and I'm really sorry."

My mom reaches out a hand and rubs my back. "Thank you for saying that. But you were just trying to make your own way. Find a little direction. We weren't giving much to you, after all."

I shake my head. "But you *were*. You've been doing it this whole time. I've been hard on you because I've been frustrated that you seem so set on standing still, when you deserve more. But this place . . ." I nod toward the chicken coop, and turn slowly toward the house. "This house, and you guys, you made me what I am. So I'm going to change the chicken coop back to its original glory."

My mom hesitates before she speaks. "Well, maybe you should hold off on that for a second."

I frown. "Why?"

"Because I have a lot of work to get done if I'm going to be in Elaine's show this summer," she says, and I squeal.

"You're doing it?" I ask.

"You were right," she says. "We were standing in our own way. We got into a rhythm, maybe even a funk. And while we do love our life here . . . there's a lot more of it we have to live."

"And there's some more news." My dad tries to smile, but there's a certain sadness behind it. He goes to speak but struggles to find the words.

My mom puts an arm around me. "Your dad is going to move out for a little while," she says.

My eyes widen. "Wait. Seriously?"

My dad nods. "It's for the best. We have to figure out who we are, without each other."

There's a long look between my parents then, one that makes my heart practically break open. My mom notices but doesn't know what it's for. "Are you sad?" she asks.

I nod, tears coming to my eyes. "Actually, yeah. I can't believe this all happened so fast," I say, my voice breaking, as my mom embraces me in a full hug.

We share laughter and tears.

"If we're being honest, this has been in the works for a while, we just needed to come to it on our own time and in our own way," my dad says. "You always think you have everyone mapped out, but human beings are complex. You need to have more faith in people."

"Do I not normally?"

My mom shrugs. "Not everyone holds themselves to the same standard as you do, babe. You can be kind of tough on people."

I bite my lip. "Yeah, I'm beginning to realize that."

♡ ♡ ♡

A little later that morning I pick up Lulu and drive her out to the old industrial building once again. This time, when Lulu is getting out of the car, I make a split-second decision that I hope I won't regret.

"Are you an alien?" I blurt out, instantly embarrassed by how dumb the words sound coming out of my mouth.

Lulu whips around. "What?" she asks, her words blending into a laugh.

"Sorry," I say, shaking my head. "That's really not what I wanted to ask." I clear my throat. "It's just, where are you going? Where do you go every Sunday? I really wanted to respect your privacy, but I've watched you walk into this old building time and time again, and I just . . ."

Lulu looks nervous for a second. Then she gets a funny look on her face. "I'm not an alien," she says. She gets back in the car and slowly opens the box, carefully turning it around to face me. Inside there isn't a book, or a pillow, or spray paint, or an alien control center. Inside is a classic chess board and a full set of chess pieces.

"What in the . . ." I whisper. "What are you doing playing chess by yourself in an old industrial building?"

Now, Lulu giggles. "I'm not playing by myself! And I'm not hanging out alone in an old industrial building, either." She nods to the right of the building, and I notice a path leading up to the back entrance of the senior community center. "I'm going there."

I make a face. "Your *big* secret is that you go to play chess with senior citizens?" I ask.

Lulu shakes her head. "I mean, sort of. My big secret is that I go and play chess with my grandma."

I frown. "Well, why is that a secret?"

Lulu shrugs. "My mom and my grandma don't get along. They haven't for a while. But I love my grandma, and she's all alone. So I go and play chess with her on Sunday mornings.

I don't want my parents to know. Not yet anyway. I think it would hurt my mom too much. I need to figure out a better way to tell her."

"Wow, I can't believe that's what it's been, this entire time," I say.

"You know, I would've told you, if you'd just asked," Lulu says. "I didn't mean for it to be so weird. I just didn't know how to talk about it, and after a while, it felt like it was too late."

I turn around in my seat. "You're right, I should've asked. But Lulu?"

"Yeah?"

"You should tell your mom. About your grandma. It'll be hard, but it's important to have hard conversations."

"I know," Lulu says. "I'm working my way up to it."

After Lulu gets out of the car, I watch her walk up the path to the community center, and then I just sit there for a while, thinking about how you could see someone every Sunday for months and they could still be such an enigma.

I take a deep breath and take out my phone, staring at my text messages for a while. Then I type.

> **CHARLIE:** I know things are weird right now, but I just found out where Lulu Cooper has been going every Sunday.

I hold my breath and watch as three little dots move next to Andre's name. My heart starts beating wildly. I always think it's so crazy the way our body responds to things even if our mind isn't willing to admit it.

Then the dots stop moving.

I wait there a little longer, bracing, hoping, to see what comes in.

Nothing does.

CHARLIE'S BACKSEAT REVIEWS

★★★★★ Always there when you need her. No matter what. —Lulu

Chapter 33

ON WEDNESDAY AFTERNOON, AFTER SCHOOL, I'M standing on a piece of land overlooking the river where the foundations of ten mini houses are being laid.

"Charlie," Mr. Minasian says, walking across the field in a pair of work boots, a big smile on his face. "Thanks for coming out. What do you think of our spot?"

"I think it's beautiful," I breathe, looking around. "Especially this view! I never . . . I never imagined we'd have anything like this in the Berkshires. A tiny house community."

"It wasn't the easiest thing to get approved, but thankfully, at the end of the day, this community cares about each other. If this puts roofs over people's heads, then the town was all for it. Hopefully this is just the first of many."

Mr. Minasian takes me over to a small trailer, where plans are laid out.

"When we're building something like this, we want to

make it the best version of itself we can, but we also need to think about the process. How will we make these better, faster, and cheaper to buy, in the future?"

I look over the plans with him as he shows me where things go, the small kitchen, and a back porch that is just as big as the house itself, to utilize the outdoor space.

"What would you add or change, if you could?" he surprises me by asking.

I swallow and, after glancing again at Mr. Minasian to make sure he's serious, I study the plans and the model.

"I'd add another window here," I say. "The smaller the space, the more light you want coming in."

"Good idea, I was thinking that too."

"And, I don't know what you're intending to do for the interior, but I'd keep the colors nice and light, natural wood if you can, but not just bright whites. Different muted tones to break up the space while keeping it open. Under-the-bed storage would be a good idea, too."

"That's excellent Charlie." Mr. Minasian nods.

"So, what's the schedule for these?" I ask. "When will people be able to move in?"

He groans. "We're running a little behind. It's been a busy year, and we're pretty stretched."

I smile. "Well, I can think of a way to go faster. Hire an extra set of hands."

Mr. Minasian studies me. "You asking for a job, Charlie?"

I nod. "Definitely."

Mr. Minasian tilts his head, confused. "I thought Andre said you were going to New Mexico?"

I shake my head. "That didn't end up working out, in the end. I want to do something around here. I want to contribute to the community."

Mr. Minasian studies me. "I've never hired someone as young as you before . . ."

"But you've already seen what I can do on the barn," I push. "I'm self-sufficient, and proactive. And . . . well, I'm also kind of a workaholic."

Mr. Minasian laughs. "Okay, okay. I think we might have a deal here. We'll try it out and see how you do. But only because you're such a talent."

I clap my hands in glee. I never imagined I'd be able to do something like this around here. "Don't tell Andre yet, okay? I want to break it to him myself."

♡ ♡ ♡

In the days that follow, I check with Tessa on the barn's availability, and ask her to keep one Friday night open. When she asks why, I say it's a surprise.

On Friday afternoon I head over to the barn, make it especially cozy, stock the mini fridge with ice cream and seltzer and all the other ingredients of the Chester Fizz. I line the shelves with local popcorn, and order a couple of pizzas, just the way Tessa and Sydney like them. Then I string up twinkle lights outside and lay out a picnic blanket on the lawn.

"What is all this?" Tessa asks, hopping out of the car when Sydney drives her down the dirt road.

"We brought our pj's and toothbrushes," Sydney says. "But I just want to say right now that I am not sleeping outside."

"I thought we could all use a night with just us," I tell them. "And it's kind of a thank-you. I know I've been absent lately. Like, even when I've actually been *here*. I guess I thought that a specific kind of place or life could make me who I was supposed to become, but in the last couple weeks I've realized that only I can be responsible for the kind of person I become. And I'm already doing that now."

"Well, we've always liked you the way you were," Tessa says, leaning a head on my shoulder.

"I know, and I just want to thank you guys for that. Even when I've felt out of place or unhappy here, I've always felt at home with the two of you. So . . ." I wave my hand at the barn. "I wanted to have a good old-fashioned sleepover, the kind we used to do, the kind that inspired this whole place."

"Charlie!" Tessa exclaims. "This is so sweet. And you know we love you, always."

"Point me in the direction of the ice cream," Sydney says.

♡ ♡ ♡

A few hours later, after stuffing our faces with pizza and dipping our toes in the pond, we're upstairs in our pj's, lying on the beds.

"These are actually really comfortable," Tessa sighs, stretching out.

"I know, even I would stay here," Sydney says as she applies a sheet mask to my face. I peer over to where I notice Tessa staring at the wall, lost in thought.

"Are you okay, Tess?"

She shrugs.

"Thinking about Marcus?"

Tessa nods slightly. "So many memories here," she says. "I can't believe we're over, just like that."

"You don't know that," I say, and both Tessa and Sydney look at me.

"You're the one who always says high school romances have an expiration date, and we have to look ahead to the future!" Tessa exclaims.

I shrug. "I know. But the truth is, we just have no idea. We don't know what's going to happen down the road. Maybe you'll stay broken up forever. Maybe Marcus will finally grow up and be worth your time. Maybe by the time he does, you'll have already found someone more amazing. People change. We're only seventeen."

Sydney and Tessa glance at each other. "Is this the beginning of a horror movie? Did someone body-snatch our friend, and is now coming for the rest of us?"

"I actually think I'm excited to be on my own for a bit. I mean, talk to me in a year, when it's time for prom, but right now, I'm excited to spend the summer working on the farm. Being with Marcus was exhausting," Tessa admits.

"Is it going to be weird though, with me and Tucker?" Sydney asks, biting her lip.

Tessa shakes her head. "We've all been friends for so long, we're better than that. Don't worry. As long as you're happy, I'll deal with it."

Sydney grins. "I *am* happy. He makes me really happy."

"What about you?" Tessa gives me a nudge.

"What about me?"

"Have you talked to Andre at all?"

"He doesn't need me for rides anymore, now that his car's fixed, so we haven't been in touch."

Sydney gives me a look. "You know that's not what she meant."

I close my eyes and exhale a long breath. "Okay, so I miss him. A lot. But I screwed it up. I tried to text him something the other day, but he never even wrote back to me."

Sydney and Tessa lean closer. "Well, what exactly did you say?"

"Just something about one of my riders."

Sydney gives an exhausted look and flops backwards. "*That* was what you chose to say after weeks of silence?"

"What?" I ask. "I know, okay? I know I messed it up, but I don't know how to fix it!"

"I do," Tessa says. "It's called an actual apology."

"As long as you mean it," Sydney cautions.

I frown. "Why wouldn't I mean it?"

"I mean, if you take it back, if you apologize . . . are you really going to be ready for a relationship?"

This surprises me. I think about how hard it was the last time around. How unsure I was of how to be in a relationship. How scared I was of being tied down. Sydney has a point. If I go through all of this, an apology, and let him down again . . . well, he will never forgive me.

I swallow, feeling tears come to my eyes. But at the same time, I know what life is like without him. I don't want that. I want Andre. "Yeah, I think I'm ready for a relationship, as long as it's with him."

Sydney and Tessa give me moony eyes.

"But you guys . . ." I say, rolling over to one side.

"Yeah?" they ask, climbing into my bed with me.

"What if he doesn't forgive me?"

"Charlie," Tessa says. "You do realize that this whole time, all Andre had to do was report you to Backseat, and he would have been totally within the law to do so? But he didn't, because . . ." She looks at me imploringly.

"Because he cares about me?" I ask.

"Well done," Tessa says.

"And besides." Sydney grins. "We just have to make it a really good apology."

Chapter 34

IF THERE'S ONE UNIVERSAL TRUTH ABOUT ANDRE, IT'S that he never misses a good party, and when it comes to my apology, we choose to use this information to our benefit.

It's Reggie who remembers when Andre's birthday is, and Tessa confirms with her parents that it's okay to have one big last hurrah at the barn, as long as nobody actually goes inside, except for the surprise part, and as long as everyone behaves themselves to a moderate degree. I confirm with the guys on the lacrosse team that they'll be attending, and I also invite all of our riders. Dennis, Lulu, Shara, and even Michaela (though she'd show up regardless). Reggie, who was thrilled to have an actual, official invitation to a party for once, and all the other people Andre gave unsolicited, but nevertheless truly helpful, advice to. And with each guest who accepts, I am more in awe of how it is possible for one person to be so universally loved.

The only rule I ask them to follow: do not breathe a word of it to Andre.

At four p.m. on Friday, just as the sun is starting to get lower in the sky, I position myself in my car down the road from Andre's house and, like clockwork, and with the help of his mom, I receive a ride alert:

Andre Minasian has requested a ride.

He is frowning at me as I pull up outside his house, before I even put the car in park.

"Hi," I say, with my best smile. I let Sydney help me pick out an especially cute prairie top for today, and even do some of my makeup. She called me her greatest success story yet.

"Hey," he says, wiping the frown off his face.

"Not like you to request a ride now that your car is fixed."

"Car trouble." He shrugs. "My battery died, which was really weird." He squints at me. "I take it you're going to the party at Tessa's?"

I smile. "Hop on in."

♡ ♡ ♡

"So, when do you leave for New Mexico?" Andre asks, after we ride for a few moments in silence. When I don't respond right away, he adds, "Don't tell me Ava said no. The barn is perfect. If she didn't offer you a job, she's insane."

"Well, the thing is . . . I turned it down?"

Andre's brows go up. "You did what?!"

I drum my fingers nervously on the wheel as we start moving again. "I realized I wasn't sure what I was really going out there for. So I actually got a different job this summer."

"Where?" Andre asks.

I clear my throat. "Um, here."

Andre's face seems to be fighting between confusion and happiness. "But . . . I thought . . . wait, with who?"

"Your dad, actually." And when I see Andre's shocked face, I explain. "I'm going to be helping him with the community housing project."

Andre's expression is now completely unreadable. "That son of a gun," he whispers. "Both of you kept this from me?"

I smile. "Yeah, so . . . maybe we could hang out?" I clear my throat. "Also, I got an internship at MaCA one day a week, and I'll keep it through next year, so maybe we could even meet up there when you're at Wilson." It takes me a moment to look at him after I say this, but eventually I do.

And I find him looking down awkwardly at his hands.

"What?" I ask.

"Well, actually," he starts to say, and my heart wobbles.

"Or not . . ." I try. "Sorry, I know next year is a long way away."

"No, that's not it." Andre shakes his head. "I just, I haven't decided if I'm going there yet. To Wilson. They're giving me a few more weeks to decide."

"And you're not sure?"

He shrugs, a slow smile creeping over his face. "I met this girl recently who told me I should get out there and see what the rest of the world is all about. I was actually thinking about heading down to Tulane, checking it out."

I blush. "That's awesome, Andre. I'm happy for you."

"Yeah," he says, looking down at his knees again. I've never seen Andre like this before. So awkward. "Thanks."

We ride in silence a little longer, and the anxiety is killing me. It feels like every cell in my body is firing. *"Do something!"* they say. *"Make your move!"*

We've reached the top of the hill now, and the sun is just starting to set. It's beautiful, and before I can think twice, I pull the car over to the side of the road. I get out.

"Charlie, what are you doing?" Andre asks, getting out too.

"I don't know," I say. "I had a plan. I was going to show you all the things I love about Chester Falls. The things *you've* made me love, Andre. But then it just felt . . . like it wasn't enough."

Andre tilts his head. "What is happening."

"The thing is, it scared me," I say.

"What scared you?"

"You and Jess. When I thought . . ." My breath catches.

Andre looks away from me. "I'm sorry," he says, looking back. "Like I said, if you'd just talked to me about it, I could have explained the visit before this got so out of hand."

I shake my head. "That's not what I mean. I mean, it scared me because it scared me. Ugh! This is not coming out right."

"Take a deep breath," he says. "What scared you?"

"This!" I say, my arms out wide. "Us!" I move my hand rapidly back and forth between us, pointing. "It scared me because it showed me how much I like you, Andre. But also, how quickly things can go wrong. I have so much going for me right now, and I've worked so hard for it. I didn't want to wonder what it would be like to lose you. And I didn't want to lose any part of myself. And I started to feel like that, when we made this official."

Andre looks off to the side, thinking. "But what I don't get is, why do you have to lose yourself to be with me? Why can't you have both?"

I swallow. "I didn't know I could. But I do now. Now I know that I'm the only one who's responsible for the kind of person I become. Not my town, or where I go to college, or who I'm in a relationship with." I shrug. "Though I can't imagine anyone better than you."

I steal a look at Andre, and he isn't looking at me. He's looking at the sunset. He turns to me slowly.

"So take me," he says. "Take me on Charlie Owens' tour of Chester Falls."

♡ ♡ ♡

I drive Andre past the stop sign where he first got in my car and refused to get out. I drive him past the Little League fields where we sat and ate granola and drank Chester Fizzes. I drive him past Jacobson's Hardware, where he quietly put a peppermint patty on my armrest when he knew I needed it. And I drive him past Lanes and Games.

"This place?" he says, laughing. "But that's where we got into a fight!"

I shrug. "It's also where I realized just how much I cared about you."

And of course, I drive him past the car wash, where we had our first kiss.

Eventually, my car pulls in by Tessa's barn. The place that started it all.

It's quiet when we get out. Too quiet. Andre is concerned.

"Hello?" he calls. Then he turns to me. "Where is everyone?"

One, two, three, I count silently in my head. Then, with a rush of screams, the barn door opens wide.

"Surprise!" Everyone jumps out from inside the barn. "HAPPY BIRTHDAY!!"

Andre's face is a mix of confusion and happiness. "What is going on?"

Everyone clamors to Andre, giving him big hugs and patting him on the back.

"But . . . who . . ." Andre asks.

Tessa nods in my direction. "Who do you think?"

"What have you done?" His eyes are suspicious, but his mouth is smiling.

I can feel everyone's eyes, which makes me want to barf, but I force myself to take a deep breath.

"Andre, you've had a rough couple of years. And through it all, you've been everyone's champion. Everyone's best friend. So tonight, we're all here for you. We just wanted to show you how special you are."

Andre looks bashful. He stuffs his hands in his pockets. "You did all this for me?"

I take a step forward, and I nod. Andre takes a step forward, too.

"Pretty sure you're worth it." I grin as a twitter goes up in the crowd.

He reaches out a hand, runs it up and down my arm. "So, what are you saying?"

"I'm saying it's you and me. That's all that matters."

He's so close now, I can smell him. Then he nods. "You're right." He leans forward and kisses me. I lose myself in it, in his warmth, my arms coming up to encircle his neck, so much so that it takes me a little while to realize that everyone is cheering.

"Happy birthday," I say as we pull apart.

♥ ♥ ♥

After a few hours of partying, of laughing and dancing, of convincing a whole group of people to jump in the lake in their clothes, Andre finds me in the barn, where I'm just putting the candles on his birthday cake.

"You aren't supposed to see this!" I exclaim, as he comes up and wraps his arms around me from behind.

"I was thinking . . . maybe you'd wanna come with me? On my trip to Tulane?"

I smile. "Really?"

Andre nods. "And we could map out houses to see along the way. You could have your architecture road trip, and I could tag along."

I think for a minute. "I'd have to ask your dad for a week off."

"Think I can help out with that." Andre laughs. "I just have one condition."

"What's that?"

"I'm driving."

I make a face. "Yeah, I don't know about that."

"Take it or leave it," he says. "I can do the road trip without you."

"You wouldn't dare!" I exclaim, as he takes me in his arms. "I mean, do you even know how to drive outside the state of Massachusetts?"

Andre grins. "Man, have I missed you," he whispers. Then he leans down and kisses me.

Epilogue

IF YOU WERE TO ASK ME ABOUT MY HOME, CHESTER Falls, Massachusetts, if you were lucky enough to know it existed, I'd tell you first and foremost about the people who live there.

I'd tell you about the salty Massachusetts ladies at the diner.

I'd tell you about the old men who never miss a Little League game.

I'd tell you about the farmers who are willing to sacrifice just about everything to keep their family legacy alive.

I'd tell you about the peaks and valleys so beautiful, with such gorgeous light, that you'd think you were having a religious experience.

I'd tell you about the people who believe there are aliens here, and yet who still believe there is no better place to call home.

And, most importantly, I'd tell you about the girl who's

still trying to find herself here. But each day, she's getting better. Building houses helps her find her place. And so does the boy with the big smile, the one who can't sit still. He's the one who's dying to get to know you, and to help you get to know yourself.

And he's the one who showed her where she belonged.

Acknowledgments

I'd like to first thank Emilia Rhodes for thinking of me for this project, Elizabeth Agyemang for sharing not just her incredible notes with me, but this concept itself, and Nicole Sclama for all her initial guidance. To all three, thanks for being open to the ways I could take this amazing idea and make it mine.

To Pete Knapp, thanks for hanging in there with me, and for all you do to keep me motivated. I'm so excited for everything that's in store.

To the friends I made moving back to New England who inspired so much of this book—Emily, Rose, Alice, Stacey, Julia. Thanks for helping me find a home again. To Caleb Dean, for the notes that saved me! To Mom, Dad, Mike, Andy, Shannon, and Laura, for their creative ideas, quick answers to my emails, and constant encouragement. To Nora, Stuart,

Angus, and Caroline for their unwavering enthusiasm and unconditional love.

To Toby, the *most* special, who really believes I can do anything.